MW01702069

Ancient Matriarchs
Book Five

Out of Darkness: Imma: Wife of Noah

Angelique Conger

SOUTHWEST OF ZION PUBLISHING / LAS VEGAS

Angelique Conger/Southwest of Zion Publishing
7401 West Washington Ave
Las Vegas, NV 89128
www.AngeliqueCongerAuthor.com

Publisher's Note: This is a work of fiction. Names, characters, places, and incidents are a product of the author's imagination. Locales and public names are sometimes used for atmospheric purposes. Any resemblance to actual people, living or dead, or to businesses, companies, events, institutions, or locales is completely coincidental.

Out of Darkness: Imma, Wife of Noah/ Angelique Conger. -- 1st ed.
ISBN 978-1-946550-37-8

To all who survived the 2020 pandemic
Wondering if it would last as long as the flood.

CONTENTS

CHAPTER 1

Breathe

I had not thought to become the wife of a man, especially not a man like Noah.

Noah lived many years before I came into the world. He already had a wife, sons, and daughters. His legacy as son of the prophets, descending through the prophets directly from Adam and each of the other prophets, frightened me. I never expected to be with a man of such renown.

~ ~ ~

The newborn child refused to wail as Mama handed him to me. "Do what you must to make him breathe," she commanded in a hissing whisper as she turned back to the woman in front of her.

She turned back to the babe's mama. "Do not stop fighting, Keshet. It is not your time to leave this earth."

Keshet had slipped in and out of awareness for more than a span as Mama worked with her to bring this child into the world. She burned. Now, her eyes rolled up into her head, then fluttered open again.

"My baby," she moaned. "Will he live? Have I given Noah another son to help him?"

"You have another son who needs his mama. You need to get well, so he can be strong like his brothers."

"Good," Keshet whispered. "Another can feed and teach him. I am not long for this world."

"Fight, Keshet. It is not your time! You must live for your son."

As wife to Noah, Keshet had given birth to many children. Mama had warned me that this would be a difficult birthing. "I am a good healer, I rarely lose a mama or a baby," she had told me, "but I fear for Keshet. I heard from her last healer that more children would not be good for her."

Now, after many spans of trying to bring this child into the world, my mama's wisdom proved correct.

I listened to Mama reassure Keshet with one part of me while I whispered similar words to the infant boy. I rubbed his back as I held him face down across my arm, pushing the mucus from his mouth as I had done with other babes Mama had helped to bring into this world.

I had seen babies who were blue at birth, but after their first breath and lusty scream, their skin changed from blue to pink. This child did not. He whimpered — a little. His shallow breaths never filled up his lungs. The blue lightened, briefly, before deepening again.

"It is not time for you to leave this world, little one," I whispered. "Breathe. You have a loving papa and a mama who need you. Breathe."

I held him by the ankles and dangled him upside down. This had startled other babies into inhaling that first breath, and then screaming their displeasure at being held upside down. This little one took in only a shallow breath. His weak cry worried me.

I bent over the child and blew soft breaths through his nose and mouth, encouraging him to breathe. While I breathed into him, his color improved. When I stopped, his breathing slowed and the blue returned.

I rubbed his back and slapped his buttocks. His tiny complaint drew little more air into him. It seemed he did not want to live any more than his mama.

"Keshet!" Mama shouted. "Do not give up. Your husband needs you. You are needed on this side of the veil. Do not go!"

"Baby boy," I mimicked, "do not give up. Your family needs you. Your mama and papa need you on this side of the veil. Do not go!"

The child shuddered and blew out his air. He did not suck in another lungful. My tears dripped onto his little naked body. I wrapped his limp little body in a blanket, wiping away my tears.

I glanced toward Mama, whose tears dripped off her nose onto the body of the child's mama. She pulled the cover up over Keshet's body and gently closed the staring eyes. They had inhaled their last shuddering breaths at the same time, neither breathing again.

"We will need to find a mama to feed the babe. His cannot," Mama said.

"No. He will not need to eat. He would not fight to breathe. He, too, is gone."

I set the child next to his mama with her arm around him. They looked natural, as if they slept together. They did sleep. They slept the sleep of death. I covered the two with the blanket, covering her face once more.

"Will you tell Noah?" I asked Mama.

Her eyes fluttered from the scene of mama and child to my eyes. "He will need to be told. How do we tell him both mama and child are gone? He will not take it well."

"I do not envy you the task," I murmured.

"You will be by my side. He will ask about the child. You worked with him."

"Me? I have never spoken …"

"You will today. Noah will want to know why the child is not in the nursery being fed by another woman."

My eyes fell to the floor. "Yes, Mama." I did not like it, but she spoke the truth. Noah would want to know from me, not her.

I had never spoken with the great man. He had been chosen to be a prophet as a child. I believe he expected this son to have the same privilege. His other sons had not stayed obedient to Jehovah's commandments. Now, he had lost the son he hoped for and the wife who could bring him more children.

I sighed. Mama had brought me along to this birthing, surprising me. She usually took my older sister, Dodi, but she nursed a sick child and could not attend. Mama sighed and took me.

"You must be quiet. Do as I say. This is the prophet's wife and child."

I had nodded, less happy to be there than Mama was to have me join her.

As an unmarried woman, Mama thought it to be unwise for me to be there for the birth, and kept me away when she could. However, I had helped her with birthings before when Dodi's family required her more than Mama's needs. She only took me to the neighbor women. Never to important women like Keshet.

I had watched Mama massage newborn infants' throats and smack them on their bare bottoms to encourage the first breath. She then handed the child to me to clean and wrap in a blanket. I suppose Mama trusted me to encourage this child to breathe. She had been much too busy with his mama.

Mama stared into the distance, past the near wall. I knew she saw nothing. I had seen this stare before. She considered the words to use to tell Noah that his wife and son had not survived the birthing. I had never heard her utter those words. She seldom needed to use them.

Her skill in helping women birth babies had spread far beyond our little village of Lior. Men sent messages from far away lands, begging Mama to come to help them. Many sent gifts of gold, silver, or jewelry. Mama rarely accepted the gifts, and she did not often leave our village to assist the women of other lands.

When the message came from Mamre that Keshet required her assistance, Mama could not refuse. The child Dodi cared for had been ill for only a day or two and still required her. That left me, for Mama had no time to seek another.

"You will see," Mama said at last. "I have begged Jehovah for the words to give to Noah. I will have the correct words when he asks." Mama plunged her hands into the hot water in the pot near her feet, washing away the remnants of Keshet's life, and indicated that I should do the same.

"When will that be?" I asked as I toweled my hands dry of the child's blood.

"Now. Follow me, Imma."

I ran my fingers through my hair, attempting to look decent for the prophet and the news we brought. Mama did not. She threw the door open and marched through it.

Noah stood from his chair near the fire and turned to us, his face stretched in a frown. "I did not hear the lusty cry of my newborn son. Why are you not with him and Keshet?"

Mama lifted her gaze to the great man. "I am sorry. Your son … your son …" She touched my arm.

"Your son did not have the strength to take a deep breath," I said.

Noah's frowning face paled. "What are you telling me?" he whispered.

"He tried but could not get enough air into him to fill him. I worked with him. I breathed into his mouth, filling his lungs for him, bringing pink to his face. But when I stopped, the blue returned. As his mama breathed out her last breath, your little son shuddered and expelled the last of the air I breathed into him. He did not attempt to breathe in again."

"My son did not live? How can I bear it?" Noah cried out. "And my Keshet? I must go comfort her."

Mama set a hand on Noah's arm. "No, sir. Perhaps you did not hear Imma. Keshet breathed her last breath as your little son breathed his last. They are both gone."

Shock and pain filled the big man's face. He stared at Mama. "Both? I have lost both?" He dropped his head and shook his great mane. "Jehovah warned me. Why did I not listen?"

Many breaths filled with tears and sobbing later, Noah lifted his head. "I need to see them. I need to see my wife and son."

Mama turned on her heel and softly led the big man into the room where his wife and child lay in the bed. I followed behind.

~ ~ ~

I did not expect to play any part in the discussion. I came from outside the family, as an assistant to the healer. I had nothing to do or say about the family of this great prophet.

Noah stared at the mama and child in the bed and spoke with my mama about the cause of Keshet's passing. Her body no longer had the strength to struggle to push a child from her womb. She had been sick even before the time came for his birth. She could not push him out.

Mama had demanded that I press on Keshet's stomach while Mama encouraged her to push from her position between Keshet's legs.

"She did not have the strength or the will to continue," Mama said, concluding her sad story.

"I saw that in the last days. She feared this son would desert the faith for daughters of men. She has been weak for much of the time she carried the child. I suspected her strength would not be enough for the challenge of birth." He turned from Mama to me.

"You took my son. Tell me about him."

I told him once more of my efforts to help him breathe and to encourage him to live. Tears washed my face as I repeated the story. "The child tried to breathe. He struggled to fill his lungs with life. He did not have the strength to keep breathing. Even with my assistance, he could not fill his lungs and keep them filled. He left this earth at the same time his mama did. That greatly surprised me."

Noah gazed at his wife and child. Tears dripped through his beard onto the front of his tunic. "Thank you for your assistance," he said to Mama. "Keshet would have lived yet a while, if I had not desired another child. You did all you could to care for her."

He turned to me and took my hands. "And thank you, too. You helped my son live, if only for a brief time. Thank you for encouraging him to stay."

I nodded. What could I say to him?

"Your name?" he asked, still holding my hands.

"I am Imma, daughter of Ket and Hana," I said, nodding toward my mama. "We live in the village of Lior."

"Papa tells of visiting small villages near here. He mentioned speaking in Lior before the last rains."

I smiled at the memory.

Noah's papa, Lamech, and grandpapa, Methuselah, had visited our village to share the commandments of Jehovah with us. Few of us joined them in our little sanctuary. Most had found an excuse to be gone.

"We have heard these commandments before," they said.

"We have no need to be harangued again about the commandments."

"We are obedient."

"We have no need to hear from those ancient men."

I sat among the few who gladly entered the sanctuary early, to hear the words of Jehovah from the mouth of two of the great prophets. We sat in a small group, welcoming them and listening to their words.

They had not disappointed us. They taught that Jehovah had grown weary of the wickedness of his people. Too many of the children of Adam had turned away from the believers, finding beautiful women among those who no longer followed Jehovah's commandments.

"Jehovah will grow weary of this disobedience," Methuselah had warned. "He told my papa, Enoch, that all life would be destroyed in a great flood. The time nears when that will occur. We do not know how long our God will be patient with the children of men. He grieves over His children. Be obedient. Call upon Him in your trials and in your joy. Do all you can to prevent the final destruction that will come upon you."

I had no man, no husband. The men of my village had gone to nearby villages with more beautiful women to find wives. Many of those wives came from families who no longer worshiped Jehovah, but I knew the truth of the prophet's words.

When would the Father choose to end our lives? Although I hoped to be among the few chosen to be protected, I laughed at the thought. Only those close to the prophet would be saved. How could I be one of those? My beauty did not entice the local young men. It would not entice the young men of a prophet's family. And few of his family, even, continued to believe.

"Yes. I heard them preach words of obedience. Few came to hear them."

"A mama and her coming babe required my attention," Mama interjected, her usually calm face flushing red.

"They said many people had other important events requiring their attention," Noah said, releasing my hands from his.

They suddenly felt cold. A breeze played across my knuckles and I dropped them to my skirts, seeking the warmth of my body.

"It is good you listened to them," Noah continued. "What do you think of their warning?"

"I fear it will happen sooner than any would like. My brothers and sisters believe they can live their lives without fear, that Jehovah will not destroy His children."

Noah barked a short laugh. "Too many believe they can continue in disobedience." He turned back to his wife and child. "Their bodies must be cared for. I will go dig their graves. Could you —?" He glanced at Mama and me. "No. You bring life into this world. I would not ask you to prepare them for burial."

He reached into the pocket at his side and withdrew coins. He gave coins to Mama. He gave me one, as well. "I promised payment if you would come to help my wife and son. You did all you could. I thank you."

He turned back to gaze at them while Mama and I gathered her supplies and returned them to her basket. We nodded to Noah before we left. I do not know if he noticed us leave.

We mounted our mules and rode the distance from Mamre to Lior without speaking much. Both Mama and I were in deep thought.

CHAPTER 2

Visitor

Three years later, a message came to Papa from the village of Mamre. Papa read the message three times before he called for me.

"What have you done?" he demanded.

"What do you mean?" I retorted. "Done? Where? When?"

"We have been called to travel to Mamre to visit with the prophet, Noah."

"We? Who? You and Mama?" I asked.

He waved the message around as he sat in his comfortable seat, never allowing me to see what it said. I stood and waited for more information.

"Me, your mama, and you. We are all called upon to travel to Mamre. The crops will be ready to harvest soon, and the 'great Noah' asks that we travel to see him. He can come to see us if it is important. I will not go," Papa growled, his voice growing louder.

I shrugged. I had a blanket on the loom, and Dodi had left her youngest child with me to care for while she and her husband traveled to a wedding a week away. "It is your decision, Papa."

He waved a hand toward me to leave. I left his presence as he took another sip of wine. Papa had forgotten the command to live a clean life. He sipped on the wine more often each day.

I returned to my loom and to the care of Dodi's babe, who slept in my small room. The addition of a small child with her small sleeping mat and toys reminded me that I occupied the smallest room in my parent's home.

As the youngest, and a daughter, it had not crossed my papa's mind that I should be given one of the larger rooms, now that Dodi and my other sisters had moved into their own homes with their husbands.

I sometimes wondered if Papa purposely left me in the smallest room of the house to encourage me to leave. But where was I to go? Women did not build homes and move into them without husbands. I had no husband. I would be relegated to this small room until I did. Perhaps Papa did not want me to leave.

I sighed and returned to my weaving.

I continued to carry on as I had in all the twenty-seven years of my life, helping Mama and Papa, weaving, reading the Book of Commandments, and striving to obey. I attended

Sabbath meetings on the Seventh Day, though the numbers of other villagers attending dwindled.

I did my share to harvest and winnow the grains. I helped dry the vegetables and herbs and store them along with those that did not require drying to withstand the long days of rain. We stored tubers in the part of the storehouse that had been dug into the earth. Other things we hung from the rafters. Some were placed on shelves.

We admired the fullness of the storehouse before Mama closed and latched the doors. We carried food for our next meal with us as we strolled into the house.

Dark clouds hung over the land. Lightning ripped through the sky with a crackle as we reached our front door. Thunder followed almost immediately. We hurried into the house and closed and locked the shutters against the rain. As I closed the shutter in my room, the last one needing closing, the rain fell in torrents, splashing against my face. I pulled the shutter closed and locked it.

I wanted to light candles to brighten my loom. Instead, I pulled my door closed and hurried to the kitchen to help Mama with dinner. Dodi and her family were coming to eat with us.

As we sat at the table to eat that evening, we heard a pounding at the door.

Papa gazed at me. "Well. Are you going to answer that?"

I stood and grumbled quietly to myself as I hurried down the passageway from the kitchen to the front part of the house.

The pounding continued. I opened the door. A huge fist came toward my face, as the man began to pound again.

I ducked as the fist drew back.

"I am sorry," a voice from the dark of the porch said. "I did not know if you heard my knock."

"Everyone in this house and three houses down could hear you pounding on our door," I said. "I had to come from the kitchen. We only now sat down to eat."

The man stepped toward the light of the house. Noah.

"Oh," I said, bringing my hand to my mouth. "We were not expecting you."

"No. Imma, is it not?" he asked.

I nodded.

"Your papa refused to come to Mamre. My messenger told me he was busy. If I wanted to speak with him, I could come to Ket's home. I am here. I knew the rain would come soon, but I did not expect it today." He shook his great head from side to side.

I opened the door wider. How could I refuse entrance to the prophet? I looked behind him, expecting others to be with him.

"I am alone. While hunting, I decided I would come to speak with Ket personally. He demanded that I come to him, so, I am here."

Though a huge man, he spoke in a low voice. "May I meet with Ket now?"

My mouth hung open. I closed it with a small pop and took his cloak. Mama would not be happy with me if I allowed him to walk across her clean floors and drip muddy water.

"Would you remove your shoes? Mama cleaned the floors this afternoon …"

Noah laughed softly. "My mama expected me to remove my shoes when I came inside, as well. No mama likes their clean floors to be muddied by a man or a boy."

He bent and removed his boots and left them standing beneath his cloak. "Am I dressed properly to meet with your papa now?"

"We can set another plate for you. Follow me," I said as I led him through the dimly lit hall toward the kitchen.

Voices echoed down the hall, wondering if I had become lost and who our mysterious visitor may be.

Noah put a finger to his lips and whispered, "Let it be a surprise."

My eyes flew open wide, but I nodded in agreement.

He signaled for me to enter the room first.

"You are back at last," Papa growled without glancing my way. "Who was banging at our door. Did you tell them to go away?"

"No, Papa. I did not send him away." I stepped around the table toward the cupboards to get another plate. "You told him to come here. Here he is."

"Who?" Papa roared, finally turning to see our visitor.

Noah stretched out his big paw to take Papa's hand in his. "I am Noah. I asked you to come visit me. You told my messenger to come here if I wanted to speak with you. I am here."

Papa knocked his chair over as he stood. "W-w-welcome, Noah. I did not know you would come on the first day of rains."

"I was already halfway here when I decided to come the rest of the way. I knew I would be wet if I returned to Mamre or if I came on here to Lior."

Mama stood, directing Dodi's family to move around the table to make room for Noah to join us. I set the plate and spoon on the table and retrieved an extra chair.

"Please join us," Mama said.

Noah stepped over to help me move the chair into place. "Thank you. I will," he said as he set the chair between Dodi's husband and me, and then sat on it.

Dodi silently handed the empty plate over with a sparkle in her eyes and a questioning look. I shrugged and set it in front of Noah. My cheeks burned. Why would he choose to sit beside me? Perhaps so he could better see Papa when they spoke together?

~ ~ ~

While we ate, my stomach clenched and released, making it difficult to eat. This had never happened to me before. Why did my stomach rebel today, when one of Jehovah's prophets sat eating the food I helped to prepare, at the table with my family and me?

I could not understand why I would be so nervous. I had no reason to expect that he had come to Lior and my home to talk about me. Or did I?

I remembered what he said, "If I wanted to speak with him, I could come to Ket's home." Before the harvest, he had sent a messenger. Who had he wanted to see then? Papa, Mama, and … and me, Imma. But what reason did he have to request to see me?

That question disturbed my stomach. It disturbed my thoughts. It disturbed my ability to sit still. Unable to show my disturbance any other way, my toe bounced within my slippers.

Somehow I managed to choke down the food on my plate. I glanced at Noah. He had no problem eating. He had accepted second helpings of most of the food on the table, and now gladly accepted a serving of the fruit compote I had made for dessert.

"This tastes wonderful," Noah said. "Which of you lovely women should I thank for the fruit compote?"

"Me," I squeaked. I cleared my throat, then spoke again. "I made the dessert. I am happy you like it."

Noah flashed a smile my direction. His smile warmed me like sunshine after rain.

Dodi's baby began to complain. "I am sorry, Mama. Her teeth are coming in. Please excuse us. We will come visit again tomorrow if she is acting better then. It is good to meet you, Noah."

I grimaced as Dodi and her family left, darting through the rain toward their own home, leaving me alone with Mama, Papa, … and Noah. Papa would be able to discuss Noah's purpose for coming to Lior. I suddenly found it difficult to breathe.

Papa invited Noah to go with him to the sitting room.

Noah nodded. "Hana and Imma will be interested in this discussion. Please join us."

"We have dishes to clean —" Mama began.

"They will wait for what I have to say," Noah said. "Please join us in the sitting room at least for a short time."

I glanced at Mama. At an almost imperceptible nod, I set the dishes I had gathered next to the pot of hot water and followed Mama and the men out of the kitchen and down the hall.

Papa offered his best seat for Noah to sit in. Noah shook his head. "That is your favorite seat. I can tell. I will sit over here. This seat looks comfortable."

Mama sat in her usual seat, leaving the seat near Noah for me. I silently took in a deep breath as I sat.

"What can we do for one so important as you, Noah?" Papa asked.

"I sent a messenger before harvest time, asking you three to come see me. I gave no supporting information. I thought you would just come because I called. I learned that I must give more information. Just because I am Noah, a prophet of Jehovah does not mean I can be demanding and vague. I must be more considerate when I request that others come to see me."

"I had crops to harvest. We could not leave then. Our food would rot in the fields and we would have none for the coming rain times and until the crops can be harvested next year."

"When my messenger returned, I was unhappy, extremely unhappy," Noah said with a grimace. "I am not comfortable with people saying 'no' to me. For so much of my life, people have done as I asked with no questions."

"I am sorry —" Papa began to say.

"No. I am sorry. I did not think about your life and the things you are required to do to live. I was prideful."

"No —" Papa said.

"Yes. I was. I forgot that I am your servant. I had begun to think you were mine. Since that day, I have had reason to spend hours in prayer and repentance."

I peeked toward my papa. Would he consider repenting of some of his unkind ways after speaking with a prophet? I doubted it.

Noah spoke once more. "I came for two reasons. First, to apologize for treating you like a servant. Please forgive me and my prideful way."

Papa glanced at Mama. One of those looks that married couples share passed between them. I knew many words and decisions passed between them in that glance. Would I ever share thought and decisions with a glance as they did?

"We forgive you," Mama said.

Papa nodded.

"Second," Noah continued, "I have a great favor to ask of you."

Papa nodded once more.

I inhaled and held my breath. This would involve me. I could sense it.

"Three years ago, you, Hana, came with your daughter to assist in the birth of my son. Instead, you were there to assist them in their passage from this life into the next."

"For that I am truly sorry," Mama said. "I should have been able to keep them both alive."

"Living and dying are the responsibility of Jehovah. We do our best to live as long as we can. But, when it is time, we are taken home to His presence. I know that. If you have read from the Book of Commandments, you will understand that."

"I do not like losing the women I assist when they bring children into this world," Mama said.

"That is what makes you good," Noah said. "Your caring and desire to keep every mama and every child alive. Some of the others who help with birthing are not as concerned about life and health."

Mama ducked her head. "I thank you for your kind words."

"I saw how your daughter, Imma," Noah turned to me, "wept at the loss of my son. I saw she did everything she could do to help him live. My thoughts have returned to you over the last years. I have considered your kindness."

He smiled at me. I quivered at his kindness.

"I questioned your village leader," Noah continued. "Imma is not yet betrothed to another man. She attends Sabbath worship each week. Is this true?" His stare focused on Papa.

I knew the truth of his words. No man had asked for me to be his wife. Warmth rose from my heart toward my cheeks.

"Our village leader speaks the truth. No man has asked for our Imma. I have found no man who would prefer her to one of the more beautiful daughters of men." Papa's words cut through me.

"I have come with a proposal." Noah swept his eyes around the room, stopping briefly to stare into each of our eyes. "I lost my wife on that day you saw me last. All my sons have chosen to follow the ways of man and Satan, rather than follow the path of peace and freedom offered by Jehovah. I have no sons to pass the line of authority through."

My jaw tightened.

"I have come to you for this reason. I need a wife to give me honorable sons. Sons and daughters who will obey the commandments of Father. Sons who will not wander into the world of men seeking a wife who does not understand nor worship the one true God."

"And?" Mama said.

"And, I would like to ask permission to ask Imma to be my wife."

I gulped. "Me? I am much younger than you. My grandpapa would be your age."

"Would that be a problem for you?" Noah turned to gaze into my eyes. "I remember what it is like to love a young woman. I will treat you with kindness. I would not abuse you. I would be a gentle lover."

"You are still able to provide my daughter with sons and daughters?" Mama asked. "She will be an excellent mama. I would not want her to lose out on that opportunity, even for the opportunity to be the wife of a great prophet like you."

"Jehovah has promised me more sons and daughters. I have taken this decision to him over the last three years. I have not considered this lightly. Imma, would you consider becoming my wife? I believe we can find love."

A prophet of Jehovah wanted me to be his wife? My face warmed again at the thought, even though he had lived many hundred more years than me.

"Would you provide her with the good things of life? Would she be called on to sacrifice because of your call to be a prophet to the people?" Papa asked.

Noah shook his head. "I have not been asked to sacrifice the good things of life. I have a nice home. Imma saw it when she came … when she came three years ago. I would ensure that she has all she needs."

"And," Papa cleared his throat. "And her mama and I? Would there be compensation for the loss of her assistance in our home?"

"You would lose her to a man eventually."

"I would, but I would require some compensation for her loss."

Noah grunted a laugh. "I am prepared to discuss compensation when the women return to the kitchen to clean up our excellent dinner."

Papa stroked his beard. "I suppose it will be Imma's decision, then."

All the other faces in the room turned toward me.

"What? You want an answer now?"

"That would be nice," Noah said.

"I cannot give you an answer so fast. I need time to think about this. I need … I need to pray."

"Ah. That I can understand. How long do you need?"

"I do not know. Can you give me a span?"

"Only a span? I expected you to ask for a week or a month. I can easily give you a span. Go pray. Think about my proposal. Your papa and I have much to discuss."

CHAPTER 3

Questions

I threw on my cloak and stumbled out the door, forgetting that the rain had come. I did not care. Rain would cover my cries and my tears. I walked around the house and on towards the barn through the rain. I could find solitude there with the animals.

Inside the barn, I removed my cloak and fell to my knees. My arms lifted into the air and words tumbled out of me as I begged Jehovah for understanding. I wanted to marry. But Noah could easily be my grandpapa. Could I be happy with an old man? He had given Keshet a child. He could give me one.

I shared the storm of my confusion with Jehovah. Slowly, the cloud cleared. I learned that this would be for the best — best for me and my future children. Noah could provide me with a comfortable home where I could use all the skills Mama had taught me. Better, he would give me children.

A thought pierced me. "When Jehovah determines this world is much too wicked to protect, you will be safe with Noah."

I dropped my hands to my lap. *When, not if, the world can no longer be protected.* I considered the men and women in my little village of Lior. Most of them still pretended to honor and worship Jehovah. But few joined us in worship on the Sabbath.

Many of the men had women they visited, believing no one else knew. Searching for gold and wealth filled their thoughts and dreams rather than hopes for life with Father and Jehovah. Worse, men began to choose other men to be with rather than women. Even women were choosing other women. How could they create more children?

You will be safe with Noah. Noah would protect me from the evil that prevailed. I would not need to fear men who wanted women for their own pleasure. I would not fear those who invaded to steal women and children as their slaves. I would not have to fear the coming destruction.

I lifted my arms once more. "I thank thee, Jehovah. I give thanks for understanding. How can I, a poor, unwanted woman, have found such great mercy?"

After I completed my prayer of gratitude, I sat absorbing the love of my God for a time.

I became aware of the cattle softly lowing, asking for their evening rations. I stood and filled their mangers with hay and oats, before pulling my cloak around my shoulders. I opened the barn door, prepared to tug the hood over my head.

The rain had stopped. The sun shone through clear sky over my head in a circle of light surrounded by black rain clouds.

I tilted my face upward to embrace the sun before I scurried through the mud to our front door. As I reached the door, the clouds filled the space and rain returned, pounding the ground as hard as ever.

I offered a silent prayer of gratitude, then pushed open the front door.

Mama stood in front of the door, her cloak over her head, and her arm outstretched to pull open the door. "Oh. There you are. We were worried about you out in that terrible storm."

"I went to a quiet place out of the storm." I removed my now dry cloak and shoes before returning to the sitting room.

"It has been a span," Papa said. "Did you decide?"

I looked at his hopeful face, then peered toward Mama. Her face, too, expressed hope. She stood beside me with a hand on her hip. Last, I gazed into Noah's eyes. I did not see love shining through. But how could he love me? We did not know one another. Still, I saw a kindness.

I remembered his concern for Keshet at her death. Would he learn to care for me as he cared for Keshet? I would have to depend on that, for Jehovah had given me an answer.

I nodded. "Yes. I have decided." I gazed at Papa and Mama, whose hands now twined together in the love I had always wanted. "I dreamed of a young man who would come and carry me away from your home to a land of beauty and love. It has not happened."

I moved my gaze to Noah, who now leaned forward, his hands resting on his knees. "You are not a young man. I doubt any of the young men near here know of my existence. They are drawn to the women of nearby villages, blinded by the hope for wealth and status."

I brushed a lock of hair from my face. "I know I am no beauty. I am honored that you would choose me to be your wife. If all the negotiations between you and Papa are completed, I accept."

Noah surged to his feet and grabbed me beneath my arms to twirl me around the room.

When he set me down, I stood breathless, wavering a bit. Noah kept his arm around me, steadying me.

"Jehovah is great," Noah said, speaking so softly only I could hear.

"He is," I replied.

Noah pulled me to sit next to him. "When shall we have the wedding?"

Mama stared at me. "We could be ready …"

I bit my lip. I did not want her to drag this out. I suppose I feared Noah would change his mind. "How soon can we get someone here to marry us?"

"I thought we would be married at my home. It is larger. I have sons and daughters …"

"No. I think here. With my sisters and brothers. Small. I do not think I would want to be introduced to your children at our wedding."

Noah chewed on his mustache. "I can understand that. My children are not always nice. But you will have to meet them."

"I know. But I'd rather meet them as your wife, not as the young girl you are sporting with."

"Me? Sporting with young girls? Never!" Noah exploded.

"I know. You know. But would your children know?"

He stopped growling and sucked in a deep breath.

"I am much younger than you."

He expelled his breath. "Yes. You are. And my children would not think of me as a serious man if I brought you to them before we wed. You are correct."

"Who will come to marry you to my daughter?" Papa asked.

Noah shoved his blond hair back from his face. "Papa Lamech will come to marry me. I would consider Grandpapa Methuselah, but it is difficult for him to travel in the rain. It is not much easier for Papa. Are you certain you want to be wed here? We could go to Papa's home."

I shook my head. "There would always be talk if we did that. I cannot give the unbelievers more reason to argue with you about the word of Jehovah."

Noah agreed, though I could see reluctance in the way he held his body.

"We could … possibly … travel to your home," Mama said. She twirled a lock of hair around a finger as she always did when she was solving a problem. "We could travel to your home, before the roads become impassable in the rains. We have a sledge and oxen … They could carry all of us. But I would need time in your kitchen. I always make a —"

"You would do that?" Noah asked, his voice lifting. "It would be lovely to have you use my kitchen. Papa lives near to Mamre. It will be easier for him and Grandpapa to come to the wedding there."

Noah's enthusiasm lifted the whole room.

~ ~ ~

Ten days later, I stood in front of Methuselah beside Noah, wearing the cream-colored dress Dodi wore when she married Itzik.

I had dreamed about the dress I would wear for my own marriage. I thought about the flowers I would pin to my hair. There had been no time to sew a new dress. Flowers were unheard of in the pounding rains.

I listened to the words of the rite, so simple yet so profound. They made me forget the new dress and flowers — almost. I had wondered if Methuselah would remember the words at his great age. He had celebrated his eight hundred thirteenth birthday during the past summer. Few lived as many years as he did.

He remembered the words, and he spoke them clearly. I glanced up through my eyelashes more than once to be sure the old man still spoke the words and a younger man had not taken his place.

We had suffered through the rains on our way to Mamre. It beat on the heavy cloth that covered the sledge and blew through the openings. I began to question my willingness to marry a man so much older than me, especially when I had to travel in such weather.

What made the journey worse was my brothers and their wives. Their comments about me going to be married to a man older than their grandpapa. I knew why I had agreed. They did not. They would never understand.

Noah had not kissed me before our wedding rite. His kiss surprised me. As I looked back on it, I expected a small, chaste kiss, much like Papa gave me on the cheek before I went to bed each night. Instead, he took me in both arms and kissed me. As my surprise receded, I kissed him back. He may be much older than Papa, but his kiss promised he would be able to give me children.

We greeted the guests who had braved the storms to join with us that cold, rainy day. Mama, unsure of what Noah's kitchen could provide, had brought with her the necessary supplies to cook a banquet. One of his daughters assisted in preparing food for all to eat and more.

We sat at long tables in Noah's large eating room, which would now be mine as well, and shared the meal. We were quiet at first. We did not know those of the other family. That did not last long.

Papa stood to greet his new son. He rolled his eyes at the word, and laughter ensued. Even Noah joined in laughing.

Noah put an arm protectively around me and whispered in my ear. "Let them have their fun. We know why we were wed this day."

I gazed up into his sky-blue eyes. "Because Jehovah desired it?"

"Exactly. And we will make the best of it. I am older than you, but I can help you in ways you would not think. I like you. I hope you like me." He smiled at me.

I returned his smile. "I like you. I wanted to love my new husband." My emotions bounced everywhere at that moment. I had hoped for a man, a young man, to want me. I had not expected it to be this old man, even if he was a prophet.

Noah's grip on my hand tightened. He could not miss my confusion. "That will come with time, my dear. You will learn to love me, and I will learn to love you. Jehovah has blessed our marriage. Now it is up to us to make it as beautiful as the words that bind us."

He bent to kiss me. I expected a kiss on the cheek or forehead, but he kissed me on the lips.

I gazed up at him. "I could grow to like that."

"Good," he chuckled. "We will be happy together."

Later that night, when we were alone, Noah kissed me again. "I cannot promise constant happiness and joy. Not in this world. But I can promise you that I will protect you from those who would hurt you. I can promise to be gentle and kind. I will try to never hurt you, and if I do, I promise to apologize and make it better for you."

"I cannot promise I will always be full of joy. I have had times of sorrow and soul searching. But I promise I will do my best to treat you well, to keep your home clean and presentable for others, to prepare tasty meals, and bear you children."

"Will you also promise to try to learn to love me?" His voice took on a wistfulness.

I leaned close to him. "I will try to learn to love you." I kissed his full lips. "And will you love me?"

He took me in his arms. "This is one way to learn that."

The next morning, we waved goodbye to my family. The clouds promised more rain, but it was the time of year for rain. They expected it.

"We hope to be close to home before the rain falls," Papa said. He put his arms around me. "If Noah is not good to you, let me know."

"And what would you do to him if he is not?" I asked.

He shrugged. "I do not know. You are his now. Be a good wife to him. Give him many children." He climbed into the seat of the sledge.

"Do what you must to maintain a quiet home. A quiet home can become a happy home," Mama suggested. She hugged me tighter than she had in many years. "Come see us, but not often." Papa gave her his hand and helped her into the seat next to him in the sledge.

Brothers and sisters and their families snuggled into the blankets under the heavy covering cloth. They waved goodbye knowing they would soon be lulled to sleep by the movement of the sledge. I had heard them late into the night enjoying the wine my new husband had provided for them. They would sleep most of the way home.

We waved goodbye to Noah's parents and grandpapa, who rode in a small covered buggy, pulled by a team of black horses. One of his sons drove the buggy, allowing the older people to relax out of the storm.

Noah put his arm around me and walked with me into the house. It felt unusually quiet with everyone gone.

"Would you like something to eat?" I asked. "I am certain there is food left from last night."

He directed my steps toward the kitchen. I found food for us in the cool part of the storage room.

We ate. He showed me around the house, opening closets and cupboards. "Nothing is forbidden to you. You are the mistress of the house."

I reminded myself to take time later to explore more thoroughly. For now, however, Noah had other plans.

CHAPTER 4

At the Well

Noah treated me well as he had promised. Over the years, I learned to love him in ways I never expected, even in my dreams. His gentleness surprised me. I learned to love him, and he loved me.

The women of Mamre, however, were much more difficult to love. I struggled to like those women. Each day, I had no other option but to meet them at the community well.

My first morning at the well after Noah and I were married, I spoke to the women as Mama had taught me. Women met and gossiped at the well each morning and evening. I had often visited with the women in Lior. I had expected to find and make friends with the women in this new village.

None of the women responded to me. When I spoke to them, they turned their back to me or pretended to see through me. I waited for my turn to draw water up from the well. I knew the conventions of the well. Each woman drew up water according to when they arrived.

Not in Mamre. A hidden code of priorities, unknown to me, determined who went next. Women who arrived after me, and after others who arrived earlier, walked to the well as soon as they arrived and drew their water.

Almost everyone had drawn water. Everyone who arrived before me sat around the well, gossiping about one of the young women of Mamre.

Since none of them would speak to me, I took my jar to the well, set it on the ground, and dropped the bucket into the water. I pulled on the rough rope to bring up the water, expecting to pour it into my jar.

"What do you think you are doing?" the woman who sat near the rope as I pulled the bucket from the well.

"Drawing water for my home," I said and turned to pour the water into my jar.

The woman knocked the bucket from my hands. "It is not your turn."

"How do I know when it is my turn? I waited for everyone who arrived before me to fill their jars. It is my turn," I said. I admit, my voice raised more than I like.

"You are newest to Mamre. You are last. Always last."

"But my husband has been here for many years."

Another woman spoke up. "His wife had first in line privileges until she died. Now you must wait."

"How long?" I suspected I would never have a turn.

The second woman lifted a shoulder in a shrug. "After all of us are gone. You should not even be here when we are."

I sucked in a deep breath and bit my lip to prevent the retort that threatened to explode.

I waited for another span before the women finished their gossiping and walked toward their homes. Some made a point to bump into me. One even bumped into my water jar, spilling the little I had managed to pour into it.

I remembered the lessons from the Book of Commandments and refused to argue with them. It would do no good for me and would make it take longer before I could get water.

That afternoon, I hurried to the well before I expected the other women to arrive.

I arrived too late. Once again, the women snubbed me and refused to allow me to get water until after they had all left.

The next morning, I left my home earlier than the day before, hoping to arrive before the women of Mamre. I wanted to dip up my water and be home before they arrived.

Once more, other women were earlier than me.

They changed the way they treated me. Rather than ignore me, they began to talk about me. They did not speak to me, only about me.

"She thinks she is better than us because she married Noah."

"She is a loose woman. Why else would a woman so much younger than Noah marry him?"

The very words I feared. They spoke them — and more.

"No man your age wanted you. Why else would you marry a man five hundred years older than you?"

He is not even five hundred years old yet. He is only four hundred and a few years older than me. I wanted to laugh, but that would make the women angrier. I followed their example and refused to respond.

That morning, I waited for two spans before the women grew tired of afflicting me and returned to their home. I sighed as I pulled up the bucket of water.

"You are late getting water," a woman's voice said.

"I am sorry," I said, hurrying to pour the water into my water jar before she knocked it out of my hand. "Did I take your turn?"

I felt the sarcasm in her laugh. "No. I don't have a turn any more than you do. I am Sigal." She leaned forward to brush her lips against my cheek.

A friend? I hoped she would be. "I'll bring some water up for you after I finish filling my jar," I offered.

She leaned against the rock wall of the well. "You do not need to get water for me. I am able to pull on the rope and bring water up for myself."

I swallowed away my nervousness. "I am happy to help. You are the first woman of Mamre to speak kindly to me."

I turned toward the well and sniffed back the tears that threatened to spill from my eyes. I heard a splash as the bucket hit the water. I took my time drawing the water up from the depths of the well.

She set her water jug near mine and touched my shoulder. "They are cruel to me, as well."

"How long have you been in Mamre?" I asked, turning to pour the water into my jar.

Sigal frowned. "I have been here two years. You would think they would accept me by now. But they have not. I have learned to wait to come to the well long after they have left. It is safer."

I nodded. "I will remember that. I do not like to be treated as they have treated me."

"Smart woman," Sigal said, dropping the bucket into the well. "Where do you live?"

I turned and pointed toward the home I shared with Noah. "Over there."

"You are the one who married Noah? I expected someone … well, someone older."

"Yes. I'm younger than him. More than four hundred years. But he treats me well." I held my breath, waiting for her to say something cruel.

"Better four hundred than five hundred," she quipped.

I stared at her, then joined in her laughter.

When I could finally control my laughing, I said, "I have been here much too long. I must return home."

"Meet me here before sunset," Sigal said as she waved goodbye to me.

~ ~ ~

I met Sigal most days long after the other women left the well. On the days when I had no choice but to go to the well, the other women of the village sat and gossiped, often about me. I sat far away from the well, as if I had no interest in the women or their gossiping. I told myself I did not.

After one of these mornings, I stood in my kitchen sobbing. Noah had been gone for several days to teach people of Jehovah in neighboring villages. I did not expect him to return for another three days. Noah's youngest children had gone to stay with an older sister. I stood alone in my home.

I felt safe standing in the kitchen crying. No one would see or hear me.

Suddenly, hands took me and spun me around. I found myself in Noah's arms.

"Why the tears?" he asked, brushing my tears away.

"The women …" I choked the story out through my tears. "They treat me … They won't let me draw water …"

"They what?" Noah demanded. His voice edged with anger.

"They will not allow me to draw water for the day's use until all of them have what they want, shared their gossip, often about me, and have left the well."

He huffed a breath out through his nose. "They treat my wife rudely? I founded Mamre. I dug the well."

I cried louder. He put his arms around me. "This will end. You will see."

"How?" I asked, sniffing my tears away.

"I will discuss it with the village leader."

"Are you not the village leader? You settled Mamre."

Noah grunted. "I gave up being leader long ago. My responsibilities to Jehovah take me away much too much to be responsible for a village and its people. I sometimes struggle to care for a wife and children."

His frown deepened and he pushed a lock of hair away from my face.

"That makes sense. I thought you were gone for three more days?"

"Jehovah warned me I was needed at home. I see that I was. What am I going to do for you?"

I wiped my tears from my face and stepped close. "Since you are home ...?"

He smiled. "Would that make you happy?"

"It will not solve my water problems, but it will make me happy to be loved by you."

He giggled. "I told you. I promised you that you would learn to love me."

I stood on my tiptoes and kissed him. "You told me. And you were correct. I am learning to love you."

"Just learning?" His eyebrows rose into peaks.

I giggled. "Yes. Are you learning to love me as you loved Keshet?"

He responded with a long kiss.

Later, when I returned to my cleaning, I remembered Sigal's words and waited until long after I expected the women of Mamre to have drawn their water from the well before I went to get the water I needed for the evening.

Noah went into the village as he often did. I thought nothing of it. When he returned, he wrapped me in his arms. "I think you will stop having problems getting water."

I turned in his arms toward him. "What did you do?"

"I spoke to Zakai, the village leader. He agreed that the women are overstepping their bounds, claiming a right that isn't theirs." He bent to kiss me.

"I will see what happens tomorrow. I have all the water I need for today. Perhaps I will go tomorrow morning." I allowed my head to drop and look at the floor.

"You are uncomfortable still?" He gently took my chin and tilted my head up.

"They say such terrible things about me. I expected them. I am more than four hundred years younger than you."

"Ah. And four hundred years better practiced than all those other little boys." He kissed me again.

"I have learned to like being the wife of a four-hundred-year-old man," I tittered.

"You may change your mind in the next weeks," he said.

I looked into his eyes. "Why?"

"Most women become ill for a time after a babe is placed within them."

"I carry a child? How would you know?"

"I have had many years of experience seeing women after they first become with child." He grinned. "Besides, Jehovah told me you were with child."

"Oh! I cannot keep any secrets from you."

"You knew?" he asked.

"I wondered. I had a difficult time eating this morning."

Noah's grin grew. "We are to have a child already."

"And if it is not a son? Will you be angry with me?"

He kissed me again. "I have both sons and daughters. I will be happy with whatever Jehovah sends to us."

CHAPTER 5

Warning

I did not go early to get water the next morning. Noah teased me about it, but I could not bring myself to go face the unkind words the women would use.

After he almost pushed me out the door with my water jug, I walked down the streets toward the well, quivering inside.

My stomach hurt more than usual. Yes. It quivered from anxiety. Worse, it had been quivering and wanting to expel everything I ate from before I crawled out of bed.

If I had been less sick, I would have laughed. Noah's prediction of my sickness came faster than I expected.

Even though I arrived late enough that the other women should have been through with their gossiping, they sat around the well, waiting for me.

One woman stood and bowed toward me. The others followed her example. "You think you are so special. You have your husband talk to ours. We have no say in this. You can get water whenever you like. But we do not have to like you."

The hostile eyes warned me they were not happy to have been warned to change their ways.

I brought my fist to my chest in a sloppy salute and pushed past them. I ignored their stares that felt like someone had lit hot fires in their eyes and sent them blazing toward me.

I filled my water jar and set the water bucket back on the well. I picked up my jar and walked through them back toward my home. Their hot eyes focused on me all the way home.

"That is the last time I am doing that." I set my water jar on the floor in my kitchen and turned to stare at Noah.

"They allowed you to get water?" he asked.

"Yes. But they were angry that their husbands were brought into a woman's problem."

Noah's eyebrows crunched close together. "Brought into a woman's problem?"

"Homes and wells. Those are the domain of women. Women set the rules. Men do not."

Noah lifted his hands in front of him, in mock protection from imaginary fists. "I did not know."

"In all the years you were married before, you did not know there were women's domains, women's rules, and women's leaders who take responsibility for them?"

"Keshet never had problems she shared with me. She led the women for many years." He dropped his eyes. "I had no idea. I guess I made it worse for you?"

"Perhaps." I shrugged. "I am a big girl. I can figure this out. Thank you for trying. It shows me you care for me."

All of a sudden my stomach revolted. I clapped my hand over my mouth and rushed out the kitchen door. Everything in my stomach landed in the bushes.

Noah followed me out and rubbed my back until I stopped. "It happened faster than I expected. When did you bleed last?"

He led me into the house and poured me a cup of water. I drank the water and rinsed away the flavor of the sickness, counting back the weeks since my last bleeding time. "Six weeks."

"Six weeks?" Noah asked. "We were only married twelve weeks ago."

"You told Papa you would be able to give me children. Did you not expect to give me a child so soon?"

Noah grinned. "I hoped to give you a child soon. It came faster than I expected."

I clapped my hand to my mouth. Noah handed me a bowl. "It is easier to use this than to run outside every time."

I did not manage to clean or work on the blanket I started earlier that day. My stomach revolted too frequently. In the times when it did not, I sat with a cool, damp cloth over my eyes.

"Jehovah is always correct. It is good I came home early," Noah said, as he brought me a plate of flat bread and an apple he had cut up that evening.

"Would you question Jehovah?" I asked. I lifted my head from the back of the seat I sat in.

He shook his head. "No. When I was young, I would forget. It is hard to be given such great responsibility as a child."

"How old were you?"

"Grandpapa Methuselah came to me when I helped in the fields in my tenth year. He called me away from the others and asked me questions that confused me. He said he had been commanded by Jehovah to ordain me to the priesthood."

"At age ten?" I dropped the cloth and stared at him.

"Pretty tough for a ten-year-old boy. I never played and teased like my brothers before the ordination. When I sat in front of the family and Grandpapa set his hands on my head, I felt a weight fall onto me. It settled onto my head and filled my whole body. I have not yet lost that weight."

"When did you first hear from Jehovah?" I asked, leaning forward.

Noah closed his eyes. I watched multiple emotions cross his face.

"Grandpapa Methuselah and Papa both have asked me that question. I never had the courage to tell them the truth. I told them of a time sometime after Grandpapa ordained me. I kept the first experience close to my heart, telling no one."

I leaned back in my seat. "Do not tell me. Not if it will betray your trust with Jehovah."

Noah's eyes popped open. "You are willing to forgo hearing my experience?"

"Yes. I understand. Some things are given to us for our own use. Never to be shared with others. Some of the things Jehovah gives us can be shared with a few. Very few are to be shared with large numbers of people, or with all the world." I wiped my face with the damp cloth.

"You are the first to understand. Keshet did not understand. Grandpapa and Papa should have understood. They received their own messages and visions from Jehovah. Maybe because I was so young when I received the responsibility for teaching Jehovah's word, they thought they had a right to pry into my spiritual history."

"They do not." I set my hands in my lap. "No one has the right to pry into your life or even my life. Some things we are expected to keep to ourselves. I do not want you to share unless it is acceptable with Jehovah."

"You would do that?" Noah asked.

"I would."

"I have something I need to tell you. For now, it is for you and me. My Grandpapa Enoch received the warning, as I have. My papa and grandpapa know. No one is left on the earth who knows. I will share it with others when Jehovah tells me the time is right."

I straightened my back and stared at him. "What is it?"

"Jehovah has given me to know that he is angry with men. If they do not repent, he will wash the world clean of men."

"All of us?" I gasped.

"All but the few he chooses of men and animals will be destroyed. He will wash life from the earth and begin again."

"How is this something I should know?" I asked touching the spot where our tiny child lay.

"He will not destroy me or my family. He promised Enoch that when he washed the world clean, he would save his family. Grandpapa Methuselah told me I would be the one to carry man into the next world, a world away from the sin and wickedness of this one."

"And me?"

"Yes. I will take you with me. We will be protected. Jehovah told me that the life of man would be reduced to 120 years. Men will no longer live to the great age of Adam, or my grandpapa, or even me."

"Men and women must repent?"

"And be baptized. They must accept the words of Jehovah and obey them."

"Or he will destroy us all?"

"Almost all life." Noah leaned back in his seat. "It is sad to consider."

"Does that mean man has 120 years to repent?"

"I do not know. I only know that men's lives will be shortened."

~ ~ ~

I spent the next five weeks struggling to keep food inside me. I knew I needed to eat to help the child within me grow, but it became difficult when more than I liked found its way out.

I made a point to go for water only after the other women had returned to their homes. I did not have the energy to deal with them and the things they said to me.

After a week, I showed up at the same time as Sigal.

"Where have you been?" she asked after giving me a fast hug. "Ugh. You stink."

"I have been trying to keep the food I eat in my stomach," I said.

Her gaze questioned my illness.

"I am with child."

She grabbed me and gave me a bigger hug. "A baby? Already?"

"Yes. Already. And he is making me sick."

"Did you not know that I am a healer?" she asked.

"A healer? No. I did not know. But I am not ill. I carry a child."

"No. But you are being sick with your child. I could give you something for it." Sigal shook her head at me. "Did you not know that?"

"I have been too sick to even wonder if there is something to help me feel better." I rolled my lips inward and fought the nausea.

"I will return." Sigal left her jar with me and hurried back toward her home. I dropped the bucket into the well and pulled it up, full of water. As I dumped the water into my jar, Sigal raced back toward me. She carried a plant in a container in her hand.

"This will help," she said.

"What is it?"

"Peppermint. I see you are sick now. Take this." She pulled a leaf from the plant and handed it to me.

I took it, wondering what I should do with it.

"You chew it," Sigal said.

I put it in my mouth and chewed. It stopped the nausea almost immediately. "Oh." I said with a sigh.

"Take this plant. You can chew on a leaf or make a tea. You do not have to be sick to enjoy the tea. But, if you are sick, the tea will help."

I dropped the bucket back into the well. "I will get your water for you. You helped me. I will help you."

"You do not …"

"Yes. I do." I pulled on the rope, bringing back the bucket full of water.

Sigal set her jar close to the well where I could pour water into it.

I took the plant from Sigal. We picked up our water jars, and I lifted the peppermint plant, and carried them down the path until time to separate.

"Stay well," Sigal said. "If you need me, send someone."

I nodded and continued along my own path.

Noah had been called to preach in other lands. He had not been happy to leave, but he obeyed the call from Jehovah.

I entered the house, ready to enjoy the quiet and the lack of nausea.

Noah stood in the kitchen, waiting for me.

"You still avoid the women?" he asked.

I lifted a shoulder in a shrug. "It is easier this way. They allow me to draw water from the well when I arrive, but their laughter and crude jokes sting. I would rather wait. I have been too sick to face them."

"We are different from them," he whispered into my ear. "We were brought together by Jehovah."

Indignation filled me. "That does not protect me from their laughter and crude jokes. I will go get water when they are gone. I do not want to face them while I am sick with the baby."

He took me in his arms. "I would help, if I could."

"I know. Your prayers have lessened the sickness. I just met Sigal at the well. I did not know she is a healer. Did you know?"

"No. I did not know a healer lived in Mamre." He stepped back. "Is that why you have a plant in a pot?"

"Yes. It is peppermint. Sigal had me chew on one small leaf. It stopped the nausea. I struggle to understand how it works, but it does. She told me to brew a tea from the leaves."

Noah stroked his beard with one hand while keeping his other hand on my waist. "I think I have heard the peppermint will do that. I should have remembered. Your mama should have told you."

"I have not told Mama and Papa about the child yet. She can sometimes be as bad as the women of Mamre." I set the plant on the table where it could get some sunlight.

"Your papa is not much better. Between them, they could cause a plant to wither in the sunshine," Noah said with a grimace.

"Mama is not that bad," I said with a little laugh.

"No. Not that bad, but I understand why you would not want them to know yet."

"I will tell her after the child moves. By then, I will not be able to hide it."

"And by then, she will have found a reason to come visit. You cannot avoid her request for an invitation forever. We will have to visit your parents or invite them here before long." He sat in a chair and pulled me onto his lap.

"I would like to ignore them. But I am not being fair. Mama brought food and prepared a wonderful wedding meal for us."

"And she made certain everyone in the room knew it," Noah said. He ran his fingers through my hair, gently loosening the tangles.

"She is a good woman …"

"With a sharp tongue."

"I think she forgets that she speaks to people whose capacity to love can be damaged. She says whatever is on her mind, regardless of how it will hurt. In her mind, it is truth, and truth must be shared."

Noah worked on a difficult tangle, working to separate the hair without pulling. "You are probably correct. I have had discussions with others like her. Not all of them are women.

Some men have the same challenge. They do not know how to soften their words and still speak the truth."

"Do you have that problem? I have not heard you call others to repentance."

"Sometimes, I do. There are times when I must speak bluntly. The spirit of Jehovah will not allow me to soften my words."

"Does it ever help?" I asked.

"Not often. They become angry, usually. Sometimes they repent and obey for a short time. Rarely does it change them for long."

"I wondered. How else can you reach some of those with such hard hearts?" I leaned into his chest.

He shrugged. "I cannot reach them, even with harsh, blunt words. Some of these men are past hearing."

CHAPTER 6

Surprise

A few days later, some of Noah's grandsons appeared in my kitchen early in the morning, along with his three younger sons born to Keshet. Even the youngest, at only ten years old came.

I let them in and fed them. Noah paced around the space behind my kitchen door for a short time, then stabbed a stick into the earth.

"Dig here," he said.

The young men took their shovels and began to dig. Some of them laughed behind their hands, saying their grandpapa had lost his ability to think clearly. He would never find it.

I had no idea what what they were looking for. It surprised me that they would dig in back of the house. One grandson dug out a bush that grew too close to the hole they were digging and set it carefully aside to be planted later.

I returned to the house and retrieved my water jug. The women would be gone from the well and I could go and return without trouble from them.

When I returned, I poured some of the cool water into a pitcher. I took a cup and the pitcher outside. "Would any of you like a cool drink? It is hot out here."

The young men came to take the cup and drink cool water before returning to their work.

"What are you searching for?" I asked one of the young men.

"You do not know?" he answered.

I shook my head.

"Then we cannot tell you. I think Grandpapa would like to surprise you."

I watched them dig a while longer. They no longer grumbled behind their hands.

"Damp gravel!" one exclaimed.

"I thought he lost his ability to think clearly," another said.

"We were wrong."

I tried to push through to see what they saw, but one of the grandsons turned me back. "This is a surprise. You need to go inside and rest, Grandmama."

"I am not an old woman," I cried.

"No. You are not," Noah said, suddenly appearing at my elbow. "But you are with child, and I would like this to be a surprise. Shall we go inside out of the sun?"

I sighed. The grandsons would not allow me to see anything, so I led the way through the kitchen door. Noah led me all the way to the front of the house.

"Sit here," he said. "Be patient in waiting on me."

"That sounds like something …"

"The Lord said to me. Yes. Jehovah has told me to be patient more times than I can count. I am learning patience. I do not know how He can be so patient with these sons of men. They refuse to listen. They refuse to repent and be baptized."

I reached into the sewing basket at my feet and retrieved a tiny tunic. I found the bone needle and stabbed it through the material, stitching the last seams together. I held it up for Noah to see.

"Is that for our child?" he asked.

"It is. I have much to prepare before our child is born."

"You will get it completed, especially now that your nausea is better."

"Not better. Only under control. The peppermint tea stops it. How long will you be home before Jehovah calls you to teach again?" I folded the tiny tunic and set it in another basket.

"Not long enough." He gazed toward me. "Will you be upset if I must leave soon?"

"No. I knew of your responsibilities before we married. I have heard of your preaching throughout the land. Where will you go?" I dragged the sewing basket into my lap and searched through it.

"What are you looking for?" Noah asked.

"The pieces for another tunic."

"For a son?"

"Yes. You need a son. That is why you married me."

"But this may be a daughter."

I glanced up to stare at him. "A daughter? Jehovah would not do that to you?"

"He would not? All those young men digging up our garden are sons of my daughters. Daughters who chose to live among the sons of men, rather than find good men who listen to the commandments and obey."

"Are there many who do obey? I did not see many in my small village."

"True. The Destroyer has gained a hold on the hearts of men. He entices them away with tinkling brass and shining bits of metal. Everything he offers is shallow. None will withstand past this life."

"I thought gold is an eternal metal. It can be changed but not destroyed." I found the pieces I had been searching for and set them on the table next to me. I put the sewing basket on the floor once more.

"Yes. Gold is much like our souls. We will go through fires and change. After enough fire, all the impurities will be burned away. The goldsmith of our lives will pour out molten lives and souls into the mold of his choosing, and we will be His forever more."

"Goldsmith. I had not considered our lives in that way." I fingered the gold band he had placed on my finger on the day of our marriage. "Is that why you gave me this band?"

"That is one reason. And, it marks you as mine. No other honorable man will attempt to entice you into his home and his bed."

"A beautiful marking. I have seen the marks burned into the skins of cattle. I have heard that some slaves have marks burned into their skins to identify them as slaves. Those are permanent marks. I think I prefer to be marked by a gold band."

One of the young men hurried into the room and whispered into Noah's ear. He whispered something back, then nodded at the reply.

"I must go inspect your surprise. Sit here and work on our little one's tunic."

My hands fell to my lap and I watched him leave. What surprise was he creating for me from the dirt and mud in our back garden? I considered the puzzle while I returned to stabbing the needle through the edges of the fabric, stitching together the pieces.

Before he returned, I set aside the small garment and returned to the kitchen. I needed to provide these young men with a midday meal since they were working so hard for me.

I mixed flat bread and set it in the fire to cook. While it baked, I cut fruit and cheese and sliced meat from our dinner the night before. I set these on trays before pulling the loaves of bread from the fire. There would be food for Noah's grandsons and young sons.

~ ~ ~

"Mama Imma," his youngest son, Kalil, exclaimed after thanking me for preparing them food, "I thought Papa wanted us to dig to please you. I thought it would be futile. Who expects to dig a well of water so near a home?"

"Water?" I teased. Inside I gulped. They dug a well for me? "I did not know why your papa would have you come dig a hole in the ground. I thought you were planting flowers for me."

"Oh, Mama Imma," the young man giggled. "You knew he wanted to find water for you."

I did not, but I would not be the one to tell him that he had ruined his papa's surprise. "I did. I did not expect you to find water so soon. I have learned that if your grandpapa is determined, he will find a way."

"I did not know getting water was a problem for you. One of us could have brought water to you from the village well. I would gladly have done that." His face lit with a silly grin.

I touched his arm. "I can get my own water, thank you. I may be your mama now, but I am still young enough to collect my own water."

He tipped his head to the side and pulled wrinkles into his face. "Why would Papa want you to have a well closer to your kitchen?"

I inhaled a deep breath. "He wants me to stay closer to home where I will be safer," I replied. I did not want to admit that the women of Mamre had not accepted me or my marriage to Noah.

By dark, the young men had completed the project. Noah, not knowing Kalia had ruined his surprise, covered my eyes with a towel and led me out the kitchen door. Laughing, I allowed him to lead me.

I heard a splash. Water dripped on my toes. A damp cup pressed against my lips. I drank of the pure, cold water and gasped.

Noah pulled the towel from my eyes. "Your own well — with your own water. You will never again be forced to carry water from the community well."

I threw my arms around his neck. "Thank you! You do understand my needs."

"I promised I would try," he said, kissing me.

The young men giggled.

"What? She is my wife," Noah said to them. He kissed me again.

The next day, I dropped my new bucket into the well and heard it splash. I pulled the bucket up and tasted the sweet water before I poured it into my water jar. No more waiting for water. No more would I be forced to listen to the other women tell crude jokes about me,

I walked to Sigal's home after Noah left again to preach. She opened the door and stepped out as I reached her porch.

"Oh," she cried. "I did not expect you on my doorstep. How can I help you? Are you ill again?"

"No. I came to offer an alternative to waiting so long to get your water for the day."

Her eyes opened wide. "And how would you do that? I am not going to subject myself to those women and their rude behavior."

"Come with me. I will show you."

She pulled her door closed and walked with me. When we passed the turn toward the community well, Sigal touched my arm. "The well is this way."

"I know the community well is that way. Come with me."

We strolled down the path toward my home.

"How am I to get water this far away from the well?" she asked.

I led her around to the back of my home and opened the gate into the back. "Come in. You will see."

Sigal entered and took a few steps into our back garden while I pulled the gate closed. The bushes hid our new well. "What is here that I can get water?"

I pushed past her and led her around the bushes to the well.

Sigal gasped and dropped her water jar. "What is this? How did you get a well?"

"Noah."

"What did he do?"

"He called in his grandsons and sons and showed them where to dig. They dug deep enough to find clear, cool water. They did this yesterday."

I pushed the bucket into the well. I heard it splash, and felt the bucket weigh heavier, before I began to tug on the rope to pull it back up. Sigal pushed me away.

"I will do this. The water is for me. You should not have to draw my water."

I stood back and watched her pull the bucket up and pour the water into her water jar. She tasted the water.

"Better than the water at the community well. Where is Noah? I want to thank him. You deserved a safe place to get water."

I smiled. "Gone. He left this morning. He must preach repentance to all the world, or most of it. He will be back in a month. I knew he would be gone often when I married him."

"Will he stay home when it is your time to give birth to this child?"

I lifted a shoulder. "He says he will be home. I trust him to be here when I need him. I hope you are here to help me. Regardless, you are welcome to come get water from my well whenever you need it."

"You know I will be here to help you."

We visited for a short time, then Sigal left.

I returned to the house and set the warp on my loom to begin weaving a blanket for the baby.

CHAPTER 7

With Child

Noah returned in three weeks and felt the babe move within me before his call to preach took him away from me again.

Late one morning, not many days later, Mama and Papa came to visit. I still had not sent them a message telling them that I would be having a child. Mama stared at my growing stomach.

"Do you not think I should know these things?" Mama asked, a frown filled her face as she stood in my doorway. "How am I to know to plan to come help you when it is time?"

"How are you to know anyway?" I asked. "In my limited experience, babies decide to be born when they choose, not when a mama or a grandmama chooses."

Papa reddened and lifted a hand as if to slap me. "You should not speak to your mama like that."

"Perhaps not, but how do we know? Yes, I know. Children often come in about 40 weeks." I lifted a shoulder. "Some come much earlier, some come much later, and every time in between. What is important is that you and Mama know that you will have another grandchild."

Mama hugged me close. "May we come in?"

I stepped back. "Of course! Please come into my home. Noah should return in a day or so. He went north to teach the people there."

"Is he always gone from home?" Mama asked. "How did you ever get a child?"

I laughed. I refused to listen to her barbs. "He comes home often enough." I touched the roundness of my stomach as the babe kicked me.

"He must!" Papa chuckled and sat down. "Have you been healthy?"

I glanced toward the peppermint plant in the window. "Since my friend gave me a peppermint plant. Before then, I did not go far."

"Stomach sickness?" Mama asked. "If you had let me know of your condition, I would have warned you to get a peppermint plant."

I lifted a shoulder. "I could not send a message. I was too sick. Would you like a drink of cool water?"

"Yes," Papa said. He sat with his arms tightly folded across his belly.

"I would not want you to have to make an extra trip to the well," Mama said.

"I have water," I said.

I walked to the kitchen and poured a pitcher from the jar. I set in on a tray with three cups. Before I lifted it to take it into the sitting room, I glanced at the pot of soup I put on earlier for dinner. It would be enough for three.

I carried the tray with the water and cups back into the sitting room and set it on a low table near them. I poured each of them a cup of water and handed one to Papa. He grimaced as he took it. I gave one to Mama. She nodded her thanks and took a sip.

"This is cold water on a warm day. Did you draw this recently?" she asked.

I smiled. I knew she would notice. "Yes. I brought the water in as you knocked at my door."

Mama looked to the right and then to the left, as though she stood outside our door. "I did not see you along the path."

"No. I no longer go to the community well for my water. Noah asked his grandsons to dig a well for me in our back garden."

"You have a personal well?" Papa's frown deepened. "Why?"

I chewed on my lip. "Noah did not want me to walk so far to get water with the baby."

Mama stared into my eyes. "That may be true, but it is only half of the answer."

I blew out the air I held in my lungs. "The women of Mamre are unkind to me. They refused to allow me to draw water, even when everyone there had all the water their jars would hold. Noah came home one day and found me crying."

"He should have gone to the village leader. He would have spoken to their men," Papa announced. He set his cup back on the tray.

"More?" I asked.

He shook his head, no.

"Noah did."

Mama gasped.

"Even at his age, he had no understanding of women's laws. The well is controlled by the women. Men have no right to say anything about anything that happens at the well. After their husbands insisted that they allow me to draw water, they did, but their jests and unkindness increased." I rolled my lips inward. I had already told them more than I wanted to tell them.

"I can understand that. I would not be pleased to hear your papa try to tell me what I am to do or not do at the well." Mama's frown sunk almost as low as Papa's.

"I thought you would be happier that I have a well." I huffed out a breath.

"We are here for only a short time," Papa grumbled. "Your mama needed to know you are alive and well."

I lifted my lips into a false smile. "I am well and happy. Would you like to come inspect my little well?" I stood, expecting them to follow me from the room.

The young men had done a good job with our well. I knew there was little Papa could find fault with when he inspected it. He searched for something, but there was nothing he could fault.

"It is a small well," he said at last.

"Big enough for me and Noah. When we have children, it will be big enough for all of us. If I am the only one using it, the water will stay sweet and pure."

Mama dropped the bucket into the well. I heard it splash. She pulled on the rope until the bucket rose out of the well, full of cool water. Mama took the cup that sat on the edge of the well and dipped up a drink. She handed it to Papa.

Papa drank from it without saying a word. He handed the empty cup back to Mama. She dipped it into the bucket and drank the water.

"It is sweet and pure," she said.

We wandered through the garden. Mama commented on my roses and other flowers. Papa sat on a bench and pulled a narrow jar from his pocket. He opened it and drank from it. I smelled the alcohol in his drink. My lip quivered at the odor.

"What?" Papa growled. "It cools me. Would you like some?"

I shook my head. "No, Papa. I do not want any of your drink." His harsh laugh rung in my ears and in my memory.

While Papa sat in the garden, I went inside to mix flat bread. Mama joined me, sitting at the table to visit while I mixed the bread. We visited.

She shared the gossip from home. I listened. I had not wondered about the family since I came here. I spent my time working to keep the house clean and to weave blankets and sew little articles of clothing for my coming child.

Only one of my brothers or sisters had treated me well, Dodi. I asked about her.

"Oh, Dodi. She is to have another child. The child moved two weeks ago. When did you feel your child move?"

"He moved three weeks ago," I said. "Our little ones will be of a similar age."

"I do not know if I can come to help you with the birthing of your child. Dodi will need me."

"I will send you word. If you cannot come, I will understand," I said. "My friend, Sigal, should be here to help."

"I should be here to help with your first child."

"If you cannot come, I will be in good hands. Sigal is a healer."

~ ~ ~

Mama arrived a few spans before our first child came into this world. She cried when she saw a girl rather than a boy. Noah hugged me, grateful to have a living child. Mama shook her head.

"Your Noah does not know," she grumbled.

"He knows. He told me we need good women to marry our good sons. We are happy to have a child."

Mama shook her head. "You will want to have a son soon to keep him interested in you." Her voice lifted until it became harsh and strident.

"Mama," I cried, "we will have a son. Noah has been promised an honorable son. I do not fear. I trust in Jehovah."

Mama snorted. "Have you seen what is happening in the world outside this little village?"

"I have heard of the hatred and fighting. Noah tells me when he returns." I lowered my voice in opposition to her stridency.

"Your Papa has forgotten Jehovah. He drinks wine and other spirits through the day, sitting in a stupor while I do what I can to keep us alive. It is good your brothers help in the fields and share the crops with me. Some of our neighbors have sons working in their fields who do not share with their parents."

I gasped. "It is getting worse."

"Every day it is worse. Stay here in Mamre as long as you can. Stay safe from the ugliness that is out there."

"I will. Noah will keep me safe."

Mama left for home three days after Nava's birth, when my brother came to take her home.

Her leaving left us with a quiet home again. Even the occasional crying of the babe did not disturb our peaceful home as much as Mama had with her ordering Noah and his other younger sons around and banging in the kitchen as she cooked.

We sighed with relief after she left, enjoying the quiet.

"Where did you come from?" Noah asked me one afternoon soon after Mama left, as I sat with Nava in the sitting room. "You are nothing like your Mama."

"I watched her from when I was little. I hid in my room when she shouted at my brothers and sister. I cringed when she called my name. I knew the time would come when she would forget to be gentle."

"Did your mama ever hit you?" His face reddened.

"No. But she shouted at me enough it felt as if I had been slapped. I promised myself I would never shout. I would never treat others in a way that would frighten them as she frightened me." I glanced down at my little babe and touched her fuzzy, light hair. "I never want my children to fear me."

Noah leaned forward over us and kissed me. "That is why I noticed you. You spoke softly. You spoke the truth of what happened that day. You offered your sorrow on my behalf." He rolled his lips inward. "However, you never lifted your voice, never once made me think that this had happened because of something I may have done or expected from Keshet. I did not receive that same gift from your mama."

He took my hand and held it next to his face.

"I learned then how different you are from your mama. But you are so much younger than me. I never thought you would accept me as your husband. And I believed I had done all I could for this family." He leaned forward in his chair.

"Why did you finally come for me?" I asked.

"As I returned to my empty home from teaching one day, the boys were with their older sister, I was thinking about losing Keshet and the babe. I fell to my knees in prayer. 'Am I to always live alone?' I prayed. 'Is there a son for me to follow your commands as I follow them? Is there a woman who will have me?'"

"What happened?" I leaned forward to touch him.

"I heard a quiet voice speaking to me. It told me a young woman waited for me. I should search my memory. I would know which young woman would agree to be my wife." He took my hand in his.

"And?" I squeezed his hand.

"I searched my memories. There were only two young women who may have met my needs. You, and another who lived in Zikleg."

"This girl in Zikleg? Is she prettier than me?" I asked.

"When I went by her home on my next visit to that part of the world, she had been taken by a man of her village. He had a wife, but believed he deserved another. I saw her on my last journey. She looked sad and worn, with little children clinging to her skirts."

"Did you prefer her?" I do not know why I asked, but I needed to know.

"No, my love. I remembered your patience, your kindness, and the grief you felt at the loss of my Keshet. I knelt in prayer, asking Jehovah if you were the woman for me, or if another woman waited for me."

"And?" I asked once more.

"'Go to Lior where you will find the woman who will bear you sons who will obey my commands,'" he repeated. "I sent a message to your papa. He refused to come to me. I thought that to be the end. Until I rode my horse into the forest the day the rains began." He brought my hand to his lips. "Jehovah's voice filled my mind. 'Go to Lior. Your wife waits for you.' I knelt in prayer to thank Him, then mounted my horse. Before I arrived at your door, lightning slashed the air and thunder echoed. The heavens opened and rain gushed from the dark clouds."

"The rain that day came heavier than I can remember for the first day of rain."

"It did. And then, you opened your door. I knew you were the one Jehovah sent me to. I did not know if you would accept. You are young, and I am old. Would you have me?"

I smiled and pulled his hand to my lips. "And Jehovah gave me the answer that you would protect me."

"And you agreed. I am happier now, as an older man, married to you than I ever was with Keshet. She should have been the love of my life. I should continue to grieve for her. But I cannot. I have you, my Imma."

"And you have a daughter, not a son." I said.

"We will have sons together, you and I. Jehovah has promised it. I trust my God."

CHAPTER 8

Sons

Children came to our home about every six or seven years after Nava.

Mama did not arrive for the birth of our first son, Japeth. To be honest, I did not send a message requesting that she come soon enough. Sigal lived close. As a healer, she knew how to help bring a healthy child into the world as well or better than Mama.

Mama arrived three spans after Japeth's birth. She stayed, cooking and cleaning, and helping until my brother returned to take her home. Tears fell across little Nava's face as the wagon rolled out of sight.

I knelt beside her and put my arms around her. "You will be able to see Grandmama again."

She flinched. She began to sob.

I hugged her close. “What is it?” I said softly into her ear.

“Grandmama …” she stuck a finger into her mouth and sucked on it.

“Grandmama what?” I asked.

“Scares me.”

“Oh?” I lifted her onto my lap. “What about Grandmama scares you?”

“She shouts and stomps around the house. She told me to get her water. You told me to stay away from the well. I did not want to be in trouble. Whatever I did, I would be in trouble.”

“Did you get her the water?” I kissed her on the forehead.

Nava nodded and cringed. “She shouted at me.”

“Yes. Grandmama shouts sometimes. Sometimes too often.”

“Are you angry with me?” Nava lifted her blond curled head and gazed into my eyes with her blue eyes.

I shook my head. “No, Nava. You had no choice. When Grandmama insists and shouts, you must do as she demands, as long as it is not something we have taught you that Jehovah would not like.”

I hugged her close to me. “Do you know why I do not want you to get water?”

“The well is high. I had to climb on the edge to get the water from the bucket.” Nava’s lower lip trembled.

“Exactly. It is not safe for you to climb onto the edge of the well. I do not want you to fall in. When you are bigger, you can get water. Not yet.”

"Good. It scared me."

I remembered Nava's fears when our next child, another girl, came. I did not call for Mama until I could supervise my own kitchen.

Mama did not like that I did not call her. I knew she would not, but my children were more important.

I sent a message to tell Mama and Papa of the birth of another grandchild. I did not want to see her disappointment in me with the birth of another daughter each time five more daughters blessed our home.

Nava did not find a man who loved Jehovah to marry. One of the young men from a nearby village began to visit. We cried when she chose to become his wife. More because they asked their cult leader to perform the rite. She did not want the blessings offered by Jehovah.

By the time she married, our fifth daughter, Adiva, celebrated her first birthday. Japeth held her close to him after witnessing her marriage, begging the child to stay close to mama and papa and listen to all they taught.

He loved all his sisters and wanted them to be happy.

"Mama," he said to me one evening, "the only way to be happy is to obey Jehovah's commandments. How can Nava be happy if she separates herself from Jehovah?"

I hugged him. "I do not know. She will deceive herself into believing she is happy. I have seen other young women who have done the same thing. Later, they find the laughter and happiness was false."

Japeth began to travel with his papa to help him teach of Jehovah. In one of the small villages to the south, he found a young woman whose family still followed Jehovah. After three trips to her village, he brought Amina home to be his wife.

Noah blessed his marriage using the covenant words given to Adam so many years ago when Father married him to Eve. They are simple yet powerful words. Those who have left the fold of faith have tried to improve on them. Their attempts are clumsy and complicated. Many take away the love between the young couple, replacing it with subservience. How sad.

Although my stomach grew large with another daughter, I assisted Sigal as Amina gave birth to her first son.

"Watch what I do," Sigal told me. "I will not always be here to help with the birthing of your children."

"You will always be with me. You are my first and best friend," I said.

"No, dear friend," Sigal said. "My husband has determined that we can no longer live in Mamre. We are no longer welcome."

"You can continue to draw water from my well," I said.

"I know, but that is not the problem. The leather Ahaz tans is stinky. When the people of Mamre were kind, they did not mind. They used the leather and the vellum as much as any other. In the past years, however, they have become less willing to suffer the smell of tanning. We leave after your child is born."

"But who will help deliver my children if you leave?" I asked.

"I will teach Amina. She will have to help you. Or you can send a message to your mama."

"And if there are problems? Will Amina be able to help?" I asked.

"You may want to call for your mama sooner if you fear problems. I will be gone."

Japeth and Amina's child came easily into the world. They had a beautiful little son.

I, too, hoped for a son. I had yet another daughter. A week after Chiba's birth, Sigal and Ahaz loaded up his tools and her healing supplies, along with all the furniture that would fit on the wagon.

I hugged her close and cried. What would I do without my best friend?

~ ~ ~

"Are you certain you are not unhappy that we have so many daughters?" I asked as I waited for our next child to decide to be born.

"No, dear. I know that we will be given a son. Some of my grandparents were asked to wait more than a hundred years before an honorable son came to their lives. So far, we have Japeth, who loves Jehovah."

"And Eve and Adam had Abel. He did not survive."

"Japeth will survive." Noah hugged me close.

"Are you certain?" I asked.

"We can never be certain about anything." Noah replied.

"I hope this child is a boy. We need another son."

"Yes. We do. And Jehovah will give us another son." Noah's arms around me comforted me.

That child came within the next week, a boy. Mama came to help with the birthing. She cheered that we had another son. We named him Telemon.

We were happy to have another son. He grew strong in his early years. Japeth's son, Eidi, and Telemon were good friends. They played together and got into trouble together.

When my next child came, Telemon bounced beside the bed, excited to learn that he had a baby brother.

"A brother, Mama? I have a brother?" Telemon asked.

"Yes, Telemon. You have a brother. But look?" I lifted the blanket for him to see the babe. "He is tiny. He will not be able to play with you for a few months. You can talk to him and be gentle with him, but you cannot be rough like you are with Eidi."

Telemon frowned. "I have a brother, but I cannot play with him?"

"Not yet, son. Give him a few months. He will be ready to play with you soon."

Telemon kissed his brother on the cheek, then called his dog to go play with Eidi.

We named this little brother Shem. Noah stayed home for more than a month this time. He took our littlest son to the family altar, as he had each of our other children. He offered a sacrifice to Jehovah in gratitude for the birth of this son. He named him Shem, meaning conspicuous or important position or name.

With three sons, he hoped to have a son who would honor Jehovah and receive the blessings and responsibilities of the Priesthood. I knew of his desires. My joy came in a beautiful little son.

Mama and Papa could no longer criticize or berate my choice to marry the older Noah. I had given them six granddaughters and three grandsons. They could no longer complain about my marriage.

Shem grew quickly. He joined in Telemon's games with Eidi as soon as he could crawl behind him. He pulled himself to his feet and started running after his brother and cousin before his first birthday.

I became with child one more time near the end of three years after Shem's birth. This child would not be as easy to carry as the others. Within only five months of knowing I carried another child, I began to bleed. I feared I would lose the babe. Noah placed his hands on my head, calling on Jehovah to bless me and the coming child.

He sent for my sister, Dodi, to come help with our children. He did not leave to teach others during the time before the child's birth.

Each time I rose from my bed to return to my duties in my home, the bleeding would return. In order to keep the child safely within my womb, I had to lie in my bed or on a seat in the sitting room.

Noah sent a message to Sigal, begging her to come to help me heal. Only she had the knowledge to protect our child. We had heard of another healer. One who lived far away in Nod, the land of Cain and his children. Would Shamgar be able to come to me?

Noah considered it. He sent a message to Nod, hoping to find her. The messenger returned with sad news. Shamgar had left Nod years before. The messenger found her. But she had died a year before. She had trained other women, but none were available to come to us.

The struggle to stay down was reinforced when cramping and bleeding returned each time I attempted to return to my normal activity. Only my desire for a healthy child kept me in my bed.

By the time the Noah's messenger returned with the news of Shamgar's death, Sigal had come in time to assist me.

I had kept the child within my womb for nearly eight months when the familiar crushing pains of childbirth filled my stomach. Noah sent Telemon to run for Sigal.

She arrived quickly, but still too late to stop the early birth of our last son. Noah took him in his arms in less than a span after his birth, praying that Jehovah would bless this little son and named him Ham. He also set his hands on my head and called on Jehovah to bless me that I would live.

Telemon brought Shem in to see the baby as soon as Noah and Sigal allowed it.

"This is your little brother, Shem," Telemon announced. "He is tiny. Show him, Mama."

I lifted the blanket to show Shem Ham's tiny body.

"He is still tiny. He will not be able to play with you like you play with me and Eidi. Not yet. But soon. He will learn to crawl, then he will play with you. That will be in a few months. You can talk to him and be gentle with him. Do not be rough like we are." Telemon glanced up from Shem's eyes to mine. "Is that right, Mama?"

I beamed in pride with my small son. "You have it exactly right, son. Ham is especially little. He came sooner than he should have. He will need a little longer to grow than you or Shem needed. Give him time, though. He will be strong and ready to run and play sooner than we expect."

The boys gently kissed Ham's little head, then left my room, ready to run and play and be noisy.

Ham and I lived. It took me many days to regain my strength, and it took Ham many days to grow. His tiny body had little energy to even eat. Sigal helped me to express my milk. She dripped this milk into Ham's little mouth, helping him to eat, gain in size, and grow stronger.

Ham soon grew. He did not run behind his brother as soon as Shem, but he did not wait long. Soon after his first birthday, Ham followed behind his brothers, trying to do everything they did.

CHAPTER 9

Problems

Over the years after that, I never found myself with child again. I wondered why no more children were sent to our home. However, I found joy in the children and grandchildren Jehovah blessed us with, as well as Keshet's children and grandchildren. Our home seldom felt empty. Still, I wondered why I no longer could enjoy the sensation of a child's first movement within me or his kicking as he grew.

One evening, when Ham had gone to spend time with his brother, Japeth, in his home, and quiet filled our home, Noah set his hands on my head to offer me a blessing from Jehovah.

"You are blessed to be the mother of all nations, as was Mother Eve," he told me in that blessing. "Because of you and the children you have already borne, nations will come forth after the destruction. You have done enough in this time. You are to teach and bless the lives of these children. Help them to choose obedience to my laws. In this, you will be blessed."

More was given to me. But like Noah's first meeting with Jehovah, those things are sacred. They are for me, not for the world. I keep them in my heart, knowing that Jehovah loves and blesses me. Since then, I have done other things to help our children grow in knowledge of Jehovah.

Japeth built a home near ours. He wanted his children to experience the love and direction of his papa. Amina often joined me at our well. We watched our children run and play in the garden, safely fenced away from the dangers of the outside world.

In Mamre, we faced dangers, for many of the residents of our village only tolerated Noah. His family had settled in this land many hundred years earlier. In those early days, most of the people were baptized and followed the commandments of Jehovah.

Now, however, some only pretended to obey the laws of Jehovah. Most did not even attempt to pretend. Men searched for gold and other wealth. Some had gone beyond hiring servants to help in their homes, now purchasing slaves from other lands. Men took more than one wife, or kept women without marrying them.

Noah told me of warring men who rampaged through the lands, seeking women and children to be their slaves or to sell as slaves. Noah warned me and the others of his family to be extra careful when we left the safety of our walled-in home compound. The women in Mamre could be cruel, as well, as I had learned many years before when I first came to be Noah's wife.

One day, Noah returned home from teaching in the east, many weeks after he had promised he would return. His face and body had been bandaged from injuries he received when attacked by the giants of Coos.

"They hate me, Imma," Noah told me as I washed his wounds with nettle tea. "I entered their land to teach them of Jehovah and to offer them the opportunity to be baptized. They captured me and locked me in a dark storage house that had been emptied of all but rotten squash and tubers."

"Did they feed you?" I asked.

"No. I received a little water and no food."

"How did you survive?" I cut the leaf of an aloe plant to drip its thick fluid into the wound.

He quivered. "I was forced to scrounge through the rotted food to find tubers without rot to gnaw on. They kept me there for many days. In the dark, I could not count the days."

"How did you get out of the storehouse?"

"I prayed for Jehovah's blessings. I wanted to return to you. I did not want you to be left alone. Jehovah heard my plea. One evening, the giants dragged me from the storehouse. I knew from those who came for me that they planned to kill me."

I gasped.

"I did not fear, for I know that with Jehovah, I am able to do all that He requires."

"How did you escape?"

"With the blessings of Jehovah. As they brought me into the center of their village, a great cloud blew up. Winds blew, drowning out their words. They tied me to a pole in the middle of the village square and withdrew to their homes. They expected the lightning to strike and kill me."

"Did it?" I asked, washing a wound on his arm.

"It did. Rain and strong winds lashed at me. Lightning flashed. Thunder echoed. My lashings stretched in the moisture, and I managed to break my hands away from the ties. While the Coos giants hid in their homes, I dashed away from their village. I will never again attempt to try to teach those people of Jehovah."

I raised my eyebrows and widened my eyes. "Will Jehovah allow this? I thought you told me your assignment is to teach all people throughout the land of His commandments?"

Noah chewed on his beard. "I have discussed this with Jehovah. I have been given permission to leave these people. I am no longer required to attempt to teach the giants."

It took many weeks for his injuries to heal. I enjoyed having him home with us.

In those days, he directed our sons and grandsons to build walls around our homes, creating a safe home compound for us to live in.

"The time has come to protect you, my love," Noah told me when he told me of his plans to build the wall. "Wicked men devise plans to hurt you and my children. I cannot allow that to happen."

Telemon had married a woman from Mamre, Nirit. She had listened to him and Noah and said she trusted Jehovah. Their home had been included in the family compound.

Shem found Edna, a woman among the men who still honored and obeyed the laws of Jehovah. Noah performed the marriage ceremony for these two. The men of the family built a home for these two within our new compound.

A year later, Ham brought home a woman from Parin, Channa. She, like Nirit, spoke of loving the blessings and commands of Jehovah. However, I often wondered how much she cared for the things Noah taught in our family worship services. Her attention roved elsewhere during Sabbath worship.

~ ~ ~

During the next three years, I learned more about the women who married my younger three sons. At first, they were kind and gentle with me, willing to spend part of the day with me.

They worked with me in the garden, learning about feeding their family and finding plants that can be used to heal others. Japeth and Shem taught me about caring for the animals. Channa joined me in the barn when I went to help deliver a foal, talking about the beauty of the process. She loved horses and other baby animals.

All three joined me in weaving blankets for babies and others who needed them. We sat together stitching together new clothing and mending our torn clothes. I grew to love them. I do not know even now if Nirit and Channa really loved me or if they were good at pretending.

As time passed, they began to ask questions about Noah and me.

"Why would you marry a man so old?" Nirit would ask.

"What is it like to sleep with an ancient man?" Channa asked another day.

"Were there no young men who would have you?"

"Did your papa sell you to Noah?"

At their first questions, I spluttered, trying to answer them, though their questions were rude. Later, I turned and pretended to not hear. My age, a little more than one hundred years, allowed me to feint missing their snide comments.

They stopped coming to visit me as often. They seldom came to help in the garden. Channa stopped joining me in working with the animals. Nirit no longer helped with weaving. I missed them.

Though they professed to believe in Jehovah and obey his commands, they slipped away every month or two during the full moon. I saw them slip away on nights when both Telemon and Ham were off teaching the words of Jehovah with Noah. Neither of the women had children yet, and they spent too much time together.

Generally, being together would be good, but for these two young women, I saw a problem. After their visits away from the compound, their attitudes toward the others became … ugly. Their taunts began as small jibes about our activities. Each time they left, the taunts and jibes became more pointed.

They withdrew from the family more each time they left for their secret meetings.

I asked Noah what to do about these wives of our sons. As a younger woman, I would have asked them about their activities. I did not want to cause problems with their husbands, my sons. However, I feared they would cause greater problems for Telemon and Ham.

CHAPTER 10

She is Gone

One day Nirit left and did not return. Telemon searched through Mamre for his wife. He forced his way into homes whose occupants did not want him to search. He did not find her.

After searching every home, and after two weeks of looking, one of the young women in the village told him where she went.

"Mama," he cried to me that afternoon. "She has been visiting the cult of Asherath. Anna says Nirit left with one of the priests. She did not tell me she planned to leave."

"What would you have done if you knew?" I asked. I sat at the table, cleaning vegetables for dinner.

"Kept her home with me. Locked her up. I do not know. I do not want to lose my wife."

"Even when we are taught, we should allow others to make their own choices? Would you have kept her with you?" I peeled some tubers.

"I would have treated her better. I would have …"

"There is little you could do about her choices," I said. "She has the right to make her choices. I watched her leave almost every month when you were gone. She leaves when there is a full moon. Did you know?"

"I did … not. I suspected she may be leaving."

I got up and retrieved another tuber. Telemon would be joining us for dinner. "Your papa suggested to me that you may know. He would not allow me to share with you. I saw Nirit leave or return almost every month. She sometimes left even on the weeks when you were home."

"How could I miss it? I noticed she had left. She said she went to the well early. I believed her."

"Which well would she go to?" I pulled out my knife and began to cut the tubers into a pot.

"That is what made me wonder. Your well is close. She could get water any time of the day or night she needed it. Yet, she suggested she needed to go early to the community well.

"If she wanted to join the other young women in gossiping, she would have wanted to go after the sun had risen. Not in the middle of the night."

"As I suspected. I wanted to believe what she said to me. I love her, Mama. What am I to do?"

"I do not know. If she is gone from Mamre, it could be a problem. Where did Anna say she may have gone with the cult priest?"

Telemon wiped away the tears that began to drip from his nose again. "They went south. Anna suggested they were going far to the south."

"Far to the south? And she has been gone for several days already." I began to chop up carrots and handed one to him.

"I am going to go after her. She will stop somewhere. I will find her."

"Do not go until you speak to your papa. He will give you assistance."

Telemon stood to pace around the kitchen. "Papa left to teach in the north. He went the opposite direction of where Nirit went. I cannot wait for him. I must leave."

"Your papa has not left yet. He will be here for dinner. Join us for dinner. Papa can help your search."

"I will pack my things. I will be ready to leave after I speak with Papa. I will return." Telemon stomped out the back door.

My stomach roiled. I feared he would not find his wife. I feared he would. I feared what he would do if he did. Would he do something that would break Jehovah's laws?

Noah came into the kitchen later. "Telemon is upset about his wife. She left him," I said.

"I know. I feared she would. What is he going to do?"

"Rescue her. He believes the priest took her without her permission."

"That is not good."

"Do you believe she was taken?"

Noah shook his head. "I do not know. Not when you tell me you saw her leaving home when Telemon was gone. I suspect it was her choice to leave." He poured a cup of water from the pitcher on the counter.

"I do, as well. I should have told Telemon."

"No," Noah said. He drank the cup full of water, then refilled it before sitting at the table.

I mixed a flat bread for dinner as we spoke together. "I should tell Ham."

"Perhaps. Channa may have had the opportunity to leave with Nirit. She did not leave."

"I pray she will not choose to leave us. I love her, though I have not appreciated the way she has treated me in the last few months."

"She has been influenced by the cult priest. I hope Channa is not being influenced the same way." Noah traced the lines of the wood in the table.

"What can we do?" I held my flour-covered hands in the air and dropped into a chair across from Noah.

"Pray for Nirit. Hope she changes her mind and comes home."

"Is there nothing more we can do?"

"Telemon would want to gather his brothers and nephews to follow her and bring her home. I do not believe it would help."

"What do you suspect?" I asked.

“I do not want to say.”

“Tell me. I would not want to think the worst of Nirit. I do love her.” I set my elbows on the table and leaned forward.

“I fear they have taken her as a sacrifice to their god.”

“He would accept the sacrifice of a human?”

“Yes. Especially when that human is the wife of one of my sons. Many people hate me.”

“Would they carry that hatred to our sons and their wives? To … to me?” I touched my chest with hands covered in flour.

“They may. Especially the cult priests. They are disturbed by the truths of Jehovah.”

Noah leaned forward and kissed me on the nose. “This is why I ask you to stay close to home, within our compound unless you have one or more of our sons or grandsons with you.”

“I knew there were problems …”

“I did not want to frighten you.”

~ ~ ~

Telemon left before we ate dinner. He took flat bread with him, not wanting to stop to eat. One of Noah’s grandsons went with him.

“I must rescue her, Mama, Papa. I do not want to live the rest of my life thinking I could have done something for her if I had gone. I cannot stay here. Even if she left on her own. I must know.”

“You know you may find her happily a part of their cult?” Noah asked. “She may even have been taken to be sacrificed.”

"Even if she left with them willingly?" Telemon asked.

"It is possible. We do not know why they enticed her to leave with them. We only know that she has changed in the past few months."

Telemon hung his head. "I know. She may have left because she chose to leave … or she may have been enticed away. I must find out for myself. I could not live with myself if I ever learned I could have saved her."

He kissed me on the cheek and took his papa's arm and hugged him. "I must go now. I must hurry to find Nirit. I love her. I must save her."

He rushed out our door.

Ham came into our kitchen with Channa not more than two spans after his brother rushed from the compound.

"Mama, Papa," he said. "We have good news to share with you."

They sat at the table with us.

"Would you like some of this fruit while you share?" I asked.

They agreed. I dished some into a bowl for them.

"Now, what is your good news? We could use some of that," Noah asked.

"We are…" Ham started

"I am having a baby!" Channa finished.

Noah and I whooped with joy. We jumped up and gave them each hugs.

"When?" I asked.

“I felt him move this morning,” Channa said. “It has been about seventeen weeks since I bled last, if that helps.”

I calculated the weeks until her child would be due to come. “So, in about twenty-five weeks. That means he should be here about harvest time.”

“That is what I thought,” Channa said with a smile.

“Have you prepared anything for the babe yet? Blankets? Clothing? Tunics?” I picked up my spoon to eat the last of my berries.

Channa waved her spoon around. “Not yet. I have not wanted to do anything that would tell others of my condition. Not until today. Now, however …” she pulled her dress around her stomach showing a bump, “I will not be able to keep it a secret much longer.”

“I will start a blanket tomorrow. I love to weave blankets for babes.”

Noah and Ham stared at us and shook their heads.

“The things that excite women,” Ham said, chuckling.

“Let them talk. When the child is born, you will be happy they do what they must now,” Noah said with a chuckle.

Channa and I put our heads together, talking about babies and making things for them. Noah and Ham spoke about men’s things.

Ham’s words settled into my ears. “…Telemon running around this afternoon with his pack. He left suddenly with Dao. Do you know what is happening?”

I jerked my head toward the men. Noah’s eyes met mine. He raised his eyebrows. I shrugged.

Noah nodded and turned to Ham. “Yes. We know.”

“And?” Ham asked.

Channa focused on Noah.

“Nirit went missing earlier. You may not have noticed,” Noah said.

“How could we miss it? He was wild with grief,” Ham said.

“He searched in our home for her,” Channa said folding her arms across her baby bump.

“What is different about today?” Ham asked.

“Anna told him that Nirit went with the cult priest of Asherath. He left with Dao to find and rescue her.”

“If she left with the priest, she left by her own choice. She has been talking about it with me,” Channa said.

“And you did not think to tell me or Telemon?” Ham asked.

She shrugged. “It is her business. Not mine. I am not going to share with him. I thought she would send a message to him.”

Ham stared at his wife. “Would you tell me if you planned to leave?”

She grinned at him and allowed her eyelashes to close and open rapidly. “Why would I do that? You would do like Telemon and chase after me. It would destroy all the fun.”

“Channa?” Ham’s voice rose in pitch and volume.

“I tease you. I will not leave you. The cult priests would not take me now, anyway. I carry your child.”

My eyes met Noah's once more. A knowing passed between us.

"It would have been a kindness for Nirit to have left a message for Telemon," I said. "He is certain she was taken against her will." I dropped my eyes to the table in front of me. "I would want to know."

Noah took my hand. "As would I. It hurts when one you love leaves with no warning, no message, and no hope they will return."

"I am not leaving you, my love," I said, lifting my eyes to his. "You are stuck with me."

"Good," he whispered and kissed the back of my hand.

Ham and Channa left soon after that. I could see Ham's unhappiness at Channa's response to his need to know. He, too, would want a message.

"Are you certain Nirit did not leave Telemon a message?" I asked Noah.

"She may have. Her actions may have been a warning. He has complained that she has not been as loving lately. Perhaps that is why he is so wild to find and rescue her. He needs to prove to himself and her that his love is enough for her."

"I hope he finds her, and she comes home with him," I said.

Noah tapped his fingers on the tabletop. "I hope he finds her before it is too late."

We did not see Telemon again.

CHAPTER 11

Channa's Child

Channa returned to visit more often after the night Nirit left. We wove blankets and sewed little things for the babe to wear. Once more, a bond of love developed between Channa and me.

We began to watch for Telemon to return to his home. One morning his door swung wide, allowing the wind to blow through the house.

Noah had left again. He felt driven to teach everyone he could.

I took my broom with me to close the door. A broom did not give me much protection, but I could hit someone if they tried to hurt me. Channa met me as I neared Telemon's door.

"Who do you think has been here?" she asked.

"Telemon? Nirit? I do not know. Our walls are high, and our gates are locked at night. How would a stranger come in?"

I led the way into the house. We searched in all the rooms. No one responded to our calls. No one stepped into the room with us. Telemon's home was empty. It even felt empty.

I swept away the dust that had accumulated on the floor and blown in by the wind while Channa dusted the tables and chairs. Telemon had left dishes in the sink. Water remained in the water jar, so we washed the dishes and put them in the cupboards.

"I miss Nirit," Channa said as we pulled the door to Telemon's home closed behind us.

"She was your friend. I hope Telemon finds her and brings her home."

"I do, as well. I do not think she will return willingly."

I raised my eyebrows. "Oh. Why?"

Channa lifted a shoulder in a shrug. "She left for a reason. Unless that reason is resolved, she will not return."

We parted at the path to her home. I went to the vegetable garden to dig the weeds from it and see what had ripened to eat. She returned to work on some tunics for her coming child.

Ham stayed home with Channa more often, even though Noah asked him to travel with him. I believe Ham feared his wife would leave as Telemon's had. Instead, Noah took Japeth and Shem with him, leaving Ham to lead the grandsons to protect us in our compound.

Recently, armies had marched past Mamre on their way to attack other cities and villages. We stood quietly on the top of our wall watching them march past us. I thanked Jehovah for our walls.

We received a protection greater than the walls, for the armies who passed would sometimes stop and force the young men of Mamre to join them in their war making. None attempted to force those who lived within our compound.

Ham argued that he did not know how to fight against an enemy determined to take us. Noah reminded him that Jehovah protected us, our families, and our homes. They were there as a visible barrier between those who would want to hurt our families and us.

Channa trembled as she stood on the wall beside me, one day while she could still climb the ladder. "They will see us," she whispered.

"They do not even know we are here," I whispered back. "They march with their eyes forward, not looking toward us or our walls."

"How does that happen?" she asked.

"Their eyes are blinded by Jehovah. Our God protects us as no other god can."

"Are you certain?" Channa asked.

"Definitely. I feel his presence here with us. Do you not?"

Channa rolled her eyes up. "Perhaps… I feel something… Maybe."

I set my hand on her hand that rested on the wall. "I feel a warmth in my chest, here." My other hand moved to my chest.

"A warmth?" Her face twisted, seeking to feel the warmth. Her other hand moved to her chest. "Here?"

"Yes. Some feel His presence in other ways. For me, it is a warmth."

She sighed. "I must feel it in another way."

"Perhaps."

The men marched on past us for many spans. After less than a span, Channa stepped down the ladder. I stood only a short time longer before I, too, climbed to the ground and returned to my garden.

The armies passed us often after that. Never did their eyes turn toward our walls. None of them pounded on our gates demanding that our sons should join them in their search for riches and wealth. The men in the armies no longer desired to work to obtain wealth. They planned to attack others and take the wealth their enemies had worked hard to earn.

Noah told me too many of the young and even older men had been entrapped by the Destroyer in his web of lies. They believed that if they wanted something, and another man or people had it, they had every right to take it from him, if they were strong enough to do so.

Before Channa's babe came, he frequently told me of coming across angry men who wanted to take from others. They gathered in these armies to attack and kill those they decided were enemies.

Many times, Noah was warned to hide in a cave, or behind a tree, or a boulder. Each time, the enemy passed by without seeing him. Since Noah had announced Jehovah's plan to destroy all life on earth, men sought to kill him.

I could only pray each night and morning that my Noah would be protected and trust Jehovah.

~ ~ ~

Ham ran into our home late one evening near harvest time with the news that Channa's pains had begun. I gathered the supplies I needed to help her give birth to her child and left to help.

Though her waters broke and pains gripped her, the child refused to enter the birthing canal. Channa worked hard trying to push the babe from within her until exhaustion overwhelmed her.

She began to burn. We mopped her face and body with cool water. I gave her a cool tea of the willow bark. Nothing stopped the burning.

Two days later, the child still would not move. I had done everything I could think of. Amina assisted me, pushing on Channa's stomach. I reached my hand up into her, seeking the babe. I found its bottom.

Other babies had been successfully and healthily born bottom first. Why was this child struggling?

Noah and Ham entered the birthing room. Channa lay on the bed weak and unable to move. The men lay their hands on her head and called on Jehovah to bless me and Amina to know the right thing to do to help the child come into the world. They prayed that both the mama and the child would be able to regain the strength they had lost in this birthing process.

Then, Noah said something that tore at my soul. "Channa, if your faith is strong, and if your Father in Heaven will allow it, you will come through this healthy and knowing that Father is God, and that His Son, Jehovah, will guard and protect you. All these things I promise you, if Father and Jehovah see your faith and the purity of your soul."

I had heard her questions. I had heard her begging Ham to leave Mamre and his parents. I saw her laughing with the other young people.

"The earth is a big place. How can it be covered with water?" She had jested. Seeing me, she had blushed and turned away.

Another day, I heard her say, "If it rains, we can climb a tree, or run to the mountains."

I overheard her say another time, "We will be safe. I do not believe there will be a flood that will destroy all life."

If her life and the life of her child depended on her faith, I feared for her.

I could not stop her burning.

Jehovah, bless this woman whom my son loves. Protect her and the life of her child. Cool them. Help the child to be born.

All that day and the next, I prayed for Channa and her babe and for Ham, who would be devastated if we lost her.

She grew weaker. The pains lessened and nearly stopped. I did not want to lose her to the burning.

I remembered another mama and another child, many years earlier. When Noah insisted I rest a bit, I could see the memory of her on his face. Keshet had been able to push the child out of her womb. But she had weakened and died.

Finally, the squeezing pains returned. Channa found the strength somewhere to push, and the little boy entered the world. His little blue face warned me that if we did not work fast, we would lose him as we had lost Keshet's child.

Amina did all she could to help him breathe. She cleaned out his mouth and held him by the heels. She spanked his little bottom. He did not breathe.

She bent over the boy and breathed into his mouth. From my place at Channa's feet, I saw the little chest rise and fall. Without her assistance, it did not rise again.

Amina worked on the babe, encouraging him to live, encouraging him to breathe while I spoke the words I heard my mama say so many years ago. "Fight to live. It is not your time!"

Channa's small body shuddered. She did not move again.

"Mama Imma," Amina cried. "The child does not breathe on his own."

I joined Amina beside the babe in time to see his face soften. "He will not live. He joins his mama in life with Father and Jehovah."

Amina cried out. "Live! You must live!"

I took her in my arms and held her close, allowing her tears to drench my shoulder. When she regained some control, I held her away from me.

“I have felt this pain. Many years ago, before I married Noah. Sometimes, children do not survive childbirth. Sometimes mamas do not survive.”

“But Ham loved her so much. Noah gave her a blessing to live.”

“If she had faith.”

“You think she did not have faith?” Amina stared at me.

I lifted a shoulder. I would not judge the woman. Not now. Her death seemed to do that for me.

CHAPTER 12

Ham's Grief

Ham's grief filled him. He would no longer join the other men in standing guard over our home compound. He refused to join his papa on his journeys to seek honorable men and women who would repent and be baptized.

Ham stayed in his bed for days. When he finally crawled from it, he stunk. His self-pity did not allow him to smell nor see that his beard had grown shabby.

I filled a huge tub with water and set it in the garden near the well. I convinced Noah, Japeth, and Shem to bring him to me. They found Ham sitting in front of a window, staring. They surrounded him and picked him up.

I could hear Ham's shout outside the garden. *Good. They have him.*

He kicked and shouted and fought to escape their grasp, but the three men were stronger than Ham. They brought him into the garden.

"Where would you like him, Mama?" Shem rumbled with a frown.

I pointed to the tub. "There."

The men carried the kicking and fighting man to the tub and dropped him in, clothing and all.

Ham yelped. He stood, shivering and clutching his arms.

"You refused to bathe and clean yourself up. I am treating you like the child you have become," I said with a stern growl.

"But Channa … my son …" he mewled.

"Are gone. More certainly than Nirit is gone," I said. "They are gone from this life. Jehovah promises you can be together again if you have done all you can to live in his presence again."

Ham stopped squalling and stared at his papa. "Is this true?"

"That is what Adam taught us. I have taught it many times. Were you listening?" Noah said.

"I think I forgot."

"Time to remember the things of Jehovah if you are to be a man of God."

Ham sat in the cold water. "Man of God. Me? What of Channa and the baby?"

"I do not know about Channa," Noah said. "Your son had no chance to do more than breathe one breath. He will be yours. If you live worthy to return to Father's presence."

Ham sat in the water, thinking. "Mama, can I have some warm water? I stink. I need to wash this off me."

I nodded and beckoned for Shem to follow me. He lifted a large kettle from the fire. It steamed with hot water.

"Will this burn him?" Shem asked.

"Not if he moves in time," I replied.

Shem carried the kettle through the kitchen door and into the garden.

"You may want to stand," I said. "The water is quite warm."

Ham had pulled most of his clothing off. He stared at me. "I am … I am naked."

"And I have seen your naked body since you were a tiny child. Stand and turn around or burn or freeze."

Ham stood and turned. I directed the pouring of the hot water into the tub.

"He will need more water before he is finished," I said. "If you would assist him with that, please, Shem?"

Shem giggled. "I would be happy to assist Ham, Mama."

"Noah, Japeth. Ham and Shem can get this done. We are no longer needed here." I spun on my heel and marched from the garden with Noah and Japeth behind me, giggling as they walked.

A span later, Shem entered the house. "Mama, Papa, may I present my brother and your son, Ham. I believe he is more presentable now."

I looked up from my mending. Ham's beard had been trimmed, his hair cleaned, and he wore fresh, clean clothing.

"That is what my son should look like," I said.

"You look more like a man of God," Noah added.

"I feel better on the outside. What do I do about the emptiness inside?"

Noah took him into his study. I went out to the garden to clear up the tub and the water. My actions allowed my husband and son to have time alone, time to discuss Ham's sorrow, and time to speak with Jehovah about Ham's future.

I knew that Noah had prayed about Ham and his sorrow many times. I suspected he had heard from Jehovah in the time Ham had grieved in his bed. I respected them and the covenants made between them.

I drained the tub and hung it on the peg before returning to the house. Rather than returning to my mending in the sitting room near Noah's office, I stayed in the kitchen preparing the evening meal.

Almost a span later, Noah and Ham found their way into the kitchen.

"Are you feeling better?" I asked Ham.

"I know that things happen for a reason," Ham said. He stood in the doorway to the kitchen watching me cook. "I have not reconciled myself to the loss of my family. However, I will no longer lie in bed and sorrow. I will do what I can to help the family. I will join those who guard our compound. I will help in the fields. I am not yet ready to travel with Papa."

Noah sat in a chair at the table and nodded for Ham to join him. "You must serve willingly. Your testimony of the goodness of Jehovah must be honest. Stay here helping the family until you are ready to speak your testimony of the goodness of Jehovah."

Ham sighed and sat in the chair. "I know that now. I have been selfish, lying in my bed crying about my lost wife and child. But my sorrow continues. I do not know how to overcome this grief."

"I have found work does a lot to assist in the overcoming of grief and sorrow," I said, turning from the fire to gaze into Ham's eyes. "Work and serving others."

Ham lifted a corner of his mouth. "Papa said the same thing. Did you discuss this before you sent Japeth and Shem to get me?"

"We discussed many things," Noah said. "However, we did not discuss what to say to you. We know that the spirit of Jehovah will direct our words when we seek to do His will."

"We did not say those words to each other when discussing you and your problem," I said. "Much of the time we think alike. We have lived together for many years."

"Lived together?" Ham asked. "Papa has traveled away from home for more than half the time since I can remember. When did you manage to think alike?"

I stared at Noah.

He smiled back at me.

I felt the laughter in his mind.

"I have wondered the same thing," I said with a giggle. "From early in our life together, I have connected with your papa and he with me. It surprises me that we would be as connected as we are."

Ham shook his head. "One day, if I am blessed, I will have a woman with whom I can connect and communicate like you two do."

"I hope you do," Noah said.

~ ~ ~

Ham honored his word to his papa for about five months. He took his turn with the guards who guarded the walls of our compound, separating us from the rest of Mamre. He went out to the fields most of the other days, planting, hoeing, watering, and harvesting the grains and vegetables that would feed us through the rain times.

He moved from his own home into his old room in our house, finding comfort in the safe surroundings. Noah spent much of that time of heat away, preaching and trying to teach repentance and baptism.

One morning, shortly after his papa and brothers left to teach, Ham entered my kitchen with a small frown. He carried a travel pack and his hunting weapons.

"You look like you plan to go for a hunt," I said, stirring the grains for our morning meal.

"Something like that," he said, dropping his pack on the floor beside his chair. He plopped into his seat. "I have to clear my mind. As much as I have worked hard here in

Mamre, both in the fields and guarding the walls, as much as I have served others, I continue to struggle with Channa's death. Why would she be taken from me?"

"And what do you plan to do to resolve your problem?" I asked, spooning the grains into a bowl for him.

"I plan to go hike into the forest for a short time. I should not be long. I am compelled to make a short journey."

"Do you have food to take with you?" I considered the number of travel bars I had in my storage.

"I have some. If you have a few travel bars, I would like to take some of them. I can hunt … I think."

"You know how to hunt. You are an excellent hunter." I brought our bowls to the table and sat beside him.

"I know how. I am a good hunter. I do not know that I am currently able to kill another living being." Ham's eyes focused on his bowl of grains. He picked up a spoon and began to eat.

I nodded. It would be hard.

After eating, I retrieved the last of the travel bars and some dried meat and fruit from my storage cupboard and gave them to my son. He tucked the bars and dried food into his pack. He put his arms around me.

"Be safe, Mama. I will return when I can."

"You be careful. Do not allow the angry men to find you and force you to battle for them. Your papa is depending on you to go with him to teach."

"I know, Mama. I must make this journey. I believe I will be ready to travel with Papa again when I return. This must be done." His face showed an earnestness I had not seen for many months, perhaps more than a year.

"I will tell your papa. He probably knows that you are going to journey. Where do you plan to travel?"

He shrugged. "East. All I know is east."

"Be extra careful. I have heard of men seeking to battle others in the east."

"I will, Mama. I do not desire to lose my freedom or my life. I want to find my faith once more."

I hugged him tight for a long breath. "Come back to us, Ham. We will miss you."

"I will, Mama." He picked up his pack and slung it across his back, tucking his weapons into the places he had prepared for them. He then kissed me on the cheek and marched out our front door.

I stood in the door watching him walk through our compound and out the gate. After the gate closed and he was gone, I returned to my kitchen to clear away the dishes from our meal and started food for my dinner.

I kept myself busy for the next days until I again became familiar with life alone in my home. I missed Ham. I always missed Noah. In my morning and evening prayers I expressed my concerns for my husband and sons. Each time, I asked Jehovah to keep them safe.

The destroyer knew his time in this era was limited. He fought to stop Father's plan, as he had from the time Eve and Adam lived in the garden and he offered them the fruit Father had told them not to eat. He would do what he could to destroy Father's plans now. He would fail, as he always failed.

I remembered a discussion I had with Noah years before. I had asked why Father and Jehovah allowed men to do evil.

"Do you not remember what you have been taught?" he asked me.

"About the Destroyer?"

"Yes. He has been given freedom to try to entice all the children of Adam from their belief in Father and Jehovah."

"I understand that. We have been given the great gift of choice, even if we choose to disobey, as Nava and so many of our other children have."

"Yes. And as our children and other children of men who once believed and trusted in Jehovah's words choose to disobey, the Destroyer believes he has won."

"Has he not? In our family he has won over so many of our children." I gazed into Noah's eyes, determined to understand.

"He believes he has." Noah shrugged. "How can he not believe such a thing when so many of the children of men have had no opportunity to hear and understand the words of truth and joy?"

"But you spend so much time away, teaching them."

"I can only teach those who choose to listen. When I go into a village, the village leaders often refuse to allow me to stay and teach."

"I did not know."

"No. I do not share with you the many times I have been turned away at city gates or by village leaders. I must continue onward for Jehovah has commanded me to call all the men and women of this earth to repentance and call on them to be baptized."

"How can they refuse the love of Jehovah?" Sadness filled my heart as I thought of all those women who could not turn to the one who would hear and answer their prayers.

"The Destroyer offers them cult gods with complicated rites and bloody sacrifices. He feeds their greed and pride. He teaches them to deny the miracles of life."

"How can they not see the simple miracles of birth, of a child or an animal, or the blossoming of a flower?"

"Or even the miracle of each morning or sunshine after the rains? I cannot answer you that. I do not know beyond knowing that the Destroyer has led them to believe there are no miracles."

"And the miracles of the Priesthood of Jehovah?" I asked.

"Those are denied, completely and absolutely. Violence and hatred have overcome the lives of most men and many of the women."

I understood Father's sorrow and grief at the wickedness of men. How much time did we have before he destroyed the earth?

CHAPTER 13

He Returns

Edna found me one afternoon, considering the warnings given to Noah as I wove a new blanket. "I have come to ask you a question," she said.

I looked up from my weaving. "Oh? What would you like to ask?"

"How do I tell Shem that I carry his child?"

My hands dropped the fibers as I leapt to my feet. "Congratulations! I had begun to wonder."

"How did you know?" Edna accepted my joyful embrace.

"I did not know for certain. I only suspected. You have been sick lately."

"I have. Shem would already suspect if he had not been with Papa Noah for the last month."

"They will return soon. I expect them within the next week. Shem will be happy and excited."

"He will. How did you tell Noah that Shem would be coming?" Edna walked with me to the sitting room.

I thought back. It had been a long time since Shem's birth as I sat down. "Noah knew before me. Every time I carried a child, he would tell me."

"How did he know?" She shook her head.

"I never did understand how he managed to know before me. But he did."

"I want to tell Shem in a different way. Do something more than tell him we are going to be parents."

"Do you have anything made for an infant? A tiny blanket, a little sleep robe, or a tiny dress?" I leaned forward toward her.

"I have a tiny tunic I made before we were married. I made it for a sister who lost her child before it was born." Edna frowned. "It is a beautiful little tunic."

"That would be a good way to share with him. Tell him you will have a use for the tunic soon." I leaned back in my chair.

"That would work. Or I could be making another and show it to him. When he asks who it is for, I can tell him it is for our child."

"I am excited for you, Edna. You will have to share with me how you tell him and how he responds. I am certain he will be excited. He has always loved little ones."

She stayed and visited for a time before returning to her own home. I returned to my weaving. I would have a blanket to make for them when I completed this one.

Noah, Shem, and Japeth returned home three days later, after the rains began to fall.

"Where is Ham?" Japeth asked.

"I thought he would be waiting for us at the gate," Shem said.

"I told them he would be gone," Noah said, giving me a hug.

"I thought you two would have hurried to your own homes, rather than stopping here. Do you not miss your wives?" I asked as I hugged each of my tall sons.

"We do," Japeth said, grinning at Shem. "Papa told us that Ham would be gone when we arrived home. We wanted to see if he is correct."

I glanced up at Noah's sparkling eyes. "You saw him leaving in your dreams?"

"I did. I do not know where he went. I know only that he left."

"Ham left shortly after you three left on your latest journey. He said he needed to clear his mind. He wanted to understand why Channa would be taken from him." I sat in my favorite seat and waved to the others to sit.

Japeth leaned against the edge of a seat. "Did he have a plan? When do you expect him to return?"

I shrugged. "I sent some travel food with him. He took his weapons, but he did not want to kill anything to eat. He felt compelled to make a short journey to the east."

"Short journey?" Shem asked. We have been gone nearly two months. That is not a short journey."

I bit the inside of my lip. "I know. He promised he would return. I must trust that he will."

Noah sat beside me and ran his fingers through my long blond hair. "He will return. I have seen him. It will not be long before he returns."

"You could have told us," Japeth said.

"You did not want to listen," Noah said with a laugh.

"Edna will be wondering why I did not return home yet," Shem said. "I must leave."

"Amina is waiting for me, as well. We will return later, after we have had time to be with our families." Japeth pushed away from the edge of the chair.

My sons bent to hug me, then scurried out the front door, hurrying to return to their wives and homes.

"It is good to have you home," I said, turning to Noah. "Do you think Ham will return home soon? I am concerned about him."

"I do. I have seen him in a dream. He is crossing the mountain spine. His journey will be difficult, but he will return home to us."

"He crosses the spine in the rain?" I asked with a little gasp.

Noah nodded. "There is a reason, or he would not be there."

"The spine is not safe in the warm, dry time. It will be dangerous now."

Noah sucked in a deep breath and released it. "The spine is dangerous. Jehovah will protect him." He kissed me. "I have missed you. Ham is not the only one I saw in my dreams."

I lifted my eyebrows. "Who else did you see?"

"I do not know if I dreamed or if it was real," Noah said, stroking my hair. "I woke from my sleep to be taken to a high mountain, one I had never been to before."

I closed my mouth to the questions that wanted to bubble out.

"I turned in a circle, gazing at the sons and daughters of men. I was shown their depravities and sins. I sorrowed for my brothers and sisters."

Noah sat with his fingers still in my hair.

At last, I turned. "And?"

"Jehovah spoke to me. 'All these my creations have forgotten me. I have allowed them time to repent, and they choose to ignore the messenger I have sent.'"

"You?" I asked.

He nodded. "Yes. Me."

"What will Jehovah do about this?"

"He tells me he repents of ever creating this world and the people who live on it. He showed me. I agree. Few believe in Him. Few continue to obey his commandments. They have become vile."

"When will he destroy the earth?"

Noah's hand moved along the length of my hair once more. "We have some time. I am to build a large floating home to rescue the animals and a few people from the destruction."

"Floating? We do not live near the water."

"I trust Jehovah. I do not have any idea how to control a floating home. I do not know how long I have to build it. I only know I must begin."

"To rescue the animals, your floating home will need to be large."

"Very large. Much larger than even the homes I have seen in the cities. Longer, wider, and taller than anything I have seen anywhere else. Jehovah called it an 'ark'."

"It will take you time to build it. How long did Jehovah give you?"

"He did not say. He told me to return home and begin building. I am to continue to teach and try to help the lost to be found, to repent and to be baptized."

"How many would it take for Jehovah to decide he will not need to destroy our earth?"

"I did not ask. More than will listen, I fear." He bent and kissed me. "I have time now to write the plans that were given to me. When the rain stops, I will be required to begin searching for the wood."

"What kind of wood will you use?" I asked.

"Gopher wood. There is a stand of gopher trees not far from here. I will begin to cut them down when the rains end."

~ ~ ~

Two weeks later, four of our sheep herders knocked on our door. Two of them carried Ham between them. The other two carried a young woman, a daughter of Cain.

"What happened to Ham?" I asked.

"We do not know," he said. "We found him and the woman on the road when we hunted for ewes that had gone astray. We recognized Ham."

"Thank you for bringing him home to us," I said and directed them to his room and bed.

I directed them to put the woman in Ham's old house. No one lived there now. She could not hurt anyone in the empty house.

Noah came in soon after. "I heard that Ham has returned."

"He is home, but he is asleep. A woman was with him," I said.

"Where is the woman?" Noah asked.

"I had them put her in Ham's home. She is a daughter of Cain! How could Ham have come home with a woman of Cain?"

"Are you certain?" he asked.

"I can see her. The mark is plainly upon her. She, like Ham, lay sleeping in the road. They had fainted on the road. Neither is awake to tell us what happened."

"Ham would not bring home a daughter of Cain without reason. He is an obedient son. He loves Jehovah as we do. I believe we should wait and hear what he has to say before we make a decision about the woman." He frowned at me.

"You do not look happy about me putting her there."

"No. Not in an empty house. Who can we have assist her when she wakes?"

I had not thought of that. "Perhaps one of Japeth's daughters could stay with her?"

"She should not be alone. It would not be showing our kindness."

I sighed. I did not like it. But it would not be kind, nor would it be wise to leave her alone in an empty home. "I will go talk to Amina. Maybe one of her daughters will stay with the woman."

At Japeth's home, Amina agreed that it would be wise to send one of her girls to sit with the strange woman until she woke.

"The woman has not eaten for hours, maybe days. Is there a way we can give her something to strengthen her?" Amina asked.

"Good point," I said. "Ham will need something to help him regain his strength, as well. I will make a thin broth for him to eat."

"How will we get it into sleeping people?" Amina asked.

"The same way we get medicine into a child. Dip a cloth into it and drizzle the broth into his mouth. It should help give him something good to help him regain his strength."

"We will do the same," Amina said. She called the oldest daughter who still lived at home and gave her directions to go sit with the strange woman in Ham's home.

I returned home and put some meat and vegetables into a pot to start cooking. Ham would need the broth as soon as I could get some made. I feared for him.

I went to sit next to Ham. Noah sat beside him, holding his hand and talking to him as though he were awake.

"… you need to rebuild your strength. Rest. Mama will take care of you," he said.

I set my hand on Noah's shoulder and bent to speak in his ear. "You know I will. Do you think he can hear us?"

"I have heard many things in those times I slept due to an illness. He will hear me or at least some of what I tell him."

"Should I speak to him, as well?"

"You should. I believe speaking to him will help wake him. He needs to know he is safe and home."

"I can do that while I sit beside him."

For the next two days, I spoke to him, washed his face and arms with a cool cloth, and dipped a clean cloth into a cup of the broth and drizzled drops of it into his mouth. Sometimes he choked on it. Sometimes, he licked his lips. I told him of the ark his papa had been called to build.

In the middle of the morning three days after the herders brought him home, I left his room to get more of the broth. When I returned, his eyes opened and he moaned.

"You are awake!" I exclaimed.

"How?" he rasped through a dry throat.

"Do not try to speak yet. You have slept two days and into the third since you were brought home. We have no way of knowing how long you lay in the rain-soaked road before our herders found you on the trail."

He did not try to speak. Instead he brought his eyebrows close together.

"Three ewes strayed from the safety of the barn. I never heard how they escaped past our walls. They were due to drop their lambs soon. As the herders searched for them, they found the ewes huddled next to you and a woman."

I lifted him up to help him drink some cool water. "Slowly," I said. "You have been without food."

"Many days," he mouthed.

"Why?" I asked. "You have a bow. Did you lose it?"

"Rain," he mouthed.

"Oh. I see. No animals in the rain?"

Ham began to shake his head, then stopped with a groan.

"Does your head hurt?" I asked. "I did not feel a bump on your head." I bent close and gently touched his head with my fingertips. "Ah. Here it is. Near the base of your head. No wonder it hurts to move your head."

I turned to get a clean cloth and dip it into the cool water.

As I set it against the back of his head, he croaked, "Basya?"

"The woman we found with you? I am surprised they found you with a daughter of Cain. That is unusual for you." I set my hands on my hips.

"Not."

"What do you mean 'not'? Her skin bears the mark."

"Basya."

I lowered my eyebrows. "Basya? Daughter of God? How can that be? What do you mean?"

"Name."

"Why would a child of Cain give his daughter that name?"

"Drink?"

I picked up the cup and helped him drink again.

"She." He coughed to clear his throat.

I held the cup to his lips so he could drink more of the cool water.

"She worships …," he coughed again, "Jehovah."

"*She* worships Jehovah? How can that be? The children of Cain deny Jehovah."

His stomach rumbled. Ham set his hand across it. "Food? I smell food."

"You can have broth. You have slept too long and been without food for too long for you to eat more. It would not be good for you." I stood to retrieve the cup of broth.

"Many days without food."

I turned toward him. "A good reason to begin with broth. I have some ready. I've been giving you some while you slept. I will go get it."

I walked into the kitchen to dip up a fresh cup of the broth from over the fire.

Japeth entered the kitchen. "How is my little brother?"

"He lives. He woke and is hungry."

"That is not surprising. He has slept more than two days."

"Plus all the time he did not have food as he tried to get home. He says they were without food for many days."

"He must be starving."

I picked up the cup of broth and a spoon. "He was before he came here. He is hungry now."

"And you are giving him broth instead of good food?" Japeth's voice rose.

"His stomach could not handle more than broth yet. I'll give him more as soon as his stomach is ready."

Japeth followed me into Ham's room.

"Mama says you are finally awake," Japeth said with a smirk. "Let me help you sit up so she can feed you. Back to being a baby." He turned toward me and winked.

Japeth helped Ham sit up. I stuffed a pillow behind his back to support him.

"I am weak. I will let Mama feed me." Ham grinned up at his brother and sighed.

"Better?" Japeth asked.

"Yes."

"How did you get out there on the path to the mountain spine? You were not far from home. We wondered why you did not make it all the way home."

I saw a look of sorrow cross Ham's face.

"Do not ask him questions like that now. Let him eat and get some strength. When your papa returns, you can ask. He will then only have to answer those questions once." I brought the spoon of broth to his mouth.

Ham opened his mouth to accept the broth and closed his eyes. He hummed his approval.

"You like that?" Japeth asked.

"It is food," Ham said and opened his mouth for another spoonful of it.

"You must be starving."

"I was," Ham managed before I filled his mouth with more broth.

"What about that woman? Why would you be with a daughter of Cain?" Japeth shook his head.

"Not now," I growled. "Let him eat."

Ham swallowed the spoonful of broth I spooned into his mouth. "Is Basya awake yet?"

"Basya?" Japeth exclaimed and opened his eyes wide. "Daughter of God?"

I pushed another spoonful of broth into Ham's mouth. He swallowed it.

"And a worshiper of Jehovah. Is she well?"

"Amina watches over her."

I gave him another spoonful of broth.

He swallowed it. "Your wife is a good woman. Please ask her to care for Basya well."

Japeth grimaced. "She will. Amina cares for all the strays."

Ham glared at his brother. "Basya is no stray."

"Oh, ho! Little brother has feelings for this woman of Cain," Japeth teased.

"Cousin."

"Cousin?" Japeth said in unison with me.

"Yes." Ham closed his mouth over the last of the broth. "This broth warms my stomach and makes me sleepy."

The herb that helps the sick sleep worked. "You cannot sleep now!" I cried. "What do you mean, cousin? How would a woman with the mark of Cain be our cousin?"

"She has the right to tell her own story." Ham yawned. "Is she awake and fed? See if she is, please, Japeth."

Japeth sighed loudly. "You drop hints of something that important and refuse to share more?"

"Um-huh." Ham closed his eyes as I dropped the spoon into the empty bowl.

I shook my head and pushed Japeth toward the door. "Go ask. He will not tell us anything until he knows she is cared for."

"Come tell me," Ham called after us. "I cannot rest until I know. Wake me if you must."

I turned toward him at the door. "You care for this woman?"

"I may."

I closed the door behind us. "He will sleep a while. Go check on the woman. He will not sleep well if you do not. He needs the sleep to heal."

CHAPTER 14

Whose Daughter

That afternoon while I prepared our evening meal, Amina shared with me that the woman, Basya, had woken and had asked about Ham.

"She claims to be a granddaughter of the lost children of the prophet Enos. She knows their names. I do not know whether to believe her. She does know things you would not expect a daughter of Cain to know."

"That is what Ham meant," I murmured.

"What do you mean?" Amina asked.

"Ham suggested that she is a cousin. *If* she is a granddaughter of Ziva or Nat, she would be a cousin." My stomach roiled. How could a woman carrying the mark of Cain also be a daughter of Adam, a follower of Jehovah?

Noah would have to sort it all out. I did not have time to solve the problem. I needed to help Ham heal. I had added an herb to the broth I gave to Ham that would help him sleep to heal.

"One thing you should know," Amina added, "she has no plan to run away. Her family is gone, murdered by the giants."

I gasped. I did not want to like her or feel sympathy for her. But how could I not when her family had been destroyed by the giants of Coos. They had tried to kill Noah.

"And she escaped?"

Amina shifted a shoulder. "Apparently so. We did not discuss that. She needed to sleep again."

"Did you add the sleeping herb to her broth?"

"I thought about it. I would have, but she went right back to sleep."

I nodded. Strange that she would sleep again so soon without need for an herb.

In another span, I dipped up another cup of broth and cut a slab of fresh bread and set it on a tray. I backed into Ham's room carrying the covered tray.

"I thought you may be awake and hungry again. Your friend is awake, too." I said.

"My friend?" He seemed puzzled. "Basya? Oh! How is she doing?" His face brightened with his smile.

"Better than you. She had no bumps on her head."

Ham laughed as I moved to set the tray on the table by his bed.

"She told Amina some about her family. How could a daughter of Cain also be a daughter of Adam? I cannot understand it. Can you sit up to eat?"

Ham pushed himself up to lean against the pillows enough to eat. He had already regained some of his strength. "Did she tell Amina who her grandparents were?"

I uncovered the tray with the broth and the bread.

Ham's smile grew wider.

"If you soak the bread in the broth, your stomach may be able to handle it." I lifted the bowl. "Can you eat this on your own this time?"

Ham took the bowl and bread and dipped the bread into the broth, soaking some into the bread. After his first bite, he exclaimed, "Yum! This tastes wonderful. Basya's grandparents?"

"She told a story to Amina. It is difficult to believe. Much too wild to believe." I sighed. "Descendants of Enos and Rebecca? The lost children? Who does she think she is trying to fool?"

In reality, I had no way to judge. I did not want to believe her. I could not understand and was not certain I wanted to understand.

Ham set the bread on the plate beside the bowl and gazed at me. "You do not believe her?"

I felt the sarcasm in my laugh. "How can anyone believe that a child of Cain worships the one true God, Jehovah? Those people are taught to worship idols of wood and stone."

I did not want to believe. I wanted to see what Ham thought about this woman.

"Not all of them," Ham retorted. "How can you not believe her story?" He began to push himself up. The broth rocked on his lap.

I reached for the plate and cup at the same time as Ham did. "Eat, son. We can talk about this when your papa returns home. He is in the next village, teaching the unbelievers. Perhaps he should go to Nod. He may have more success there."

Ham glared at me. "Mama! What are you saying?"

"Have you heard what your papa is suggesting now?" I wanted to change the subject of the discussion away from me and the girl from Nod.

"No Mama. I have been gone since before the rains came. You know I went to clear my mind. I missed Channa. I still miss her."

"You will for many years, I fear." I leaned forward and touched his hand. "You will miss your wife and child."

"Jehovah took them for a reason. It took days of walking alone in the wilderness before I could clear my mind." Tears dripped from his eyes and down his cheeks. "I know now why He took them from me. It does not matter what Papa is saying. He speaks for Jehovah. I stand behind him."

"Even when you bring home a daughter of Cain?" I could not help asking and bringing her back to the discussion.

Ham picked up the plate with the broth and bread and dipped the bread into the broth. "Yes. Jehovah led me to her. She helped me when I broke my arm. Rains fell hard on us.

She shared her cave with me so I could be dry. She shared her food, though she had less than me. She did not need to do any of that. I was a stranger. Yes, Mama. I trust Basya."

"That name," I spat. "How did a daughter of Cain get that name? How can she be a 'daughter of God'?"

"When you hear her story, you will know. Trust me, Mama. I would not bring an unbeliever into our home compound, not even a woman. I know how unsafe it is." He ducked his head and ate some of the soggy bread. "I lived with one," he added under his breath.

"What?" I asked. "Channa believed."

"Did she? No. She tried to convince me we should leave Mamre and go to her community. I do not think she believed. She pretended."

He dipped his bread into the broth and ate some more, watching my face.

I stared down at my hands, glanced up at him, then returned my eyes to my hands. "I can believe it of Channa. It is not hard to believe it of this new woman. I have been taught since I was little to stay away from the children of Cain. They were marked so we would stay from them. Such ingrained beliefs are hard to change."

Ham's frown lifted a little. "I know, Mama. I must speak with Papa. When do you expect him to return?"

"He took Shem with him this time. They plan to return in a day or so before Edna's child is born. She is big. The child will come soon. Papa and Shem should return in a few days."

"Edna is with child? I will need to congratulate her and Shem when he returns." He ate the last bite of the bread after sopping up the last of the broth. "I hope they return sooner than later. I have need of his advice."

"You have need to regain your strength." I took the empty bowl and stood. "You need to rest if you are to be strong enough to speak with your papa. Sleep."

"Yes, Mama." He slid lower in his bed.

I pulled the soft blanket up around his shoulders and kissed his cheek. Taking the tray with the bowl and plate on it and carried them out of the room with a soft click as the door closed.

~ ~ ~

I took Ham broth with the herb in it again that day and twice more the next. I wanted him to sleep. Sigal had taught me that sleep would best help healing.

Japeth visited when Ham woke. I left the room, giving them time to share as brothers.

The next time Ham woke, Japeth tapped on the door.

I called for him to enter.

He brought the woman, Basya in to visit Ham. She still wore the muddy clothing she wore when our herders found her. I frowned. Did she not have anything clean?

The woman glanced around the room, searching for something. I did not know what. She breathed out heavily as she looked at the shelves of books bound in calf skins and rolled. Did she know what a book was? Could she read?

"Basya." Ham spoke the woman's name. I heard a longing in his voice and frowned.

The woman turned from her examination of his books and hurried to his side. "What happened to you?" She leaned over to touch his forehead. "You are not burning."

"No. He has not burned since he woke. He refuses to eat any more of my broth. He needs to eat if he is to regain his strength." I heard the petulance in my voice.

The woman, Basya, picked up the cup of broth that sat on the table and smelled it. "Is this the same broth you brought to me?"

"It helps those who are ill to heal, especially when they have not eaten for a time," I said. I did not know why I had to respond to this woman.

"It tasted good to me. Did you give me the same broth as you are giving Ham?" I do not know why she insisted on asking the same question.

I nodded.

"Why broth? Is there an injury or illness I do not know about? He wasn't ill the morning before he fell." She bent to examine him, touching his head.

Ham flinched when she touched the spot behind his ear.

"Does that hurt?" she asked.

Ham nodded. "I think I hit my head there when I fell."

Basya hummed as she examined other parts of his head and arms. "That is possible, but the lump isn't as big as I would expect." She turned to me. "Have you been caring for it?"

I flinched. What did this woman know about healing? "Yes. I cared for it. What do you take me for?"

"You did a good job. The lump has shrunk. I expected it to be bigger."

"Are you a healer? Ham says you are." I rolled my shoulders back and stood straighter.

The woman did not stop touching my son. "I trained with Arisbee who trained under Shamgar. Have you heard of Shamgar?"

Surprise raced through me, causing shivers. "I have. She must have lived many hundred years. My grandmama and grandpapa received remedies from her parents in Kib before they died. I would not have thought she had lived that long."

Basya turned her head toward me as she examined Ham's legs. "She lived a long and lonely life. She kept busy healing others and perfecting her healing remedies. I sat with her on the day she died. Among her last words were thoughts of Jaxom, her lost love."

"I heard about him. The villagers of Kib spoke of him when Grandmama returned for another remedy. They said Shamgar had run off with him to Nod."

Basya grunted. "After they burned her home. They thought they burned her, too. She left to find honey that day. When she saw they wanted her gone, she left. Jaxom and the leader of his guard, Crites, took Shamgar with them to Nod. Or Crites did. Jaxom lost his life in battle before they reached Nod."

"This Shamgar must have been a great healer," Japeth said. "I have even heard her name."

"She was a skilled healer, always looking for better ways to help the sick and injured. Those trained by her were blessed." Basya returned to examining one of Ham's arms. "Your arm is almost healed. You will have a bump there because I couldn't be sure it was straight and in line with the other bone where we were. The bump will not affect the use of your arm."

"Broken arm?" I cried.

"Yes, Mama. Remember, I told you. I broke my arm. Basya cared for it." Ham moved his eyes from Basya to me.

"Thank you, Basya." I felt more respect for her now. Even if she could not prove her belief in Jehovah, she could prove her ability to heal.

"I heard him cry out as he tried to straighten his own arm. It happened after the rain started. I lived in a cave I found to hide from the giants and the rain. I didn't bring all my herbs and remedies with me. If I had, perhaps Ham would not now have a bump on his arm."

After examining his eyes, throat, and heart, Basya ran her hand across Ham's chest and belly. She turned to Japeth. "Can you help me turn him over? I need to look at his back."

"My back does not hurt," Ham grumbled.

"I need to see it to be certain you have no other injuries. We fell more times than I like on our trek."

Ham chuckled. A cough interrupted it.

"And I'll need to see into your throat to see why you cough," Basya added.

"There is that," he agreed.

Japeth moved Ham onto his side. "Is this enough?"

I stood back while this woman examined my son. She said she had experience as a healer. The things she did were much like the things I had seen Sigal do when she had examined our sick or injured children.

She turned her gaze toward me. "He has some scrapes and bruises. That is not surprising. He fell more than once on our hike through the mountain."

"Why did you go through the mountains?" Japeth asked.

"Rain filled my valley and my cave. If Ham had not insisted that we leave when we did, we would both have drowned."

I gasped at the thought of my son drowning.

"Valleys on both sides of the hill were filled with water. We had to hike through some high mountains.

"You went over the spine?" Japeth asked, turning toward Ham.

"We had no choice. Up was the only way out and away from the flooding," Ham said with a shrug.

~ ~ ~

"Do the rains fall that hard in your part of the world?" Japeth turned to Basya.

"Worse this year than any other year that I can remember or have ever heard of." Basya lifted her eyebrows. "This year has been different in many ways. I have not traveled far from my home in Safe Haven before this, though. I would not know if this is unusual."

"Why did you leave your home this time?" I asked.

The words she spoke next chilled my soul. "Giants. My home was destroyed by Coos giants. I almost didn't escape the fires they set."

I sucked in a noisy breath. "Noah tells me the world is becoming more wicked. Men are battling everywhere. Although I believed him, I did not understand."

"How could you understand? Your home is safe. Your village has not been repeatedly attacked and plundered. Like Mamre, Safe Haven was safe behind tall walls for many years. Only when its people began to forget Jehovah's hand in our safety did we lose His protection."

It surprised me that she could say those things with so little emotion.

"Papa warned us," she continued. "I listened and prayed. I tried to obey. My obedience did not help. One who obeys among many who refuse does not bring the blessings of heaven to a village."

"You really do worship Jehovah?" I asked. My jaw sagged lower.

"I do," she said, setting her hands on her hips. "How is that so hard for you to believe? More importantly, why have you continued to give Ham this broth?"

My head pulled back and I stood taller. "He could not eat anything more. He had starved." My hands raised to stop her questions. It did not help.

"That answer was correct the day we were found and brought to your home. He needs more nourishment now. Much more than broth and bread. Worse, however, Ham needs to waken and stay awake to heal."

"But, but—" I spluttered.

"It is not good for him to drink those herbs for so many days. It will stop his healing."

"Worse? Stop his healing?" I gulped. "I have been taught that sleep is needed to heal."

"Sleep is necessary when the body is seriously ill. If not, those herbs can cause greater problems." She stopped speaking and breathed in and out slowly. "It is not my place to lecture you. You have done well in caring for Ham and me. But the time has come for Ham to eat more than broth. He cannot heal without more food. And no more of those herbs."

I bit the inside of my lip. "I wanted him to heal faster. His papa has need of him."

"Then give him bread and a thicker soup — and more of it. He needs to eat, not starve. He has had enough of starving." Basya's voice rose at the end.

I stared at her for several breaths before dropping my eyes. "I will bring him more healthy food."

"Without the herbs that force me to sleep?" Ham asked.

"Yes, son. Without the herbs." I picked up the tray that held the broth and carried it from the room.

Would he sleep if I poured what was left of the broth into the soup? Would Basya know? I needed to be certain she knew as much as she claimed to know.

I scooped some thick beef stew from the pot of stew I made for the family into a clean cup and dumped the broth into it. I would see if this woman knew as much as she thought she did.

I sliced another slab of bread. Ham had eaten the one I took for him to eat with the broth earlier. I set everything back on the tray and carried it back to Ham's room.

"Here is food for you. There is not anything hard to eat, but something more substantial." I set the tray on the table next to his bed.

"Yum. That looks better," Ham's words were punctuated with a growl from his stomach. He reached for the spoon.

"Good," I said. "Everyone is eating this tonight. You can be first." I watched to see what Basya would do.

She took the spoon from Ham and lifted the bowl to her face. She cautiously smelled the stew. She brought it down and stared at me. "I thought you agreed? No more of the sleeping herbs."

She smelled it. "I-I-I did not want to waste the broth…" I glanced at my feet. "I did not believe it would affect him if I mixed the broth with the stew."

Basya's frown deepened. I expected her to shout at me. She did not. "It will make him ill. Do you not believe me? I trained with Arisbee who trained with Shamgar. I know. You cannot give him these herbs day after day for many days without causing him problems."

"What kind of problems?" She had not told me earlier. I needed to know.

"Breathing problems. Is that enough reason to stop giving him those herbs?"

"You are certain you are a trained healer?" I asked.

"Yes. As I have told you, I was trained by the best healers. And, Shamgar and Arisbee worshiped Jehovah. They were not cult worshipers. Shamgar's skills came from Him. I am certain more of these herbs will cause Ham breathing problems."

In the back of my mind, I cheered. I could trust her decisions as a healer. Instead, I huffed and picked up the tray. Ham grabbed the bread before I could leave.

"This doesn't have that herb in it. I can eat it while I wait."

Back in the kitchen, I started to dump the broth with the herbs into the slop for the pigs, then reconsidered it. The pigs did not need to sleep any more than Ham did. I took it outside and dumped it near the house, and poured water over it, hoping to wash away the effects.

I dipped up a clean bowl of the stew and cut another slab of bread. I buttered the bread and set it on the tray beside the stew. I covered the food to keep it warm, then carried it to Ham's room.

"Yum!" Ham said reaching for the bowl and spoon.

Before Ham could grab the bowl, Basya took it and inspected it as she had the previous bowl.

"It is a good," I protested.

Basya stirred the stew as she smelled it. "It smells like you didn't add the herbs."

"I did not. You gave me reasons to leave it out. I hope you know what you are doing."

She gave Ham the bowl, and I watched him enjoy about half of it before I left to finish preparing the evening meal.

CHAPTER 15

Healer

Noah returned with Shem the next day. He found me weaving a blanket for Edna's baby.

"Ham is awake," I said, not looking up from my weaving.

"I thought he might be. Is he well?"

"And the woman?"

I stopped weaving and turned to look at him. I wanted to see how he would accept this particular woman.

"She lives."

I held the shuttle still and turned my gaze back to Noah. "She is a healer."

He lifted an eyebrow, waiting.

"And she is a daughter of Cain —"

"Ham knows better —" Noah spluttered.

"— who claims to believe in Jehovah."

Noah stopped spluttering. "She believes in Jehovah? How would a daughter of Cain even know about Jehovah to believe in Him?"

"She claims that Nat and Ziva, the lost children of Enos and Rebecca, were her grandparents."

Noah inhaled and closed his eyes.

I knew better than to interrupt him when he did this. He communed with Jehovah. I pushed the shuttle through the warp of the blanket.

Noah exhaled.

I turned toward him once more.

"It is possible. I do not see Nat and Ziva having children together, but it is possible she is their granddaughter. That is one sure way that she would know of Jehovah." Noah's lips began to lift.

"But she carries the mark —" I argued.

"And? Do you believe those who are marked as children of Cain cannot hear the words of peace offered by Jehovah and not believe?"

"I was taught to avoid all with that mark, for they were unbelievers."

Noah put his arm around me and pulled me from my seat onto his lap. "The mark was set as a protection for Cain and his children. We, who are the sons of Adam, are commanded to leave them alone. The command came when Cain's brothers desired to find him and put him to death for killing Abel. Jehovah protected them."

I had heard that many times when the stories of old were shared. "But we have also been warned to avoid them."

"Because they do not believe in Jehovah. We also ask our children to avoid other nonbelievers. Look at what happened to Telemon. He raced away from family and our beliefs, chasing a woman who does not trust Jehovah."

"Nava is lost to us, too. She chose a man who does not believe. She and her children are lost to our beliefs, as are her sisters." I rolled my lips inward, forcing back the tears. "I do not want to lose Ham to a woman of Cain."

"Even if she is a believer?"

I kissed Noah. "If she is a believer, if her story is true, perhaps we will have to accept her. I do not know if he cares for her enough to marry her. I only know he brought her here."

"Wait to decide if she is acceptable. I will have a chat with her. She cannot hide her truth from me." Noah set me back in my chair. "When can I meet this woman?"

"When do you want to meet her?"

"I think I will go visit with Ham first."

Later, Ham passed by my door walking toward his papa's office. I went to the kitchen. We would be having a big family dinner, as we always did when Noah returned from his preaching to the world. I looked forward to hearing about his interactions with the people he met.

~ ~ ~

That evening, Japeth brought Amina and their two daughters who still lived with them. Shem and Edna arrived. Two of the grandsons, born of children born to Keshet, also joined us.

At last, Ham entered the sitting room with Basya. We were considering a move to the eating room without him before he finally arrived.

All the noise of visiting and preparing to move to the other room halted as Basya followed Ham into the room. He held her hand and led her toward Noah and me.

I stared at them, noticing the way Ham held her hand. He no longer mourned for Channa and their baby.

"I asked Ham to bring her to dinner," Noah whispered.

She hung back. Ham pulled her close. "Mama, Papa, may I introduce Basya? Jehovah led me east as He led her to the west. I believe we were intended to meet."

Before Noah could comment, Japeth hurried over and gave Basya a hug. "It is good to see you again."

Noah stood. "Welcome to our home, Basya. Ham tells me you saved him more than once in your trip from your cave back here to Mamre."

Crimson rushed up her neck into her face. It surprised me. I did not know red would show on a dark brown face.

"Because I was there when he needed help. Perhaps Jehovah sent me to be there for Ham." I almost missed the tiny shrug of her shoulder.

"And I am happy she was there for me," Ham added, gripping her hand.

"Your mama has prepared an excellent dinner for us, as usual. We should go eat while it still tastes good," Noah said.

"I would not want it to burn," I said. "We should go eat now that everyone is here." I turned my eyes toward Ham.

Noah took my arm and we led the family down the hall. I heard Edna welcoming Basya. I heard Basya's laugh echo down the hall as she responded to Edna's welcome.

As we neared the eating room, I heard them talking of helping mamas bring children into the world. I helped all the children who joined our family, except those I birthed myself. It fell to me to be responsible, since I had helped with Keshet's last child.

I left Noah at the door and went into the kitchen, followed by Amina and her two daughters. We emptied the food onto plates and into bowls to bring to the waiting family. We carried it from the kitchen into the eating room.

After we set the food on the table, Noah helped me sit in my usual seat, then moved to his while the other men helped their wives. Ham led Basya to the seats he and Channa often occupied when … I did not want to think of that last day. I inhaled and glanced down the table at the others.

"Mama Imma, this smells exceptionally wonderful," Basya said.

"I am happy it smells good to you. After you eat, we will see if you still like it," I said.

She smiled and commented to Ham on each dish as she ate it. The others were too busy eating to ask many questions. They had already visited with her before then and had their curiosity satisfied.

Noah asked a few questions. She told of the giants attacking her home in Safe Haven. She and Ham told the story of their escape from the floods that would have drowned them if they had not fled. Ham regaled us with the story of the hike across the spine.

"Mama Imma?" Edna asked. "This babe will be born in not many weeks. How many children will this make that you have helped to be born?"

I fiddled with a lock of hair as I counted all the children and their mamas. "I have helped all my grandchildren and some of my nieces and nephews. I guess the number would be about twenty children." I turned toward Basya. "How many children have you helped to be born?"

"Basya says she has helped birth at least fifty children," Edna said.

Basya's cheeks reddened once more.

"That many?" I asked. "Were they all successful?"

"No. Two mamas were sick before their children determined to come to this life. We couldn't save them or their babies. A third became ill during the delivery. We managed to save that child, but we lost her mama. It is sad to lose mamas and babies."

"It is," I replied. "I still have bad dreams about Keshet and Channa." I glanced toward Ham. "I am sorry, son."

He shrugged. "It is a bad memory for us all."

Edna cleared her throat. "I would like Basya to be with us when this child comes. Would you allow that, Mama Imma?"

"If she is here and available, I see no reason she should not be. She is a healer," I said.

I rose and retrieved the sweet cake I made that afternoon for the dinner.

When everyone had eaten it, Noah turned toward Basya. "I have enjoyed this meal and learning a little about you. But we need to know more about you and your past. You have the name Basya, Daughter of God. How would a daughter of Cain have a name like that?"

She sucked in her breath, held it in, then slowly let it out. "My mama and papa gave me my name. I come from a large family of people who love and worship Jehovah. It is not so unusual in my family."

"How is that possible?" Noah asked. "How did your family learn of Jehovah? People in your land are not allowed to even know His name."

"My family have been worshipers of Jehovah for a thousand or more years. My grandparents, Ziva and Nat were taken to Nod as children."

I had heard this story from Amina, but somehow it sounded different from her.

"Grandpapa Seth and their papa, Enos, taught Crites of Jehovah while he and his mama lived in the country on the edge of the land claimed by Cain. Crites married my grandmama, Ziva. He helped them to remember what their papa, Enos, had taught him."

"Ziva? Nat? You claim to be the grandchild of those two?" Surprise filled Noah's voice.

"I do. My grandmama, Merab, tended to Grandmama Ziva's body before they buried her in Safe Haven." She continued to share the story of her family, how they were purchased from the slave market, and how Nat had been freed. She spent more than a span sharing the history of her family.

"You tell a good story. I have to admit that," Noah said. "I will have to consider it. You do look like a daughter of Cain."

"I suppose I would," Basya said. She bit her lip. "Grandpapa Crites was the grandson of Tubal Cain, a son of Cain. Some of our other grandparents were also children of Cain's children. Who else would Ziva and Nat's children marry? Some of them left the faith. They wouldn't continue to obey. Most of the others read and obeyed the words found in the Book of Commandments."

"You say you read the Book of Commandments? Can you repeat some of the commandments given in that book?" Noah asked.

Ham stared at Noah and took Basya's hand.

She glanced at him, then turned toward Noah. "We are taught to keep the Seventh or Sabbath Day holy. Even in the early days, the servants were released from their duties in the afternoon of the Seventh Day. During the time they were gone, our families used that time to worship Jehovah."

"Were there any baptisms?" Noah asked.

"No. Grandpapa Nat and Grandpapa Crites knew they nor any of the others had been given the right or authority to baptize. We always hoped to have Grandpapa Enos or one of the other prophets come near so we could be baptized. Grandpapa Crites received the words to use to marry couples. When Kerstin came to Safe Haven, she told my parents, the words he used were the same words used by Adam and his sons."

"How would he know?" Japeth asked.

"I wasn't there. But Mama told me that Crites had prayed for the correct words and was given them."

"He was given the words to marry? And the same words Adam gave to us? How?" Noah's voice was filled again with awe.

"I was told he prayed until he had them. We didn't know they were the same as Adam used until Kerstin came to Safe Haven. She told us. Kerstin was also a granddaughter of Enos. She escaped the Coos giants, too."

"We have lost many of our women to the giants over the years. It does not surprise me that Kerstin would be taken."

"Did you know her?" Basya asked.

"When did she live?"

"She met Grandmama Eve and Grandpapa Adam late in their lives."

"So you did not know her?" Noah asked.

"No. I was not yet born when we learned that Grandpapa Adam died. Have you heard of her, then? She was born in Canaan."

"No. I knew some of my cousins from Canaan, but I did not know of Kerstin," Noah said.

"Do you believe me, then?" Basya asked.

"I believe it could be true. I must think about it and take it to Jehovah."

Ham pushed his chair back. "We have been together for a long time. I am going to take Basya back to her room."

After helping me clean up the dishes and the kitchen, Japeth and Amina and their girls walked home. Seth and Edna put their arms around each other, following Japeth and his family toward their own home. Their love filled me with joy.

CHAPTER 16

Edna's Baby

Over the next few days, Ham brought Basya to the house many times. She spent time with me in ways I had not enjoyed with another young woman since Nir-it ran away with the cult priest.

Early one morning, even though it still rained, Ham and Noah left to travel south to teach the people there about the truth of Jehovah. I stood with Basya waving goodbye to them as they rode out of the compound, leading a mule that carried the provisions they would need.

"They are gone," I said with a sigh. "We must carry on."

She sighed and turned to me. "How may I assist you?"

I invited her to join me in my house. We worked together to sew clothing for Edna's coming child.

I still did not trust her. I did not believe yet that she believed in Jehovah. Ham's certainty did not fill me. I could not know. Not yet. Nirit and Channa had left me unwilling to trust easily.

Ham had worked with Noah in developing plans for the ark. The rain had kept them inside more than usual.

"Does it always rain this much here in Mamre?" Basya asked.

"No. This heavy rain is unusual. I can almost believe Noah when he says Jehovah will cover the earth with water."

"Is that what he has said?" Basya said. "Ham told me that Jehovah plans to destroy all life on the earth. I did not know how he planned to do that."

"Neither did I, until Noah returned home while you and Ham crossed the spine. He told me that life would be destroyed. I believed we, too, would be destroyed, until he told me about the ark. I do not know how he will carry all the animals and enough people to repopulate the earth. It is beyond me." I put my hand to my mouth. "Did I say that? Those words never came out of me before."

Basya smiled. Her eyes twinkled. "I wonder the same thing. Ham told me of helping his papa in planning the ark. It will have to be gigantic to hold all the animals. How will Noah keep the lions from eating the gazelles?"

"My question, as well," I said with a little giggle. "I hope Jehovah will understand my lack of understanding. I believe. I just do not know how it will happen."

"I do not know how, either. I trust Jehovah will give the information to Noah. All I can do from now until that day that occurs is live my life in the way that Jehovah and my parents would be happy."

Did I dare trust her? I did not want to lose my heart to another woman who would lead my son away. I loved each of those my children married almost as much as I loved my children. I did not know if I could trust my heart to losing more.

Basya also spent time with Edna, becoming friends. Edna grew big, making it difficult for her to waddle through the compound.

Basya joined in our worship each Sabbath. She knew the commandments of Jehovah. It became harder for me to distrust her.

Before Noah and Ham returned, Shem ran into the house where Basya and I worked together. "Edna is doubled over. I think it is her time."

"Her time?" Basya and I chorused together.

"How far apart are her pains?" Basya asked.

"They have shortened. She says it is time." Panic filled Shem's voice.

"Do you have the things you need?" Basya asked me.

I nodded. I had put them into a little bag the week before, knowing this would happen soon. "Shall we go?"

"I have a few more supplies I gathered in my room. I will meet you there," Basya said as we went out the door.

"Please hurry," Shem called after her as she strode across the compound to the house where she still lived.

I went with him, hoping the child would be born without problems.

Three spans later, Basya wiped her forehead with the back of her hand. "Stop, Edna. Don't push." She stood at Edna's feet, doing all she could to help the childbirth. "I have to check something."

She glanced my way. "Something is not right," she murmured.

"What do you suspect?"

"The child should be born by now. I think he is laying wrong."

I nodded. "What will you do?"

"Check to see how the child lays."

She put her hand inside Edna through the channel where the child should be born. She frowned.

"He is laying wrong. Do you want to feel?"

I shook my head. "I trust you. What do you feel?" I whispered.

"A shoulder."

"Shoulder? The child is laying crooked. What do we do?" I kept my voice low. We did not want to frighten Edna more.

"Move him?" Basya said with a little shrug. "He cannot be born like this. If we do not move him, we will lose him and possibly Edna, too."

I swallowed. "Do what you need me to do."

"Can you help Edna stay calm?"

I moved from Edna's feet to stand beside her shoulders, opposite of Shem. "Try to relax, Edna. Breathe and concentrate on your breathing. Your little one is in the wrong position to be born. He did not turn far enough. Basya is going to try to move him. It may be uncomfortable for a time."

"Worse than it already is?" Edna moaned.

"It could be. She has to move the child so his head can come out. His shoulder is where his head should be."

"That is not how it should be?" Edna asked. Her teeth chattered.

"No, dear. His head should be in the canal, ready to push through. He cannot be born like this. Relax. And breathe."

"Even I know that," Shem muttered in a quiet voice.

I stared at him with my mamas 'do not say that' look. "Talk with her. Help her think about breathing until I tell you to have her push. This could hurt her more than it already has."

Shem nodded and sat in a chair where he could speak in low tones in his wife's ear.

Basya continued to try to move the child. "I need your help, Imma. Push on her stomach. Can you feel the child's back?" She pointed to Edna's protruding stomach.

I pushed on the child from the outside while Basya tried to move him from the inside. Finally, the babe moved back. We worked together to get him moved so his head engaged into the birth canal.

Basya removed her hand and breathed a loud breath. "Time to work to get this baby out of you," she called to Edna.

"You can push now, Edna," Shem encouraged.

"Push!" I called.

"At last!" Edna cried.

A pain squeezed her stomach, helping the child move downward. Edna pushed. After five pushes, Basya checked the child once more.

"Stop," she called. "Breathe. I need to help him once more."

She ran a finger around the child's head and adjusted a shoulder.

"Push with the next pain," Basya called.

When Edna's stomach clenched down, Basya called, "Now! Push!"

Shem and I encouraged her to push.

"It is almost over now," I cried. "You can rest soon."

In two more pains, the head slipped from Edna's body. One more pain and the child lay in Basya's arms. She glanced up at me.

"You have a daughter, Shem, Edna," I said.

Basya lay the little girl across Edna's belly. "Shem, do you want to help separate her from her mama?"

Shem squeezed Edna's hand and stepped to take the knife from me. I tied a red thread two finger-widths apart along the cord that connected mama and daughter.

While I directed Shem in cutting the cord, Basya cleaned Edna's body, waiting for the next squeezing pain. When it came, she pushed on Edna's belly to help push the bag of waters from her body.

While Basya took care of the bag of waters, I worked with the little girl. I massaged her back, then held her up by her heels and swatted her bottom.

"What are you doing, Mama?" Shem cried.

"She must breathe. I am helping her."

"Oh." He grabbed Edna's hand.

The little girl gasped. Then she wailed. A loud, shriek.

"Listen to that," I said. My face almost hurt with my huge grin. "Life."

I caught her head in my hand and lay her on the bed next to Edna. I dipped a cloth in the warm water and quickly washed the mucus from her body. When she was clean, I wrapped her in a tiny blanket Edna had set on a table. I handed the baby to her.

"You may want to help her eat," I said.

"How do I do that?" Edna gazed at the tiny little girl.

I helped her bare her breast and set the little girl's mouth close. The babe rooted around until she found it.

I gave Edna and Shem some privacy by helping Basya finish cleaning Edna. Shem helped move Edna while we changed the bedding and put a thick pad between her legs. I pulled the blanket over her.

I bent over to gaze at my newest little granddaughter. "You three should get some rest. This has been a rough experience for all of you."

"I will stay in the other room for a time," Basya said. "I want to be sure everything is still well with mama and daughter. We do not want anything to happen to either of you now."

"Could that happen?" Shem asked, raising his head to look at her.

"It could. But I will stay close. Nothing bad should happen. If it does, I'll be here to help."

~ ~ ~

Basya returned to her own room the next morning. Edna and her baby were no longer in trouble.

I went to visit Shem and Edna and their daughter shortly after Basya left.

"She is a beauty," I said as I held her close.

"She is," Shem said.

"I feared you would not want a girl baby."

"We need honorable girls as well as boys," Shem said. "Besides, our next child can be a boy."

"Next child?" Edna squeaked. "Not for a few days."

Shem laughed. "No. Not for at least another year."

"You saw me. You felt my pain. And you are ready for me to go through it already?"

He giggled. "No. Not right away. Maybe we can have another one in two or three years."

"You will have forgotten your pain in a year or two, probably less time than that," I reassured her. "I did."

"You forgot the pain?" Edna asked. Disbelief filled her face.

"It surprised me that I could forget the pain as fast as I did. But I did forget until the next birth."

Edna sighed. "It is good to know I will forget."

I smiled at the babe and ran a finger across her little cheek. "It is a gift and a blessing from Jehovah. Father promised Eve that children would come with pain and sorrow. Part of that pain is in their birthing."

"And the other pain?" Shem asked.

"When they make choices we would rather they not make."

"Like Telemon and my sisters?" Shem asked.

I nodded. "Like them.

"What did they do?" Edna asked.

"My sisters married men who are not believers. They lost their faith in Jehovah. Telemon, well, you know what happened to him." I gave the little girl back to her mama.

"Oh." Edna said with a sigh. "You will not do that. Will you, Lilah?"

"Lilah? Is that what you are naming her?" I asked.

"Yes," Shem replied. "Do you like it?"

"A name as beautiful as the child."

When Noah and Ham returned within a week, they were excited to see little Lilah.

"Another beautiful granddaughter," Noah cooed as he held her close.

"When can we offer the thank offering and sacrifice for her?" Shem asked.

Noah glanced up at his son. "We cannot make a sacrifice in the rain."

"The rain should end soon. How soon after the rain ends can we sacrifice?"

"Do you have a ram?"

"I do. I went out yesterday to look at the early rams. The herders promise me the one I chose is a first-born ram."

"We can sacrifice when the rain stops."

My eyes locked with Edna's. "We will want to do some planning. Family will come."

"I sent word to my parents that Lilah was here. I guess I should send another message."

"They can stay with us in the compound until time for the sacrifice," I said, "If they will want to participate in the sacrifice?" I raised an eyebrow.

"They will want to. They remember sacrifices from before."

"Will we want to send for Grandpapa Methuselah and Lamech?" I asked.

Noah nodded. "They will want to be here for the thank offering and sacrifice."

Edna and I spent time planning a feast to serve after the sacrifice. Shem collected the ram and put him in a pen by himself. He inspected the ram again, making certain it had no blemishes.

The rains ended when Lilah was a month old.

Guests began to arrive a week later. Grandpapa Lamech brought Grandpapa Methuselah with him. Some of Noah's children and grandchildren from Keshet came, as did my parents and Dodi.

The day of the sacrifice dawned bright and warm. We trekked up a small hill to where Noah had built an altar many years before. Edna carried little Lilah. Ham helped Noah set the firewood on the altar while we waited for Shem to lead the ram to the altar.

We women sat together while Noah, Japeth, Shem, and Ham performed the rites for the sacrifice. Basya sat near me. She gasped once. Then sat quietly during the remainder of the sacrifice. When Ham lit the fire that consumed the sacrifice, she breathed out softly.

"I feared they would make us taste the blood," she murmured.

I glanced her way.

She shook her head and mouthed the word 'later.'

I returned my focus to what the men were doing. After the final rite, Shem came over to get the baby. He carried her to stand near the altar. He held her close while Noah, Methuselah, and Lamech lay their hands on her head and offered a blessing.

Her blessing gave me hope. She would need the assistance of Jehovah to survive the coming flood, when it came.

CHAPTER 17

Could I

During the feast after the sacrifice and thank offering, I asked Basya about her comment.

"Grandmama Merab told me about the cult sacrifices. The cult god Lorca is the bloodiest. His priests take the blood from the sacrifice through the crowd of participants, dribbling the blood into their mouths."

I shivered. "Into their mouths? Nasty."

"That is what we all thought. How could anyone believe in gods made by men? And why would they want to taste the blood of the sacrifice?"

"Jehovah has commanded that we not drink blood. It is sacred. Life comes through blood," Ham said. "Forcing their worshipers to drink that blood is causing them to break one of Jehovah's most stringent commandments."

"The Destroyer would want his people to do that," Noah said. "He would want them to do those things that would push them farther from the presence of Jehovah, not bring them closer."

"He is shrewd," Basya said.

"He does all he can to destroy the faith of Jehovah's children," Noah said.

Basya glanced toward me. "I am happy to believe in Jehovah. I have always wanted to participate in a sacrifice to Him. All my grandpapas back to Nat dreamed of participating in a sacrifice to Jehovah. Only Nat ever did, and he was a child when he last watched Adam."

"Did you ever have to attend a cult festival?" Ham asked, taking her hand.

"No. We left Nod long before my birth. I did not have to attend. But my grandparents told me about it. They were forced to attend the cult festivals. They tried to leave, pretending to go to another festival. They traveled from one cult temple to another during the day, making an appearance at one, and then another. When it came time to sacrifice, they had left all the temples and gone home."

"How did they know about the blood?"

"Nat was a personal slave to the high priest of Lorca. He attended all the festivals until Qinten died."

"How do you know of the things that happened so long ago?" Amina asked.

"They are written for us. Nat didn't want us to forget. And our parents told us stories."

"It is easier for children to remember stories," Noah said, nodding. "But sometimes, the story changes with the telling."

"That is why Nat and the others kept a written history. Is that not what Adam did? Is that not how we got the Book of Commandments?"

"Where is this history?" I asked. "It would be interesting to read. It would prove your contention that your people were followers of Jehovah, and that you descend from Nat and Ziva."

Basya dropped her head and gazed at her hands. "Amasa, a many times grandson of Chemish, who is Nat's oldest son, kept the record. He lived across Safe Haven from me. We were allowed to read from the text, but he kept it safe inside a rocked space in his wall. I don't think it burned when the giants burned the village if he put it in the space before the fire."

My eyes burned into hers. I had begun to learn to love her, but the inconsistencies bothered me.

"How is it so bad that it is hidden away where we cannot find it?" she asked.

"Mama Imma, do you not have the books written by Eve and the other matriarchs?" Amina asked.

"I have them in my room where they cannot be ruined," I agreed.

"I do not have them." Amina waved toward Edna. "She does not have them. To read them, we must ask permission from you."

"Because I only know of mine. I know others were made, but I do not have access to them, only mine."

"Do you not see?" Amina asked. "It is the same for Basya. That record is sacred to her family. But she knows of only one copy the one that a cousin writes in and protects."

I gazed at Basya, thinking. I had not read from the books written by the matriarchs of our people for some time. They were sacred to me and other women. The books written by her family were as sacred.

"I … see … what you mean." I nodded to Amina, then turned to Basya. "I apologize for not trusting you. If the records are kept by another, you would not be able to bring them with you."

Basya gazed at her hands. "I may not have remembered them, even if they were in my home. Fires burned. Giants rampaged. My parents lay dead on the floor."

I quivered. "No. It would be difficult to remember everything you needed."

"I did forget some of my tinctures and draughts that would have been valuable to help Ham's broken arm and our starvation. I may have forgotten a record of our people. I did want to bring the Book of Commandments, but, like the record of our family, it lay in another home, too far for me to claim."

Basya's plight when she left her home became clearer. Could I have done any better? I shook my head.

"I apologize to you, Basya. I am not certain I could have done as well as you did, especially as you were fighting a fire and hiding from the giants."

"Thank you, Imma," she said.

After that day, I worried less about her. I did not yet completely trust her motivation, but I believed her story.

~ ~ ~

Noah and the boys, his sons and grandsons who still lived in Mamre, searched for the gopher wood Jehovah commanded that they use for the ark. One small thicket of the trees grew within easy reach. We knew they were gopher wood trees. They grew taller than any of the other trees.

Sadly, however, there were not many in the thicket. Ham mentioned that he had seen another small wood of gopher trees to the east, before he reached the valley where he found Basya. He did not know if they withstood the flooding.

"If Jehovah requires gopher wood for our ark," Noah said, "I suspect they will survive flooding, if they are not flooded for too many days."

The men took oxen and sledges to the gopher wood grove and cut the mature trees. I expected the wood to be dark and heavy. It was not. Though they grew tall and straight, they could be carried on two sledges. One carried the bottom of the trunk. Another, attached by a long, heavy length of hemp rope, carried the top.

Noah and the others cut off the branches, piling them on top of the trunk. One tree filled the two sledges. It took three pair of oxen to pull them from the grove to an empty field outside our walls. They brought one tree a day for six days.

"What will you do if enemies try to burn your wood?" I asked when I saw the pile of trees after the first week. "You would not want to lose all the work of cutting and hauling those trees."

"I would not want to lose this work, yet I have no way to protect it."

"A wall?" I asked.

"We cannot take the time to build another wall."

"Assign men to guard it?"

"Who? We do not have enough men to guard the trees and the wall around our compound, and still go cut more."

"What will you do?"

"For now, we will watch and see what our neighbors say and do."

"And if they try to destroy the trees?"

"I must depend on Jehovah to protect them. It is by His command that I use gopher wood. I trust He will protect the trees I find and cart home."

"How many trees will it take? Those trees are huge."

"And the ark will need to be large enough to carry all the animals. It, too, will be huge."

A noisy breath escaped my lungs. "How many animals will you bring?"

"At least two of every kind."

"Every kind? The horse and the mule? The antelope and the gazelle? They are so similar."

"I do not know yet which animals Jehovah will direct to enter the ark. Nor do I know which people it will protect. I can only hope you and I will be included."

"You are building the ark and you do not know if you will be invited to enter it?" Red rose up my neck as I recognized the shrillness of my voice.

Noah patted my hand. "Do not fear. Jehovah is kind and fair."

"And you are past five hundred years old."

He raised his eyebrows. "And? I am a prophet of Jehovah. If I am not going to enter the ark, Jehovah will call another before we leave. Do not fear."

I breathed in and out slowly, regaining my composure and my confidence. "I trust Jehovah will do the right thing."

"Always." Noah kissed me.

"What will you do now?"

"Bring the last of the mature gopher wood from the grove. I will leave the young trees to grow. I may need them later."

"And then?"

"Find more. This will not be enough for an ark as big as Jehovah demands."

"How big is that?" I could not envision the size he suggested.

He blew out a breath. "Three hundred cubits long, fifty cubits wide, and thirty cubits high."

My eyes widened with each number. "That is big. I cannot comprehend anything so big."

We stood next to the pile of logs. Noah hammered a stake into the ground and stepped out the distance of three hundred cubits from me. There he hammered another stake into the ground. I could almost see him from where I stood.

He returned and measured the distance of fifty cubits across. I could see him at the end of that measurement, but we could not speak to each other.

I imagined thirty cubits up, taller than I expected.

"I think animals will fit nicely in this," I said when Noah came back to my side.

"I agree. Numbers mean nothing until we step out the actual distance," he agreed.

Three weeks later, all the mature trees in the grove were cut and in the stack of wood outside our wall.

Ham, Japeth, and Shem lay the trees on the ground, marking the bottom of the ark as far as they went. Not nearly far enough. The trees were nearly 100 cubits long, but their width changed from the bottom of the trunk to the top.

"What are you going to do about that?" I asked Noah.

"I am thinking we can plane the trees into long slabs of wood. We do not have to use each tree as a whole."

"And you know how to do that?" my fist slid to my hip.

He nodded. "I have done it on smaller trees. It will be more difficult on these long ones."

I gazed at the tall trees and nodded. "You may need to cut them into shorter pieces."

"Perhaps. If I do, I will. But I think there is a reason Jehovah ordered us to use gopher wood. It is light, but it was difficult to cut. I hope I can plane the planks off and keep the length. I have seen no other trees that grow so tall."

It took many days to plane the trees into slabs the width of two of Noah's fists. He did not want them to be any thinner. They would have to hold out the water.

The men would take turns. They worked on planing the trees while the grains grew in the fields. By the time the early grains were ready to harvest, all the trees were stacked in a pile along the sides of the space Noah had laid out on that day with me.

"You do not have enough wood," I said in the evening as we sat beside the pile of planed wood after winnowing the wheat. "What will you do?"

Noah shrugged. "I will have to search for more gopher wood and bring it here."

My eyes opened wide. "You will cart those great trees from around the land?"

"I will do what I must to be obedient."

CHAPTER 18

Getting to Know Her

That year we stored the early grains in our storage buildings that sat half under the ground to help them stay cool in the heat of the growing times. Amina, Edna, and Basya helped me in preserving the fruits and vegetables as they ripened. These, too, were stored in storage buildings.

"Why are we storing so much food?" Edna asked as we carried more grain into the storehouse.

"Have you not heard?" Amina asked her. "Noah has prophesied the end of life in this world. That is why he is building the ark."

"Yes. I know he is building an ark to preserve the life of the species. But why are we storing so much food? We will not be here to eat it."

"But whoever goes on the ark will need food to eat while the earth is flooded. They cannot grow food on the ark." Basya moved another basket to a shelf.

"Whoever? Do you not think we will go on the ark?" Edna asked.

"I do not know. I have no reason to think I will be included." Basya glanced away from the others. "I am a daughter of Cain. Why would I be included?"

"But you love Jehovah as we do," Amina argued. "Why would you not go?"

She lifted a shoulder. "I have not been invited."

"None of us have been invited," I said. "I doubt Noah will tell any of us that until the ark is closer to being finished. They still have much work to do, and many more logs of the gopher wood to cut and drag home."

"This is true," Amina said. "If you were Ham's wife, Basya, you would be more certain of a place on the ark."

"If?" Basya said. "Would you accept me as his wife? I am different from all of you. I carry the mark of Cain." She bit her lip.

"If Ham decides you are the right woman for him, we would accept it," I said. "You have shown how much you love Jehovah in the time you have been with us. Your belief and obedience are more sincere than either Nirit or Channa pretended to have."

"You would accept me into your family?" Basya asked.

"I would."

"We would," Amina and Edna chorused.

"We have wondered for many months why you had not accepted him."

"He has not asked me for some time. I have asked Jehovah for an answer. He has not shared his thoughts with me."

"Have you thought on it and made your own decision before taking it to Him?" Amina asked.

I swallowed the same question, glad that Amina had suggested it.

Basya stared up at Amina, then glanced at me. "I have been waiting to hear from Jehovah. Must I make a decision first. What if I am wrong?"

"You must make a tentative decision and take it to Him. He will reinforce your decision or let you know it is wrong," Edna said. "Have you not made big decisions like this before?"

"Nothing so big as marrying Ham. He is such a good man, and … and he is your son, Imma, and Noah's."

"And you do not believe you are good enough for us?" Amina asked.

"I am a daughter of Cain. I carry the mark. How can I be worthy of Ham? Of your family?"

She had put in words my concerns. "It is your decision. You must choose to be his wife or not," I said.

"I would not want to be a reason to divide Ham from his family. I have seen the sorrow brought by Telemon's leaving. I could not do that to Ham," Basya cried.

"Talk to Noah when he returns home. Make your decision and take this to Jehovah. You may be surprised at what answer you receive," I suggested.

Basya lowered her eyes. "Your words mean much to me. I will have to take this to Jehovah again."

We finished storing the grains with more talking and laughter. Basya, however did not join in the laughter. She had lost herself in deep thought. We had given her much to think about.

When Noah returned from teaching and cutting more of the gopher wood, Basya entered his office to visit with him. They visited together for nearly a span.

Ham came in the house, searching for his papa.

"He is with Basya," I said indicating Noah's office with my head. "She has been there for some time."

"Do you know why?"

I inhaled. "We suggested she talk with your papa. She does not feel worthy to marry you."

Ham stared at the door to Noah's office and bit his lip. "What will papa tell her?"

"Do you want to marry her?" I asked.

His whipped his head around and his gaze turned from the door to me. "I do. I believe Jehovah took me searching to find Basya to be my wife."

"A daughter of Cain?"

"A daughter of Adam. She and her family were blessed to know of Jehovah and trust him in a thousand or more years without having Papa or any of our grandpapas teach them and help them remember what Jehovah taught." Ham's voice rose with every word.

"I admit that took courage for her and her family."

"She is special. And yes. I do want to marry her. I have met no other woman who honors Jehovah as well as Basya. And I love her." Ham's voice softened, until the last word came in an almost whisper. "I want her to love me."

Noah's office door opened. Basya stepped through it into the room.

"I do love you, Ham," she said and hurried to his side. "Your papa has convinced me that my love is acceptable to Jehovah. I feel it. Here." She touched her chest. "Do you still want me?"

Ham threw his arms around her and lifted her off her feet. He kissed her. "Yes, Basya. I want you to be my wife."

"Even though —"

"Regardless of anything you are, or say, or do, I love you and want you to be my wife."

Basya wrapped her arms around Ham and kissed him. "If you will have me, I want to be your wife."

Ham spun her around. "I want you to be my wife." He held her close, tears dripping down his face. He kissed her again.

Noah put his arm around me. "I think we will have a wedding soon."

~ ~ ~

We invited family to come to the wedding of Ham and Basya just before the end of the dry time. My mama and papa came in early enough to help cook the feast for the guests.

I wanted to put them in Ham's house. We had been using it as a guest house. Amina suggested that Ham and Basya would prefer to have his house to themselves after the ceremony. Instead, she invited them to stay with her.

Our homes were filled by all the people that came for the wedding. Both Grandpapa Methuselah and Lamech stayed with us in our home. Ham requested that Grandpapa Methuselah perform the wedding rite.

I assisted Edna and Amina in surprising Basya with a beautiful dress for the wedding. Edna had shared some of her clothing with Basya when she first came to Mamre. The two young women were similar in size except that Edna was a fist width taller than Basya.

We sewed the dress while Basya and Ham spent time together in the evening, discussing their future. I do not think Basya had any idea.

The day of the wedding the three of us went to Ham's house to help her prepare for the wedding.

"Which of these dresses should I wear?" Basya asked, indicating the three dresses on her bed.

"I like this blue on you," Amina said.

"And I like the pink," Edna said.

"But I do not think any of these are nice enough for you to wear to your wedding," I added.

The excitement in Basya's face fell as fast as rain falls from a sudden rain storm. "I don't have any other dress to wear."

"Are you certain of that?" Edna asked.

"You know all of my dresses. You gave them to me," Basya said. She plopped into the chair beside her bed.

"Yes. I know each of your dresses. You did not have much to wear when you arrived here."

"That is why ..." Amina said, reaching into her basket.

"We brought you a new dress," I said as Amina pulled the dress out.

Basya squealed as Amina lifted the cream-colored dress from the basket. "Where did that come from?"

"We made it for you," Edna trilled. "You needed a new dress to wear. You are special, and we wanted you to know that."

Basya threw her arms around us and hugged. "Thank you."

We helped her put the dress on and tied the ties on the sides. Her striking figure looked wonderful in the new dress.

"Ham will like you in this new dress," Amina said.

"You need one thing to make it look nicer," I said, pulling a string of orange and black beads from my pocket.

"Ooh. These are beautiful. Grandmama Ziva had two strings of beads much like these. Nat made one for her. Auntie Daphne brought her the second. Grandmama Rebecca gave them to Daphne, hoping she could find her missing daughter."

"And Daphne found her?"

"She did."

"Why did she not return to tell Rebecca that she had found her daughter?" I asked.

"Wicked men tried to take away the gold coins she earned as a trader. They wanted the Book of Commandments, not knowing what it was, only that it was special. When they attacked the trader's caravan, they did not get the gold or the Book. She left the gold with Uncle David. The Book …"

"What happened to the book?" Amina asked.

"Burned." Basya whispered.

"How could your family learn from the Book of Commandments if it burned?" I asked.

"Before she thought she left David behind, she made a copy for Ziva to use. Two other copies were carefully made. We had one of them in our small village of Safe Haven. Ziva left her copy in Nod. She couldn't get it before escaping."

"And the last one?" Edna asked.

"I do not know what happened to it. Grandpapa Nat sent it to Limhah, a city he built for his grandchildren."

I nodded. "It is hard when there is only one copy of the commandments available for you to use."

"Do you have more than that?" Basya asked.

"Yes. Noah has a copy, as does his papa and grandpapa. Their copies will come to Japeth and Shem when they leave this earth."

"And Ham? Will he get a copy?"

"Perhaps you can copy it for him," Edna said.

"Perhaps I can."

The orange and black beads looked beautiful with the dress. We led Basya out of the house and down the path to our home where Ham and our guests waited for us.

Those in the audience gasped when Basya walked in. The creamy dress against her dark skin looked amazing. As she walked to stand by Ham, he gazed at her as though he had never seen her before.

She smiled at him, then turned to face Grandpapa Methuselah, who repeated the simple and sweet words used from the beginning of time to marry couples. I thought about Crites, Basya's Grandpapa, who had received these words to wed his children.

After the rite, Ham and Basya greeted their guests. Mama found me.

"Where did Ham find a daughter of Cain?" Mama asked.

"Mama, I told you she came from that land. You knew."

"But you said she honors Jehovah?"

"She does. Remember, she is one of the many granddaughters of Ziva, daughter of Rebecca and Enos."

"One of their stolen children? How did Ham find her?"

"I will let him tell you the story, Mama. But not today. They will want to meet with all their guests, and they will want to be alone together tonight. Maybe before you leave?"

Mama pulled a face and gazed at the line of people congratulating the couple. "You are right. I need to serve the feast we worked so hard to prepare."

"We have others to help serve —"

But Mama had turned and scooted toward the kitchen. I shook my head. At least, she would be kept busy and not beg Ham and Basya for their story tonight.

Most of the guests had met Basya earlier. Rather than discussing her as a daughter of Cain, their conversation turned to the pile of wood that grew outside our walls.

"Why would Noah be building a pile of gopher wood?" I heard as I passed one group of people.

As I passed another, I heard, "I hear he thinks Jehovah will destroy all life on this world. What makes him think he can be one who is saved?"

"I heard Noah is building an ark?" I heard another person mutter.

"What makes him think water will reach us here? We are high in the mountains and far from the seas," another grumbled.

"Crazy. The man is crazy."

If Noah's family had these thoughts, what would the rest of the world say? What would they do?

CHAPTER 19

Jest

"Do not worry about the rest of the world," Noah said that night as we prepared to sleep. "Jehovah warned me that the world would not understand. They would not believe. If they believed, they would repent."

I sighed.

"I have a hard time listening to people who pretend to love you and who came to eat our food say such bad things about you."

"This is nothing compared to what it will be like, my dear." He pulled me onto his lap and kissed me. "This is part of the reason I built a wall around our homes. I want to protect you from the hatred of those who will hate me."

I hugged him. "I do not like the thoughts of people hating you. If they knew you as I do —"

"They would repent. But they cannot. They have accepted the lies the Destroyer has taught them. It is easier to believe the lies than to repent."

"But it is easy to be obedient …"

"For you it is. You love Jehovah. For those who have lost that love, it is easier to disobey. They like the evil and wicked behaviors. They prefer to disobey, act as if there were no commandments against their actions. Love whomever and whatever they chose."

"How sad. They love everything except the one who will make them happy."

"Yes. I see it even among those who were here tonight. They would rather jest about my ark than help me build it."

I stood from his lap and pulled the covers back on the bed. "Would you accept their help if they offered?"

"I may. But I won't expect them to offer. They will not want to have the villagers of Mamre or others who come to gawk at us taunt them. They have no courage."

"And our sons do?" I lay on the bed and pulled the covers over me.

Noah joined me. "I believe these three sons do. They have been courageous. I feared we would lose Ham like we lost Telemon."

"Have you had news of Telemon?" I asked.

"I ask in every village about him. Some saw him with an army of Tishites. Others suggested they saw him with the Shulonites. I fear he has been lost in the battles against others. Armies fight over land and gold. The invader believes he deserves everything owned by those he invades, even their lives and freedom. Rather than work to earn or create his own, he attempts to steal it."

"That is how I see it, too." I blew out the candle on my side of the bed as Noah blew out the one on his side. We snuggled under the covers. "What will you do if Telemon ever returns?"

"Invite him back. Hope he can repent of his actions."

"And if he cannot?"

Noah blew out his breath. "Love him. What else can we do?"

Love him. So simple. I hoped it would be enough. I loved Telemon and his lost sisters as much as I loved Japeth, Shem, and Ham.

~ ~ ~

Noah predicted the behaviors of our neighbors correctly. At the end of the rains, they began to come to watch Noah and the boys plane the wood into slabs of wood.

"What do you think you are building?" they would taunt.

Noah would stop for a time to teach them of Jehovah and warn them that the end would come if they did not repent.

Laughter filled the air. They would not believe.

Noah and his sons and grandsons who worked on the ark entered the gate at the end of one day covered with the remains of rotten food.

"What happened?" I asked, aghast at the food splattered across their clothing.

"The villagers decided we needed to have our gopher wood painted with rotten food, and us along with it," Ham said with a little laugh.

"What will you do to stop it?" I asked.

Noah shrugged. "What can we do? I have no time to argue with them. The food smells, but we will live."

"Cannot Jehovah protect you from them?" I asked.

"He could. But he will not. He has promised all his children the right to choose. He could stop them, but it would take away their choice."

"And allow you to be injured to give them the choice to throw things at you?" I cried.

"Perhaps. I will be protected, as will the boys. As long as it is only rotten food, we will survive."

"You are taking your clothing off out here," I ordered. "I am not having that rotten food smelling up my home."

Noah laughed. "Where shall I go to take it off?"

"Out back by the kitchen door. I will heat up water for you."

"You will let me freeze out here while you heat the water?"

"You will not freeze. It is hot. You can bring water to me from the well to fill your tub."

Noah laughed. "Now who is taking away choices?" Noah demanded.

I lifted a shoulder. "My clean house."

He laughed and headed toward the back of the house, untying the ties that held his tunic on.

A span later, he came into the kitchen again dressed in clean clothing. "Do I look any better?"

"You smell lots better. Did you empty your tub?"

"Tub?" he asked hiding a grin.

"Your bathtub. Is it empty?"

"I did not want to get wet."

"Wet! You were already wet." I turned from the pot with a wooden spoon in my hand.

"I emptied it. I know better than to leave a tub of water standing in the garden." He giggled a little.

"Will this happen again?" I asked when I joined Noah at the table.

"Perhaps. You may want to have the tub ready outside tomorrow. I fear they did not get their fill of throwing things at us today."

"Do they not have better things to do than taunt and threaten you and throw rotten vegetables at you?"

"They do. They forget that other things are more important."

"They will be hungry when it rains if they do not return to their gardens and fields."

"They will."

Once more, Noah predicted the truth. He and the others returned home covered with rotten vegetables each day for the next four days.

"This is the last day you will have to have a tub prepared for me," Noah said that fifth night.

"Why is that? Are all the rotten vegetables gone?"

"No. We have planed all the trees into long slabs. We will need to cut more trees."

"Where will you find more gopher wood trees? You have cut all the trees near Mamre."

"I know. I saw a bigger stand of gopher wood the last time we traveled west to teach."

"But there are mountains to the west. It will be difficult to drag the trees over the mountains."

"It will be difficult, but I must be obedient. Jehovah will help us."

"Will you take all the boys?"

"No. I will leave Japeth behind. He needs time to be with Amina, and you need a man here to protect you. Some of the grandsons will go with me if only to laugh. Others will stay here to help protect you."

"You think I need protection?"

"You and our son's wives need protection from those who listen to the Destroyer. You will until we all get on the ark."

"Is it that bad?"

Noah leaned his elbows on the table in front of him. "It is not bad yet. It will get worse."

"You promised to protect me all those years ago when I agreed to marry you."

"And I have. I will always protect you. When I am gone, Jehovah will be here to watch over you. But you must stay within the walls to be safe."

I took his hand in mine and kissed the back of it. "I trust you and Jehovah to care for me."

He held my hand. “I always will.”

CHAPTER 20

Protection

No one tried to enter through our walls to attack us while Noah was gone that trip nor the next. However, one of the grandsons shouted out a warning while Noah traveled the second time.

"They try to burn the wood!" he called.

I ran to the wall and climbed the ladder to stare over it at the wood.

Men with torches ran toward the big pile of planed wood. All the hard work Noah and the others had done would be gone if it burned.

Jehovah, please protect the wood. It is for the ark you commanded Noah to build.

I watched the edge of one slab catch fire and gasped.

Please protect it!

The sky darkened. I glanced upward to see dark rain clouds where there were none only breaths before. With a sizzle, lightning zipped from the clouds toward the men attempting to burn Noah's wood. The accompanying crash of thunder brought rain that drenched the men with torches and the gopher wood.

The men stared up at the clouds.

"Where did those come from?" one man shouted. He raised a fist toward the clouds and heaven. "You will not stop us. We will destroy this."

"Not if Jehovah is protecting it," I murmured. "Thank you, Jehovah."

The soaking wet men ran from the pile of wood toward their homes. The rain lessened, no longer pounding the wood and the earth, until only soft sprinkles fell. The cloud dissipated. The sun shone on us once more through blue sky.

I turned to climb down the ladder. Only then did I realize the rain had fallen on the men and the pile of wood. None fell inside our wall. My clothing, the wall, and the ladder were dry.

I hurried to my room and fell to the floor beside my bed and raised my arms in prayer, thanking Jehovah for this miracle of rain.

The men returned days later. Once again, they planned to burn the gopher wood. I watched from the top of the wall, begging Jehovah to protect the wood again.

A cold wind began to blow from the north. I wrapped my arms around myself against the cold. The men below me stared around as the fire on their torches blew out.

The man with a torch nearest the wood tossed it toward the gopher wood. He cursed when he saw the flames were gone.

"What is this?" he cried.

He turned toward his companions. Only one torch remained afire. He beckoned the man holding it forward.

"Come. You must light these on fire now while you can," he called.

The man with the lit torch stepped forward, into the gale. The fire of his torch blew sideways. It touched the clothing of another man, catching it on fire.

The burning man screamed and fell to the ground, writhing in pain as all his clothing burned his skin.

The torch bearer stared at him.

"Come now," the first man shouted. "Light this wood!"

The torch bearer broke his stare from the burning man and ran forward toward the gopher wood. He brought the flames close to the edge of the wood.

The torch flames blew in the wind.

"Light, curse you, light," the leader shouted through the wind.

Instead, the flame extinguished in the wind.

The wind increased, pushing the men who still stood toward the village. Two men lifted the burned man by his arms and half carried, half dragged him with them.

The wind pushed them past their homes. They could not break away to turn out of the wind. I watched until they disappeared into a grove of pines.

I shivered and climbed from the wall seeking refuge from the wind in my home. At the base of the wall, no wind blew. Inside our compound, we enjoyed a calm day.

I bowed my head and gave thanks to Jehovah once more.

Noah returned the next day. He came into the kitchen for a drink and to let me know of his safe return. They had passed by men from Mamre with bodies battered from a strong wind. They carried one of their men in a litter.

"When I asked if they would like our help, they cursed me. I did not hurt them. Why the cursing?"

"They tried to burn your pile of gopher wood. They could not," I said as I kneaded bread for our evening meal.

"Oh?" Noah's eyes turned to gaze toward the pile of wood, though he could not see it through the walls of our home and the walls surrounding our compound.

"Shortly after you left, they came with torches, trying to burn your wood pile. A cloud appeared above them. It dropped all its rain on the wood and them." I held up hands covered in flour and shrugged.

"Perhaps this is why Jehovah required the use of gopher wood. It lay in the rain during the last rain time, with no ill effects. It did not warp or bend."

"Perhaps. It does not catch fire easily, either. Yesterday, the men returned with torches. Like the last time, I watched from the wall, praying for Jehovah to protect your wood. You warned us men would try to destroy your work. Our men listened to your orders to watch them and do nothing. I think some of our grandsons may begin to believe in Jehovah." I plopped the ball of dough into a bowl and covered it with a towel.

"That is good. What happened yesterday?"

I sat in a chair across from Noah, my elbows on the table, and my flour covered hands in the air while I shared with him how the wind had come up blowing out the torches and burning the one man.

"The wind pushed them into the pine trees. I could see them no longer, and the wind on top of the wall bit into me. I thought they returned home."

"The wind must have blown them farther along the road, for I passed them farther away than the pine grove. It is strange. I felt no wind."

"It did not blow within the walls of our compound. It came suddenly and blew them away."

"Jehovah protects you and he protects my work."

~ ~ ~

Noah had returned with more gopher wood trees. He and our sons spent many days planing them into thick slabs.

One evening after spending the day working with the wood, Noah sat with me, Ham, and Basya on the front porch, watching the sun drop below the mountains. We loved to watch the colors of the setting sun, especially the golds and purples of distant clouds.

"I believe we have enough wood to begin the process of building the ark," he said.

"Begin? Enough to begin but not complete?"

He turned his eyes from the beauty of the sunset to me.

"Yes. We will need many more trees to complete the building of our ark. It will be bigger than any home I have seen built."

"I have heard of buildings almost as big as your ark will be. Mama told me of the homes of people in Nod. Many families lived together in them, separated into compartments," Basya said. She did not move her eyes from the display of colorful clouds in the sky.

"Huge homes, almost as big as the ark will be?" I asked.

"Papa says that the home his Grandmama Merab and Grandpapa Tiqvah lived in while they lived in Nod had three floors, one on top of the other. But their home was small compared to the big compartment homes within the city for the poor. Ah. The light is nearly gone."

Noah rocked his head back and forth in a tiny motion. "Jehovah warned us not to live so close together. It causes problems."

"I heard the violence and murder increased within those homes," Basya said, turning toward Noah.

"It would along with other greater sins."

"Oh?" I asked. "What other sins are greater than violence and murder?"

"Certainly, murder of the body is one of the greatest sins. Murdering the soul or the heart of a person is greater."

"How would one murder the soul of a person?" Basya asked.

"When they teach only the wickedness of the Destroyer, never allowing the hope of Jehovah, they destroy the soul," Ham said.

"Yes. That and teaching them to wallow in their sins. Nothing is sacred. Men and women can do as they please. I have seen that in many lands outside Nod." Noah leaned back in his chair.

"Papa tells stories of cult gods and their commandments. Men and women of Nod did not always act with freedom to do as they pleased. They obeyed the edicts of their priests."

"In the early days, all men obeyed some priest, some authority greater than themselves. That has changed over the years." Noah took my hand in his.

"How has it changed? I have been here in Mamre much of my life since I met you, and many of those years behind these walls." I squeezed Noah's hand in mine.

"Men will attack women without considering how it affects the woman or her family. They take her and abuse her." Noah's face hardened in the fading light.

"Beating her?" I asked with a gasp.

"And more. They do those things to her that should only be done with a man's wife." Noah lifted my hand and set it in his lap.

I had heard of this in the years before.

Basya gasped. "They take her for that?"

"And other things. Sometimes they take her to be their slave, to use as they please, to sell to other men to be used," Noah continued.

"Sick!" I said.

"That is not all," Ham added. "We are learning we must travel in groups. Men are doing the same thing to other men, using them as they would a woman, selling the man's body as they sell a woman's body."

My face crumpled. Basya grabbed her stomach. All the color drained from her. She rushed to the side of the porch and vomited over the rail.

I hurried inside to get cups of water for all of us. When I returned, I handed a cup to Basya first. "You will want to wash your mouth out."

She nodded. "I am sorry. My stomach has been queasy lately. I do not feel sick, except for my stomach."

I touched her forehead. It did not burn.

I gave Ham and Noah their cups of water, then returned to my seat. Noah smiled.

"What?" Basya asked.

"You are with child. It causes your stomach to turn. I have seen it many times in the women around me."

"With child?" Basya questioned.

Ham whooped. "A child! Is it possible?"

She bit her lip, her fingers twitched.

"It is possible. I did not want to hope," she murmured.

"Will it be safe? Papa tell me it will be safe for her," Ham pleaded.

"I cannot promise you anything. I do not know the future of all things."

"But you are a prophet. Can you not tell me if she will have the child safely?"

Noah gazed toward the couple. Ham held Basya's hand firmly in his own. Noah nodded. "I believe you will have many children safely. If they will stay safe in the love of Jehovah, I cannot say."

Ham whooped before hearing the last of Noah's words. "We will have a child, many children! Did you hear, Basya?"

She smiled weakly. "That will be great as long as I do not have to feel like this until the child is born."

I stepped down the steps of our porch to the overgrown peppermint plant. I picked a leaf and took it to Basya. "Chew on this. It will help."

She took the leaf and smelled it. Her nose wiggled a bit. She put the leaf in her mouth and chewed.

"What is this?" she asked.

"Peppermint. I am surprised you have not heard of it. You are a trained healer. It settles sick stomachs."

"We have none of this in Safe Haven. Many of the people I helped to heal would have been happy for this."

"It works well in a tea. I will bring you your own plant tomorrow when I can see better to take a bit for you."

"That would be wonderful," Basya sighed.

"I will give you another leaf or two to chew on tonight and tomorrow to help your stomach until I can bring you the plant." I turned on my heel and stepped down the two stairs off the porch once more.

When I returned, I handed several leaves of the peppermint to Basya.

She smiled. "Why did no one tell me that peppermint helps nausea?"

"We thought you learned from top healers?" Ham teased.

"I did. I don't know why I missed this important knowledge."

"I am happy to share my knowledge with you," I said.

CHAPTER 21

Twins

Over the next months of the warm times, Noah and our sons worked on the ark. They began to use the long slabs of gopher wood to create a great ark. It would be huge, and wonderful.

Noah would not allow me or the other women stand outside the wall to watch them work. "It is too dangerous for you to be outside the walls without men to protect you."

"But you will be there," I protested.

"I will be there, but I will be working. Not watching for men who would attack us. Men who would take you and use you or sell you as a slave."

"They would do that?"

Noah put his arms around me. "Have I not told you about what the men do?"

"You have but I did not think they were close to us."

"They are, Imma. They are. It is dangerous for you to be outside the walls of our compound."

I shivered.

"May I watch from the top of the wall?"

"You may, but you must stay within the wall where you will be safe."

I spent part of each day after that while the men were working standing on the path built below the top of the wall so guards and others could safely look out. I watched them notch the wood together, pounding pegs to keep them together, using the steam from boiling water to bend the slabs to meet the specification given.

Slowly, the ark began to take shape. I had expected them to start at the bottom and build it up the sides to the top. I was wrong. Instead, they carefully bent the slabs of wood to curve to form the bottom of the ark. The curved slabs became the ribs of the ark. The long lengths of gopher wood did not reach the distance from one end to the other end of the ribbing. It was here they notched and pegged the lengths together.

Each day, I went to the top of the wall to watch the men work. The length of the ark bowed slightly near the ends as the bottom took shape.

Noah directed them to bend the slabs of wood to round the bottom, front and back. It amazed me to see how he worked through the problems of completing the outside shell of the ark.

The men spent many of the warm days working on the ark. I appreciated the Sabbath during that season of warmth more than I had in many years. We would meet together to share our love for Jehovah and his many blessings.

Noah would discuss with us the things he had learned from Jehovah in the week before. As he worked on the ark, he received new information almost every day.

Toward the end of the warm time, he surprised us.

"I have been commanded to leave Mamre and the ark for a time."

"What are you to do?" I asked.

"I am to take Japeth and Shem to the east and teach those I find."

"East?" Basya questioned. "Toward Safe Haven and the edge of Nod?"

"Perhaps." Noah nodded toward her. "We have not been that way for many years. We did not know that your Safe Haven was there."

"If you saw us, you would have diverted around our walls. We lived on the edge of the land of Nod. We were children of Cain." Her voice no longer held the pain of being considered less than a daughter of Adam.

"Perhaps," Noah said. "We go where Jehovah sends us. Perhaps there are still men and women in your village of Safe Haven who live. Some who would like to know that there are still men and women in the world who believe in and obey the commands of Jehovah."

"That would be good," she said, chewing on the inside of her cheek.

"Is it a problem, dear?" Ham asked.

She shook her head, but even I could see her concern.

"What is it?" I asked.

"I fear the giants," she sobbed. "I have heard how they hunt you, Papa Noah. They took over my village. I do not know if they stayed there."

"The giants are not known for staying in a village after they destroy it," Shem said.

"But there were many women in the village."

"And they may have taken them to their own villages," Japeth suggested.

"Yes. They took the women to their camp while the village burned." Basya set her hand on the bulge of her stomach. The hand bounced with the kicking of her child.

"You are going to be there when it is time for the rain to come again," Basya said. "Will you be caught in a flood like Ham and I were?"

"Does it happen there often?" Shem asked.

Basya lifted a shoulder in a tiny shrug. "I do not know. I never went that far from the village before then."

"It could flood again, but I suspect that flood was unusual," Noah replied. "We will be safe, even if the giants are there. Jehovah sends us."

"You are leaving me here?" Ham asked. "I am the only one who has traveled that direction in many years."

"And your wife will be giving birth to your first child before we return," Noah replied.

"Oh," Ham said, shutting his mouth on whatever he planned to say.

"You will be gone that long?" I asked.

"Perhaps. We will plan on it. If we return sooner, all of us will be happy. I will be watching for more groves of the gopher wood. We will need much more of it before we complete the ark. We go to find wood and to teach men and women."

"When do you leave?" Edna asked in a tiny voice.

"On the morning after tomorrow," Noah replied. "Is there a problem?"

"I … I …"

"You are with child?" Noah asked.

Edna colored. "I do not know for sure. I have not been able to determine for certain." She turned to Shem. "I did not know enough to tell you."

Shem threw his arms around her. "I would have liked you to tell me when we were alone, but I am happy to hear you may have another child. Is it too early after …?" His eyes found Basya.

"She is healed. By the time the child is to be born, she will be fine." Basya touched Edna's hand and smiled.

"Do you think I will have problems like before?"

"Who knows. Every child is different."

"We can wait two days to leave. We should give Shem an extra day with his family," Noah said. He put his arm around me. "And I would not mind an extra day home with you," he whispered in my ear.

Two mornings later, Noah led Japeth and Shem out the gate of our compound. Shem and Japeth each led a pack mule loaded with supplies.

Noah kissed me. "I will miss you while I am gone," he murmured.

"Not as much as I will miss you," I replied. This had become our regular goodbye in the years since our marriage.

He smiled and kissed me again. "Remember. Do not leave the safety of our walls. For anything. It is not safe for you or any of our women to leave. Depend on Ham alone to protect you. But stay in the compound."

"I have no plans to leave our compound," I told him.

"You will be tempted. Do not give in. Stay here in the safety." He swung his leg over the back of his tall red horse.

"I will not leave. I promise."

"Remember," he said. He bent low over the horse's neck to touch his finger to the center of my forehead. "It is important that you remember."

I had no clue what he meant. I had not considered leaving the safety of the compound for years. I had all I needed inside our walls. What would lure me out?

~ ~ ~

I wondered at Noah's final warning as I went about my chores, keeping our home clean, mending clothing, weaving fabric for clothing, and sewing new clothes for Noah and myself. I went out into the sunshine and gathered in the last of the vegetables from the garden.

There was more than enough to keep me busy within the walls of our compound. I had no desire to leave.

Basya's belly grew bigger than any of us expected. I wondered if there may be a problem with her and the baby.

She tired easily, too. Much more easily than any of the other women who carried their first child. I worried, about her.

"Mama Imma," she said as she entered my home early one afternoon. "I need you to feel my baby. Something does not feel right."

I swallowed my fears. I had been afraid of this.

"I have felt many babies before their birth. Do you trust me to know the problem?"

"I will guide you. Between us, I think we can better understand what I will be facing."

"Come into my sleeping room and lay down, so I can examine you." I led her down the hall and into the room.

She kicked off her slippers and lay down. She pointed at a spot on her protruding stomach. "Here, first."

I sucked in a breath and touched it.

"Press harder or you will never feel," Basya said.

I pressed harder. I felt a roundness. "A head, or a bum. It is round."

She had me move my fingers over slowly. I felt a space, then another roundness. "How can this be?"

"What do you feel?"

"I felt a head or a bum, a space no connecting parts, and another roundness."

She bit her lip. "Feel some more. See what you feel."

I moved my fingers around, feeling the baby through his mama's belly.

"I do not understand," I said after I had poked her over all her belly, twice.

"What do you not understand?" She sat up and brushed her dark hair back.

"It is as if there are two babies inside you. Is that possi5ble?"

Basya released the air from her lungs. "Some of my grandmamas had twins. It is possible that I have twins, as well."

"Twins?"

"Two babies born at the same time."

"Oh. I have heard of that before. I have never seen it, though."

"Twins don't happen often."

"Is it safe for you?"

"The babies will grow bigger than I can hold. I do not know much more. I have never had one child before. I certainly have not had twins. And I have never helped a mama give birth to twins."

"It is all new to me." I submerged my fears. She did not need to know.

"New to me, as well." Basya pushed her feet back into her slippers. "We will have fun when they decide to be born."

"I wish Sigal still lived in Mamre," I said with a whimper.

"Is she a healer?" Basya asked.

"Yes, and my friend."

"I wish she lived nearby, too. I fear this may not be an easy birth. Where is this Sigal now?"

"I do not know. She left Mamre many years ago. I would send a message for her if I knew where to send it."

Basya sighed. "It may be you and me doing this together."

"That could be a challenge," I said. "I am happy Ham is here with us."

"Yes. We do have Ham. I wish he had training in healing."

"It would be nice if he did. Perhaps we need to teach him."

CHAPTER 22

Tiny Boys

I worried about Basya. I had not helped birth twins before. I feared there would be problems. How would I ensure two babies were breathing? Perhaps my mama or my sister? Amina did have some experience. Perhaps she could help.

Basya's stomach continued to grow as the rain began to fall. I hoped to see Noah and the others return sooner than he suspected. He had warned me this would be a longer journey. I missed him.

Much sooner than we expected, Ham came pounding on my door. "Mama! Basya told me to come get you. There is blood in our bed."

"It is too early for the babies," I cried as I grabbed the bag with supplies I had prepared only that morning.

"Basya says it is too early, too, but they are coming."

I threw a cloak around my shoulders and pulled up the hood before following Ham into the cold rain. I glanced up at the clouds. It would rain all night.

Basya lay in her bed, moaning and gripping the edge of the bed. "They are too early," she cried.

I washed my hands in the warm water Ham brought in and examined her. "I do not think the babies know it is too early. They are coming."

I could not send for Mama or Dodi. The babies would arrive long before the message would even reach them.

"Go get Amina," I said, pushing Ham out the door. "But return. We will need you."

I bent to help Basya birth her babies. Amina and one of her daughters, Yedida, came in as the first child entered the world. He did not shout his joy to be released from the constraints of his mama's womb.

"Take him," I said. "He needs encouragement to breathe."

Amina took the tiny boy and handed him to Yedida. "You know what to do," She pointed toward the stack of baby clothing on the trunk. "Ah. There is a blanket for him, after he breathes."

I had returned to help the other child find his way from within Basya. This little one decided to stay within the warmth of her mama.

"You cannot stay now, little one," I cooed to the child. "Your mama cannot keep you there. Come to me."

Basya lay on the bed, panting. "The pains have retreated."

I set my hand on her belly, now smaller than before the first tiny boy entered the world. It did not clench for many long breaths, and when it did, the strength of it had lost its power.

"What do we do?" I asked.

The boy squalled as Yedida cleared his throat. "This one is a fighter."

Basya held out her hands for him.

Yedida wrapped him in a blanket and placed him in Basya's arms.

"Be ready," Amina warned. "She may need to concentrate on pushing the other one out soon."

Yedida stood next to the bed, watching while Basya allowed the child to suckle.

Her muscles began to tighten once more. "This one will not be able to enjoy the extra space much longer," I said.

"Good," Basya replied. She handed the first baby back to Yedida. "I think I am going to be busy."

More than a span later, the baby made his appearance. I picked him up from the bed and held him in my arms.

"Another son, Basya."

Ham stepped forward to take the child.

"We need to cut the cord before you take him." I lay the babe across his mama's tummy.

I made the preparations, then showed him where to cut with the sharp knife from my supplies. He lifted the child.

"Why is he not screaming?" he asked.

Amina took the babe from his arms. "He needs the mucus to be cleared from his throat." She deftly removed the mucus and worked to help him breathe.

I continued to work with Basya, helping her body to expel the last of the bag of waters the babies had occupied over the last months. I watched Amina work on the child. She had almost as much experience as I did in getting little ones to take that first breath.

"Hey!" Ham cried as Amina slapped the babe's bottom.

The shocked babe sucked in a breath, then screamed. The blue that had begun to encroach on his face changed to pink and red as he screamed.

Amina wrapped the babe in a blanket and handed him to his papa. "You can hold him now."

Ham held him close and rocked back and forth. "Two baby boys. Can you believe it, Basya? Two boys!"

"I told you there were two. Did you not believe me?" her voice squeaked, expressing her exhaustion.

"I know you told me. Mama told me. I should have known. You were so big."

"The easy part is over now," I said. I stood with the remnants of the afterbirth wrapped in rags.

"Oh?" Ham raised his eyebrows.

"Now you get to help them grow, teach them to be honorable sons of Adam. That is the hard part."

"I had not thought about that," he said. He set the child next to his brother and leaned over to kiss Basya.

I walked from the room with my bundle that needed to be buried.

When I returned, Ham sat in a chair beside Basya. She had scooted up in the bed and tried to feed both children at the same time.

“How do I do this?” she asked. “They are both hungry.”

I helped her until we found a way both babes could eat. Amina and Yedida had cleaned up the last of the mess and expertly put clean bedding beneath Basya. There was little left for me to do.

“What will you name them?” I asked.

Basya glanced up at Ham.

“The oldest is Nat,” Ham said. “We want to honor Basya’s grandpapa.”

“And the younger one?” I asked.

Ham gazed into Basya’s eyes.

She nodded.

“Amir.”

“A strong name for a second son.”

“He must be strong to survive the coming days,” Basya said. “Nat had to be strong to survive the life Jehovah gave him. Both sons must be strong.”

I gazed into the dark eyes of each child. “I see strength.” I bent to kiss them on the forehead. I then kissed Basya on the cheek and hugged Ham. “I will leave you four alone. You need to be alone together as a family. I will be in the kitchen if you need me.”

Ham kissed me on the cheek. “We will be good.”

I softly closed the door. I hoped all would be well with this new little family.

~ ~ ~

The little ones were tiny, so tiny they fit into one basket. They held hands as they slept.

Keeping them warm became a problem. Ham set their basket near the fireplace, which helped. However, each time their clothing needed changing, or they needed to be fed, they were removed from the warmth of their little nest. Even wrapping them in a blanket as quick as possible, they chilled faster.

We used both baskets Basya has prepared. One dried and aired out while the babes slept in the other. Ham moved the baskets closer to the bed where Basya recovered, so the time between warm basket and her warm bed shortened.

Still, little Amir struggled. His strength, or lack of strength, didn't allow him to suckle long enough to get enough food to grow.

"What shall I do about him, Mama Imma?" Basya cried to me. "I have never had a tiny child who could not eat."

I remembered when she and Ham had returned from the east. Ham had been so sick. In that sickness, he slept. He could not eat, yet he needed food to help him recover. What had I done?

I remembered dripping the broth onto his lips. Could little Amir get enough food into him if we dripped his mamas milk onto his lips?

I made the suggestion and Basya agreed. Amir had become listless in his weakness. She expressed a bit of her milk into a cup as she fed Nat.

I wrapped little Amir in a blanket and sat with him close to the fire to keep him warm. With the cup in one hand, I dripped tiny drops from a spoon onto his lips. He opened his lips and allowed the drops into his mouth.

After several drops entered his mouth, Amir swallowed.

"Good for you, Amir," I cooed. "Open your mouth, here is more for you."

More milk dropped onto his lips. Some ran down his cheek. He opened his lips and allowed the rest inside to be swallowed.

After many drops, Amir closed his eyes and slept. I held him close for a few breaths more, then set him into his bed.

"I hope he got enough to help him grow," I said.

"More than he would get from me." Basya set Nat into the basket beside his brother. "He worked so hard to suckle, I do not know if it helped him any."

"All of you rest now. I will be back in a span to try it again," I said.

"I can …" Basya started.

"There is no need for you to tire yourself feeding him every span."

"No. But I can feed him some of the time. I am his mama." She stared at me.

I nodded. "You should. I will come help with Nat while you feed Amir."

"That will work. Now I must sleep."

I left the three of them to sleep and went into the kitchen to check on the meal I had started earlier.

Ham walked through the kitchen half a span later. "How are they?" he asked, kissing me on the cheek.

"We got Amir to accept some food. We will want to feed him more often. He does not get as much each time he eats."

"How are you doing it?" he asked.

"I dribbled a drop of Basya's milk at a time onto his lips. He opened his lips to accept it. I need to try it again in another half span."

"Could I do it?" he asked.

I lifted a shoulder. "I do not see why you could not."

"I am going in to see them."

"I will be there in less than half a span," I called to his retreating back.

He lifted a hand to acknowledge that he heard.

Half a span later, I entered their room. Basya had expressed some fresh, warm milk for Amir. Not as much as she had the first time, but enough to spoon some to his lips.

"It looks like you two can handle this," I said. "Nat still sleeps."

Basya glanced up and nodded.

"I will return soon."

I walked home to my own home to change clothes. I had spent most of the last three days with Ham and Basya in their home.

I stood in my kitchen, then spun around. I remembered the first day I knew this kitchen belonged to me. The same warmth filled my heart.

I sat down in my favorite chair in my comfortable sitting room. It had only been three days, but it felt like it had been many weeks.

My eyes closed and I drowsed off.

Pounding on my door woke me.

I leapt up, thinking Ham and Basya needed me. But as I hurried to the door, I realized Ham would enter without knocking, through the kitchen door.

I pulled the door open. A messenger stood on my porch.

"I have a message for you from Noah," he said.

"Noah?" He never sent messages before. "Why would he send me a message?"

"I do not know, Madam, I only know I have a message sent to you by Noah."

I took the message. He had not written it.

Imma, I read,

There has been accident. I need you to come to me.

Noah

"Where is he?" I asked.

"I received the message from him near the Salt River."

"The Salt River?" I asked.

"Will you go to him? He asked me to guide you there."

"Wait while I gather some things together," I said.

"Will you feed me?" the messenger asked.

"I have nothing to feed you. Sit on the porch, please while I gather my things."

I hurried to the sleeping room and pulled a bag from the trunk. I started to stuff a clean dress and socks into the bag, when Noah's voice filled my ears. "Remember. Do not leave the safety of our walls. For anything. It is not safe for you to leave."

The Salt Sea is south and west of here. Noah went east. Why would he be at the Salt River? This is a lie. Noah said I would be tempted.

I tossed the bag into a chair and left the house through the kitchen door.

CHAPTER 23

An Attempt

"Ham," I said as I rushed into their bedroom. "I need your help."

He glanced up from setting Amir in his bed and lifting a crying Nat. "What, Mama?"

I plopped into the chair. "Your papa warned me not to leave our compound. It would not be safe. A messenger sits on my porch. He brought me a message. Said it was from Noah, but it is not his writing. It said I should go to him."

"A messenger? Papa would not send a messenger." Ham handed Nat to Basya.

I gave the message to Ham.

"The messenger said he left Noah near the Salt River but is not the Salt River south and west of here?"

"It is. Papa traveled east. He could have circled around … No. Papa told me to watch over you. Wicked men want to hurt him by hurting you. It is not safe for you to go with the man. I do not think he is a messenger. Not from Papa anyway."

Ham bent to kiss Basya. "Can you and the babies manage while I go with Mama?"

Basya lifted Nat to her breast. "I think we can manage. Amir is sleeping."

"I'll send Yedida over. I do not want you and the babies to be alone."

"If you must," Basya said, glancing up to smile at Ham.

We strode out through the kitchen door toward Amina's home. "The messenger is waiting on my …"

"He can wait. I do not want to leave Basya alone with the boys." He stepped up on the back porch and banged on the kitchen door.

Amina answered. "Ham? What …?"

"Can you send Yedida over to be with Basya and the babies? There is a problem I must attend to with Mama. I do not like leaving Basya alone. Not now."

"I will send her over there now." Amina turned inside and called, "Yedida!"

Ham did not wait for Yedida to leave. He took me by the elbow and walked with me to my kitchen door and through the house to the front porch. He grabbed rope from the kitchen closet.

The rain had stopped for a short time. The messenger stood by the front railing, staring out into the clouds.

Ham stepped forward and grabbed the man by the wrists. He tied the messenger's wrists together and spun him around.

"Wha—" the messenger cried.

"Exactly. What are you doing here? How did you get in?"

"The gatekeeper let me in. I brought a message."

"This?" Ham said, holding up the message scroll. "It did not come from my papa. I recognize my papa's handwriting. This is not it."

"Your papa was injured. He asked me to write it for him."

"And what is Papa doing by the Salt River?"

"He said something about following the river —" He struggled to loose himself.

"You think you will hurt my papa by taking my mama? It will not happen. Mama is smarter than that. She saw through your deceit and came for me."

He marched the messenger out across the space between the house and the gate. "Stay here, Mama. This may not be pretty."

I watched as they marched toward the gate. Ham gestured wildly at the guard at the gate. The gate opened and Ham shoved the man out.

Shouting echoed from outside the gate. Ham ran up the ladder to stare out at the shouting men. Cold filled me as I watched him. I had avoided a great peril.

I bowed my head and whispered a prayer of gratitude to Jehovah. I knew that He had helped me remember the words Noah spoke before he left me.

Eventually, Ham left the wall and returned to me.

"There were others outside our walls, waiting for the messenger. They expected you to be with him. When he left our compound without you, they were enraged."

"I heard the shouting. Will the messenger be safe?"

"I do not know. They dragged him away. They were not happy."

A shudder tingled up my spine, then down again and out onto the porch through my feet. "I listened," I whispered.

"It is good that you did. You should sleep at my home again tonight. I fear those men will try to come for you again."

"I planned to do that. Little Amir will need extra attention during the night."

"We can do it, Mama. You need sleep as much as we do."

"We will see what happens. I left a clean dress and socks in a bag in my room. I will get it and come right over to your house."

"I will wait here for you. We can go together."

I kissed Ham on the cheek and entered my home.

As I reached for my bag, arms encircled me. At first I thought they may be Noah's, but they were too scrawny and thin. Noah had worked hard on the ark. His arms were strong.

My scream was cut off as a filthy hand covered my mouth. I fought to reach the hand, but he held my arms down at my waist. I bit his hand and screamed again.

The hand clapped over my mouth once more.

Ham is on the porch. Did he hear me? I prayed that he heard my short screams.

"You think you outsmarted us," he growled into my ear. "We prepared for this."

Why had Ham not come running? I bit his hand and screamed again.

His hand slapped over my mouth. "There will be no more of that."

Feet pounded down the hall toward the sleeping room. Ham heard me!

"What are you doing here?" Ham shouted.

My abductor growled.

"How did you get past our gate guard?"

"Do you think your guard is not willing to let another in for a price?"

"He betrayed us?" Ham asked.

The man laughed. His breath stank of stale socks.

I gagged.

"He betrayed you. When he let in Brun, he also let me in. He showed us which home is Noah's, so we would be able to find you. Now we can take you. Noah will have to stop his nonsense of telling the world it is going to be destroyed."

I bit his hand.

He jerked his hand away and hit me. "I said stop that."

"But it is. How can you not believe?" I shouted.

The hand clapped against my mouth once more. "How can it happen. Noah is building an ark. A huge boat? Here in the mountains? Where does he think the water will come from? Surely it will not come this far from the sea?" His harsh laugh echoed in my ears.

"If you trust Jehovah, you will know that He created this earth. He can create a flood that will drown the earth," Ham said.

"You are as crazy as your father." The man spat on my clean floor. Ugh.

"I am not crazy. I trust my God."

"Your god is as crazy as you are."

~ ~ ~

The man began to drag me out past Ham. Ham stuck his foot out and tripped him. His hands flailed outward, letting go of me as he fell. I stumbled, but I managed to run a few steps away from my captor.

Ham jumped on him. They rolled around on the floor, hitting each other with their fists. The attacker reached into his sock and pulled out a knife.

"Ham! Watch out!" I shouted.

He saw the knife and twisted away without letting go of him.

They rolled around on the floor, bumping into the bed and tables. A clay candlestick fell, hitting my attacker on the head.

He shouted.

Ham grabbed a chunk of the broken candlestick and bashed the man on the head.

Suddenly, the man slumped back, no longer fighting.

"Did you … Did you … kill him?" I asked and held my breath waiting for an answer.

Ham leaned back from the man. "I hope not. I would not want to be responsible for a man's life."

He leaned forward and touched the man's neck. "He lives. I feel the blood pumping."

I let out the breath I held with a whoosh. "I would not want you to take another man's life."

"Not even to save yours?" Ham asked as he stood.

"No. Not even to save my life. What will you do with this man?"

"I thought I would send him out the gate as we did the first one, but now I think we should hold on to him. Papa will want to talk with him." Ham handed me the man's knife. "Do not let him escape. I will go find more rope."

I shook my head and handed the knife back to him. "You make certain he does not escape. I will go get the rope. I know where to find one."

I rushed down the hall to the storage closet where ropes and other supplies were kept. I grabbed a rope and hurried back to my sleeping room.

The man still lay unmoving on the floor.

"You are sure he still lives?" I asked.

"Look!" Ham pointed toward his chest. "His chest rises with his breath."

"Good. Here is the rope."

"Take the knife while I tie him up."

We traded the rope for the knife, and Ham tied his hands and then his feet together.

"Where will you keep him until Noah returns?" I asked.

"In the root storage cellar. It is nearly empty."

"It is full of potatoes and other root vegetables. Have you not gone in there lately?"

He glanced up at me. "It is full?"

I nodded.

"I do not know where it will be safe to put him," he frowned.

"Is it safe to keep him within our compound?"

"It is not safe to put him out if we have a betrayer at the gate."

"What will you do?"

"Lock him in the root storage cellar for now. But I will leave him tied," Ham said. "I will have to have a chat with the gate guard as well."

Ham bent and lifted the attacker, throwing him over his shoulder. "If you will open the doors, Mama, I can take him out the back. Then Shammai will not see that I put him in the root cellar. I will want to chat with him, as well, so he does not break this one free."

I hurried ahead of Ham and opened the doors. The root cellar had been dug in the space behind our home. Its roof stood above the ground, but the rest of it lay beneath the earth.

I opened the door and Ham threw the man inside. The man groaned.

I slammed the door closed and Ham locked it.

"I will go see that Basya and her little ones are doing well," I said as we walked along the back path between my home and Ham's.

"Tell her I will be there soon."

"Do you think you should see if Amina's sons will go with you? You do not want Shammai to overpower you."

"I had not thought of that, Mama. I will stop by Amina's and get her son. He will help be sure we stop the betrayer."

"What will you do with him?"

"I do not know. Not yet." Ham grimaced. "It is hard to think we have a betrayer in our midst. Papa will be sad."

"All of our guards are his grandsons. He will be heart-broken."

"He will. I am, as well."

I kissed his cheek and walked into his kitchen. I stopped to wash my hands. I did not want to smell like the man who tried to capture me.

Yedida sat with Basya when I entered the sleeping room. Both boys lay in their basket, sleeping.

"How is Amir? Is he eating?" I asked.

"He was more interested in eating this time than any other time since his birth," Basya said. "I think he may be getting stronger already."

"Already? We have only fed him twice," I bent over to gaze at my twin grandsons.

"Three times. You and Ham have been gone longer than you think. Where is he?"

"He went to get Baniy to help him speak with Shammai."

"Why?" Yedida asked.

"Shammai is guarding the gate. He allowed strangers to enter. One brought me a false message. The other tried to abduct me."

Both Basya and Yedida gasped.

"Ham stopped him. He put the messenger out of the gate. We put my attacker into the dark root cellar. Tied up. He should be safe for a time."

"What will Ham do about Shammai?" Yedida asked.

"I do not know. I left it up to him. I hope Noah comes home early." I sat in the empty chair. "This has been a long trip."

"He will come when he can," Basya said. "It has not been as wet this year as it was when Ham and I left my cave in time to avoid being drowned in the flood. He should be having an easier trek."

"Should," I said. "We will not know until he arrives home. I will fear that I left him with abductors along the Salt River until he returns."

"What would take him to the Salt River?" Yedida asked. "He traveled to the east when he left. I watched."

"I know. That is what he planned."

CHAPTER 24

Prisoners

We waited for Ham to return with Baniy for more than a span.

While we waited, Basya fed both boys. Even though little Amir had only been fed three times before with a spoon, he opened his eyes and began to gaze into his mama's eyes more often. More importantly, he opened his mouth and swallowed the milk. His strength increased.

Nat continued to eat with no problems. He would be larger than his brother if Amir did not begin to eat and grow better.

I held little Nat while his mama fed his brother. He, too, turned his eyes to stare around the room. He wanted to see everything, though he was much too small to see anything well.

"He is going to be curious," I said.

"I hope he is," Basya responded. "Curious children are intelligent children."

"True. Ham and his brothers have always been curious."

The boys yawned.

I lay Nat and then Amir into the basket near the fire. I sat next to them and watched them sleep. They reached out to hold hands.

Basya held a finger to her lips as Ham stepped into the room. "You have solved the problem?" she asked.

He shook his head. "No. Shammai and Mene are certain they have a right to take Mama away with them. I could not put them together."

"Where did you put Shammai?" I asked.

"Not in the root cellar with Mene," Ham said with a sigh.

"Will our vegetables be safe with him there?" Basya asked.

"I hope they will be. Some may be destroyed." Ham sat on the bed next to his wife. He hugged her close to him.

"What will we do?" I asked. "We have no place to lock up attackers."

"It is a problem. I have asked Shammai's papa to be responsible for him. If he does something he should not, his papa Nane, will be responsible, as well. He is now in his papa's home."

"Will that work?"

"I hope it does. We have no place to put someone who is working to destroy us." Ham leaned over the baby basket and watched his sons sleep. "You must be tired, Mama. You did not sleep much last night."

I yawned. "I am. But I am also fearful of others coming to take me away."

"I thought you might be. I asked Baniy to come guard our home so you could sleep. Basya and I will take turns for the next few hours feeding Amir. You will be sick if you do not sleep."

Sleep sounded good to me. I had not slept during the night the twins were born. I spent the night checking with Basya that her children were growing and eating.

I hoped to rest some during the day, but the boys needed extra attention, especially Amir, who needed extra food.

I yawned again. "I could use a nap."

Ham pulled blankets from a chest by the wall and handed them to me. "Take these and lay on the long seat in the sitting room. You will be close enough you can help if Basya or the boys require assistance. Until then, you can sleep."

"I will stay as well. Do you have a blanket for me?" Yedida asked.

Ham opened the chest and handed her a blanket.

I wiped my eyes, peeped at the babies, then took the blankets with me into the sitting room. I set the blankets on the seat next to the one I intended to sleep on. Yedida helped me smooth the blankets out on the long seat.

I lay my head on the seat and sleep took me.

I woke to Ham's hand touching my shoulder, dark surrounded me. "I need to go check on Shammai and Mene.

Please go in with Basya. I do not want her to be alone with the boys. She needs sleep."

I stood and folded a blanket.

"Take the blanket with you. You will need it again later. Just go in with Basya, please. I must go see to our prisoners."

He hugged me and watched me walk toward the light in their sleeping room. I heard the door close softly as he left the house.

Basya held Nat to her breast when I entered the room.

"Can you help with Amir?" she asked. "He is hungry, too."

I picked the whimpering child up from his basket and took the cup of milk Basya offered to me. I picked up a clean spoon and drizzled the milk into his little mouth.

Amir opened his mouth and waited for the milk to be dripped in. He closed his lips around the milk and swallowed. Then he opened his mouth again, waiting for more.

"He will be strong enough to nurse soon," I said.

"I hope so." Basya looked up from gazing at Nat. "It will be easier to feed them at the same time."

"Probably so. Amir will get more if he is nursing than he gets from this spoon."

After the boys had enough food, we changed the wrapper around their bottoms and wrapped them in warm blankets. I lay each boy in the basket and covered them with the blanket.

Not long after, they lay closer together, holding hands once more.

Ham returned.

"Those men have no idea what they are doing to us. What am I to do about them? I cannot hold them long. They are angry men. To keep them from destroying things, they must be tied. It is not something I like to do to them."

"Would you rather they keep me tied?" I asked.

"No!" He stood still, staring toward the storage area. "I hope Papa returns tomorrow. I need his experience."

"Did Papa Noah hold a man prisoner like this before?" Basya asked.

"Not that I know of," I said.

"He never told me of needing to hold an enemy prisoner. But he may have never had men enter his home to take his wife."

"Unless it happened with Keshet, it has not," I said.

"They can be tied until morning. I need to go discuss this with Jehovah." Ham kissed Basya and left the room.

My eyes followed him. Jehovah would have the answers. Would Ham be able to listen?

~ ~ ~

Noah returned early the next morning. He pounded on Ham's kitchen door before the sun had lifted above the walls of our compound.

"Why are you staying here?" he asked as he held me close in his arms.

"Basya had her babies two days ago. She …"

"But they were not supposed to come for another two months! Will they live?" Noah asked.

"I hope so. The youngest, Amir, struggles. He has been too small to eat much on his own. We have drizzled milk into his mouth from a spoon. He begins to strengthen. The oldest, Nat, eats well. He should survive."

"Two boys?"

"Yes. Two handsome boys. I need to go help feed little Amir. Would you like to come with me?"

Noah washed his hands in the kitchen before he followed me down the hall to Ham and Basya's sleeping room.

Ham did not glance up. He changed clothing on one of the boys. "Are you here to help feed Amir?" he asked.

"I have never fed a child so young, but I believe I could do that," Noah replied.

Ham's head swiveled toward the door. "Papa! Jehovah heard and answered my prayers."

Noah reached out to take the tiny boy. "How is that, son?"

I walked to Basya's side to help with Nat.

"I prayed that you would return earlier than planned." He handed Noah a cup with warm milk in it.

"Why would you need me to return early?" Noah dipped some of the milk into the spoon. "Drip the milk into his mouth? How do I do that?"

"Drop a drop or two onto his lips. He will open his mouth. You can drip some into his mouth. Just a few drops at a time, though," I told him. I held myself back, not wanting to step in and take over for Noah.

"I need your wisdom. We had a problem yesterday. I do not know what to do with the men."

"Problem? Men?" Noah glanced up from the tiny child.

Amir's tiny cry called his attention back to dripping milk into his mouth.

"Mama received a message yesterday. Shammai allowed the messenger into the compound."

"Does he not know why we do not allow anyone into the compound?" Noah growled softly, then softened his voice. "There you go, Amir. Suck that milk in. Good boy."

"He does now. The messenger brought a message he said came from you."

"Me?" Noah's head pivoted toward Ham, then turned right back to the babe he fed. "I sent no message."

"He said he got it from you near the Salt River," I said. "It said you needed me to come to you."

"I see you did not." He dripped another few drops into Amir's mouth.

"No. I gathered a bag of supplies, then I remembered what you said before you left. Instead, I came to Ham and showed him the message."

"You listened to the Spirit of Jehovah. Good for you."

"I did. Ham caught the 'messenger' by his hands and tied him. He marched him from the compound."

"That is not something that requires my assistance," Noah murmured. "You did well."

"If that were all, I would be happy, but it is not." Ham set a hand on my shoulder. "Another man waited in your home for Mama. She returned for her bag. The intruder tried to capture her and drag her out."

"What stopped him?" Noah lifted the tiny child to his shoulder and patted his back.

"Ham came in. I do not know why he came to help me. Perhaps because I prayed."

"I heard your scream and heard it cut off. I found the man with his arms around Mama, trying to drag her away."

"What did you do with him?"

"I thought you would want to speak with him. He is in the root storage cellar. Shammai is tied in his papa's home, locked in his room."

"Why would Shammai be locked in his room?" He lay little Amir back into his arms and began to drip milk into his mouth once more.

"Shammai let the men in. He knew what they planned. They paid him a copper to convince him to let them in." Ham growled.

"Was it only the copper?" Noah asked.

"No. He believed their lies that you are lying about the destruction that is coming."

"Did he know they planned to take your mama?" Noah asked.

"He says he did not, but I suspect he did."

I glanced at Basya. I had not heard this.

She lifted a shoulder.

"What do you plan to do to them?" Noah asked.

"I do not know. That is the reason I prayed for your return. I need your advice. What do we do about these men?"

Noah dripped another few drops into the tiny boy's mouth. Amir coughed. He lifted the child to his shoulder. "Is that all you can manage for now?" he asked. He handed the cup to me.

"He ate all that?" I asked. I leaned over his shoulder, expecting to see milk all over his mouth. It had no milk on it.

"He did," Noah said. "Is this unusual?"

I handed the cup to Basya.

She smiled. "He ate more for you than he has for anyone else. He loves his grandpapa."

Noah cradled the tiny boy for a few long breaths. He handed Amir to me. "I guess you and I should go visit with our guest, Ham."

"Our guest?" Ham exclaimed.

"He is our guest though his guest room is the root cellar." Noah stood. "We need to have a chat with him."

The men kissed us and left.

"What will he do?" Basya asked.

"I have no idea. Little Amir sleeps."

"He should," Basya said with a little laugh. "He ate more than his little tummy has ever held."

I gently lay him in the basket next to his brother. Nat reached out and took Amir's hand. I covered them and returned to my seat.

Thunder shook the building. Rain pelted against the window.

"Will they send the intruder out into the rain?" Basya asked.

"They may. I do not know."

CHAPTER 25

Stop the Work

Noah and Ham returned spans later.

Haggard exhaustion filled both men.

"What did you decide to do with the intruder?" Basya asked.

The men sat with us in the sleeping room while the babies slept.

"We questioned him. Mene tried to claim that he had only come looking to meet with Papa," Ham growled. "I reminded him that I found him trying to force you to leave with him. I have cuts on my hands and arms from his knife."

Basya brought a finger to her lips to remind him of the sleeping babies.

He nodded.

"And?" I asked.

"Papa did not believe his lies. We have no place to keep someone who broke into our home." Ham's voice rose with passion, but a glance from Basya softened his tone.

"I cannot force him to stay in our root cellar. He will damage the food we are preserving for ourselves and the creatures we will save," Noah whispered.

"What did you do with him?" I asked.

"We took him to the gate and sent him away. I warned him that we would not treat him so easily if he tries to return." Noah walked to the window and watched the rain fall.

"Do you think that will keep our attackers away?" I asked.

Noah's head moved from side to side. "No. They will try to come back. They think if they hurt me or the ones I love, they can stop the destruction."

"If they are more wicked, more vile, more disobedient, they will stop Jehovah's punishment?" I could not understand their thinking.

Basya hushed me.

I spoke more quietly. "Have they no sense?"

"It is the sense of the damned. They choose to believe the Destroyer. Their end will come whether they hurt me or not. Jehovah has spoken."

Ham gazed at the little ones in the basket by the fire. Their innocence and love filled the room. "I pray these two little ones avoid the hatred."

Nat stretched. Then he sighed, sleeping once more.

"Can you two manage with the babies if I take your mama home with me?" Noah asked Basya and Ham as he took my hand in his.

"We will," Basya said. "Yedida plans to spend the night here so Mama Imma can sleep."

I opened my mouth to argue, but Basya interrupted. "You have not slept since before Nat and Amir came to us. You will be ill if you do not sleep. Yedida can help feed Amir. I think he will be strong enough tomorrow to try to suckle again."

Noah pulled me to standing. "You need sleep as do I. Come."

He led me from the sleeping room and out the kitchen door toward our own home.

"Did you teach anyone while you were gone?" I asked.

"None would listen."

He guided me past the kitchen and down the hall to our sleeping room.

"What about Shammai?" I asked.

"He says he repents."

I gave him a sideways glance. "He *says*. Do you not believe him?"

"He *says* he did not know they planned to capture you and hold you. I am not certain of it."

I put my hand over my mouth to cover my yawn.

"Neither one of us slept last night. We can talk in the morning."

He helped me pull my dress off and tugged my sleeping robe over my head and guided me toward the bed. "You need sleep. I need sleep."

"I agree," I said with a yawn.

He gently pushed me onto the bed. I put my head on the pillow and yawned again. Noah lifted my feet onto the bed. I closed my eyes.

"We need … need … to … talk," I mumbled.

"Later," Noah whispered.

Darkness filled my sight and I slept.

I woke to the early morning sunlight peeping through our window. We forgot to close the curtains the night before.

I yawned as I swung my feet to the floor.

Noah took my hand. "You do not need to get up yet."

"Not yet?"

"No. We need to visit. Here is a good place to do it."

"Visit? Visit about what?" I lay back and lifted my feet back onto the bed.

"You have to be careful. They almost took you this time." He tucked his arm around me.

"I know. I spent the night quivering. It frightened me."

"It is more than that. Shammai allowed those men into our home compound, the place you should be safe."

"What should I do?" I turned to face him. "I recognized it was a problem. I did my best to stay away. I listened to you."

"You did." He squeezed me closer. "I am happy you listened to my warning and to the Spirit of Jehovah. I would hate to have to go searching for you."

"I am grateful I was not taken away. I am needed here. Basya and the babies need me."

"I need you," Noah said. He kissed me. "I need you to be safe."

"What are we going to do to keep them away? I was in my home doing what I should have been doing. I did not run outside seeking assistance for Basya."

Noah ran a finger down my arm.

I shivered.

"We need to find a way to be safer. I hoped my grandsons would love me enough to protect you."

"They have," I said. "Until now."

"And we have had one grandson who has accepted their lies and their coin. Will another? Will he help them find you? Help them take you away? I do not know what to do about all this."

"Trust in Jehovah," I said and kissed his nose. "You teach us to trust Him. I do. I always have."

"That is why I love you, why my heart was drawn to you all those years ago when you came to help Kes— give birth."

"You loved me then? How could you? Your wife lay dead in the bed, only a few breaths had passed when you met me."

"But I knew. I did not want to know. I did not want another woman to take her place. I fought it. But I could not for long. Jehovah brought you to be with me. I needed you and I need our sons."

He kissed me again. I melted in his arms as I had that first night we were together.

~ ~ ~

Noah never left home with all our sons again. He left two to help protect their wives and me. And he seldom left the protection of our walls alone after that day.

Japeth, Shem, and Ham worked together with Noah to build the ark. It slowly took shape in the space outside our wall.

When the rains stopped falling each year, the men moved out to work on the ark. They cut tall pines to lean against the ark to support its weight as it stood in the soil.

They used all the gopher wood from around our home. Then they searched out the groves of gopher wood from other parts of the land and cut the trees and brought them to be included in the ark.

Stands of pines were cut and the wood processed to make pitch to fill in the spaces between the planks. Gopher wood did not absorb water, but if the spaces were not filled with pitch, water would leak through and the ark would sink or capsize.

Japeth's sons helped their papas build the ark. They protected the walls of our compound. Shem and Ham's wives gave birth to more children. I hoped they would listen to their Grandpapa Noah and obey the commandments of Jehovah.

Nat and Amir, along with their sisters and brothers, carried the mark of Cain. It did not matter to the people of Mamre or the others who came to taunt Noah while he worked. The women attempted to entice all the young men away. Men were enticed by the dark beauty of Ham's daughters.

As the ark grew up from the dust of the earth outside the walls of our home, people from all around the world came to gawk and laugh at Noah and our sons.

"What makes you think there will be a flood?" they laughed.

"You are far from the sea, far from any big rivers. How will there be a flood big enough to float that big ark?"

"What makes you think we are wicked? We have been obedient. You are no better than we are."

"You think you will live and the rest of us will die?"

"You are an old man, a dreamer."

"You are no better than us. If we die, you will, too."

Their jests and anger continued from early morning until late at night, long after Noah and our sons came back inside the walls of the compound.

"How can you listen to this every day?" I asked Noah one evening twenty years after he started work on the ark, as I had asked frequently before.

"I have no choice. I have learned to close my ears and not hear their voices." Noah rubbed his temples.

I moved to behind him and massaged his head. "Even the jests and taunting? It hurts me to hear the things they say to you."

"I know who I obey. I obey my God. It does not matter what these men and women say."

"How much time do we have?" I asked.

Noah ran his hand through his hair. "We have been working on the ark for twenty years now. We have cut every gopher tree we can find. The outside is complete. But we still have to complete compartments for the animals. They will be happier when they are kept separate from the others that would eat them."

"How are we going to carry enough food for all those animals, plus the family?"

"That is why you have been preserving food these last years, so we will have enough for people and animals. How much extra do you have now?"

My hands stopped moving as I thought about the storage spaces. "How many animals will we be caring for?" My hands returned to massaging his neck and shoulders.

One shoulder lifted. "I do not know for sure. Jehovah says a male and female of every kind, more of those we may eat."

"Lots then," I said. "How are we to feed the lions and others that eat only meat? We cannot allow them to eat the animals we are protecting."

"No. Jehovah warned me to gather oats and other grains for the animals. He suggested vegetables that will stay edible for a long time. I do not know how long we will be in the ark."

I had dried meats and vegetables for us, and preserved grains. "Will there be enough space for all the creatures and food for them?"

"Jehovah provided the plans for the ark. There should be sufficient space for all." Noah sighed. "It took twenty years to get the outside of the ark built. Perhaps twenty more years of working on the inside. I thought we would be finished by now."

"Your need to stop and preach repentance to those who come here to taunt you makes it take more time."

"I am commanded to try to convince them to repent. Their hearts are hard as flint. I do not believe many of them will repent. Fewer will be baptized and covenant with Jehovah to be obedient."

"If they would, your ark would not be needed," I said.

"That would make me happy," Noah said. "I have seen the things they do. I do not believe they will repent. But I could be surprised."

I patted his back then moved to sit next to him. "The rain comes again soon. What will you do during the rain time?"

"We could work on the inside rooms, if we had wood cut and planed to the right size."

"Are you ready to begin the inside rooms?" I asked.

"As soon as we finish covering the last planks with pitch. When that is done, we will have the outside completed."

"What kind of wood will you use inside?"

"Not gopher wood," Noah said with a short laugh. "We have used every tree within our reach. I fear the gopher tree will not survive our efforts."

"Perhaps the rain will wait this year while you cut trees to use inside."

"If I had some cut, I could plane them inside the ark, out of the rain …" He stopped talking as his thoughts overwhelmed him.

I held his hand and allowed him to think. He had much to do to obey Jehovah's commands.

CHAPTER 26

Building the Ark

Noah and our sons took much of the next twenty years cutting pines and tall fir to build the structure within the ark. One door that opened on the side had been built large enough even for the aurochs and mammoths to enter, another small door had been built for men to enter while they worked inside. They kept the doors firmly closed to the taunting, heckling insults of the onlookers.

Noah spent time standing on the upper deck preaching to the men and women who had come to taunt him. It took time away from his working. Additionally, they built many hundred compartments of many sizes for the animals.

Noah built several closets within the ark to store the grains and food needed for all the animals where we would be able to retrieve it easily when it came time to feed them.

While Noah and our sons worked on the inside of the ark, Amina, Edna, Basya, and I continued to grow grains, vegetables and gardens. We dried vegetables and fruits and other food to help us get through the time we would be on the arc.

"We will need enough food to last two years," Noah said after years of our putting everything extra into our storage bins. "I have no way of knowing how long the rains will fall or how long it will take the water to recede enough we can leave."

We sat together at the kitchen table.

"Even after we leave the ark, we will require food. It will take months for food to grow. We will need to have enough food to eat while we find a new home and plant gardens and fields," Noah continued.

"I wonder if the animals will require our assistance even after we release them from the ark. Will we need to carry enough food for them to eat later?" I asked.

Noah traced lines along the grain lines of the table. "I have no answer for you. It would be wise to be prepared."

"We will want to take seeds with us. It will be difficult to plant without seeds. Perhaps we will need some plants," I mused. "Grapes come from plants, not seeds."

"You should make a list of things to take with us. I would not want to leave something behind that we may desperately need." He set his elbow on the table and leaned his head on his hand. "There is so much to plan for, so much to prepare. I could not get it all done without you."

I caught his free hand in both of mine. "Who will go on the ark? Will there be enough space for everyone?"

"I have no word yet who will go on the ark. I expect you to join me. I also think our sons will join us. Japeth has been true to his faith, as has Amina."

"Their children?"

He brought my hand to his mouth and kissed it. "I do not know. Some of them have fallen away. Nat and Amir have married daughters of men who follow cults." He bit his lip. "Too many of our grandchildren take the sons and daughters of men and follow the cult gods rather than Jehovah. How have we failed them? What more could we have done?"

"We taught all our children and grandchildren of Jehovah. We worshiped with them each Sabbath Day, emphasizing the importance of living as Jehovah taught. We reminded them how necessary it is to choose a wife or husband who believes as they did at one time."

"It did not help." Noah set his elbow on the table and set his head in his hand.

"The young people did not find others to love among the believers. They turned to those who worshiped cult gods. We join with their parents in sorrowing for the loss of their children."

About thirty-five years after they began to cut logs for the interior, the rain stopped falling.

Everywhere.

Few people had stored enough food to survive a drought. They began to die.

Noah hoped they would turn away from their false gods toward Jehovah. He took time away from working on the ark to travel through all the country, preaching the gospel of Jehovah.

I insisted he not travel alone. He took Shem with him, leaving Ham and Japeth home to continue work on the ark and to watch over the women and the few children who still lived in the compound.

We had the well, still, and some water that flowed up from a spring near our fields. We used the spring to water the smaller fields we planted that year.

Amina, Edna, and Basya spent much of their time with me during that time. Their children had left the compound. They did not like being alone in their homes without children or husbands. I did not like being alone, either, and welcomed their company.

Women and men began to pound on the gate to our compound, begging for food and water. How did they know we had both food and water enough to survive?

Before he left, Noah warned me about this. The people would want to live. They would not repent. Not even for water or food.

We wanted to give them food and water, but we could not. We would be left without enough food for us for the year, and certainly not for the time we would be on the ark. We moved to the far side of the compound where we would not hear their cries when they pounded on our gates.

It felt harsh to keep the gate closed to their cries. However, we did not have enough water or food for them all.

When Noah returned, he fell into my arms. "No one would listen. No one would even pretend to obey long enough to bring back the rain. I do not know what we will do."

"We have almost enough food to last us the two years you recommended we will need when the rain falls again. We harvested enough grains for ourselves and the animals this year, and a little more, though our fields were smaller and the water difficult to push through them."

"You have more food now than before the beginning of the drought?"

"We do. We would not have enough if we had fed all those who pounded on the gates. I cried when children cried. But I could not feed them."

~ ~ ~

I have read the stories told by Eve and the other matriarchs. Most of them were written after they told their stories to the gathering of women when the family gathered to honor Eve and Adam. Other books, written by Zehira, Elia, Vida, Helsa and Qutarah, were written and shared among the women who continued to worship Jehovah. I never saw life the story of Aleeza, Lamech's wife. I suspect she never took the time to write it.

Basya had not read these books. I shared my copies with her. I knew of no other copies, except those both Qutarah, Methuselah's wife, and Lamech's wife, Aleeza kept. I did not know what happened to them.

The ark neared completion. I felt the need to write my story. I did not know who would read it. Would there be women who cared on the other side of the flood? Would women read? I covenanted with Jehovah that I would teach the children who survived the flood to read and write. Perhaps the stories of the matriarchs would assist me in teaching.

I asked Ham for vellum. He brought me a few sheets.

"Is this all you have?" I asked.

"Why do you need more? Are you writing a long message or a book?" He laughed.

"A book of my life."

Ham stopped laughing. "A book of your life? Now?"

"Yes, now. There are books written telling the stories of Eve and the other Matriarchs. I will take them and my book with me when we enter the ark. Perhaps at some time in the future, women will want to read about these last dark days, before Jehovah finally determined to destroy all life."

"All life except those who are protected on Papa's ark?"

I nodded to him. "Yes. Except those who survive the destruction. They may wonder about our lives one day, as I have wanted to know about Eve."

"Basya has been reading Eve's book. I did not know some of the things she tells me."

"Hers is the story of a woman told to women. Men no longer care about the life of women. In their concern to gain wealth and gain what others have claimed for themselves, they forget the things of value. They forget Jehovah. They forget women and the stories of women."

Ham rubbed his eyes. "I did not understand. I apologize for laughing. The stories of women, the stories of your lives are important. I will bring you a book of vellum.

While I waited for him to bring me the vellum prepared and ready for writing my story, I made notes of the events of my life.

As I write, I discover that some of the events I considered important have not found their way into this writing. I want to leave space for the things that will happen in the future.

Over the next days, weeks, and months, in the time when we should have been hiding from rain, I wrote the story of my life in the quiet of the afternoon when the other women were resting and Noah and the other men worked on the ark.

One afternoon, Noah came home early. "I have received a message from Pisgah. Papa Lamech … Papa … died two days ago."

Tears flowed down his face.

"You are surprised he is gone? He was old."

"I know. I expected it. I thought perhaps Grandpapa Methuselah would die before Papa." He sat next to me on a seat.

"Your Grandpapa is exceedingly old."

"Older than any other who has lived on this earth. I suppose this is why Papa's death is so hard to bear."

"Will we travel to the funeral?" I put my hand on his.

"The funeral is in two days. If we go, we must leave today to arrive in time. We will need to ride horses, not take a wagon, if we want to get there in time. Do you still know how to ride?"

I laughed. "I have not had occasion to ride for more than a decade …"

"Probably more than several decades."

"Yes," I said. "But I believe I can remember how to ride a horse." I stood. "I will gather a bag of clothing for us."

"I will ask Ham and Basya to go with us."

He rushed out the door toward their home. I walked into our sleeping room.

When he returned, Noah joined me and gathered some of his clothing. I folded it and stuffed it into the bag along with mine. I hurried into the kitchen and filled a basket with food to eat on the ride while Noah saddled horses.

Ham and Basya met us at the stable. We needed them to go with us. It would not be safe to ride that far alone. Even with Ham and Basya, the trip would be dangerous.

We prayed for Jehovah's protection and left through a hidden back gate, hoping no one would see us leave.

We rode into the darkness until the moon set behind the mountains. When Noah called a halt, I jerked awake. Only then did I realize I had been sleeping in the saddle.

We slept a short time, then Noah roused us to ride again. He wanted to be in Pisgah before the funeral.

We pushed onward through the morning, stopping only to eat. By late afternoon, we reached Pisgah and Grandpapa Methuselah's home.

He tottered out the door when we knocked on the door, leaning on a thick, hardened, twisted root he used for a cane.

"Noah, my son. I did not think you would arrive in time. And you brought Imma with you."

"And Ham and Basya," Noah said from the bear hug he found himself clasped in.

Grandpapa Methuselah released Noah but held onto his hand as he reached for Ham. "It is good to see you, as well." He wrapped his arms around Ham.

After a few long breaths, he released Ham and Noah, only to throw his arms around Basya and me. "It is good to see you here. You have not left Mamre in many years."

"I have had no reason to leave and Noah feared for me to leave. Since he started working on the ark, life has been dangerous for both of us."

"I remember men tried to take you."

"They did. That is why Ham and Basya came with us. It is not safe for Noah and I to be out alone."

Grandpapa Methuselah laughed. "As if another man and woman will have much effect on men determined to attack your small group and enslave you. You are here safely because Jehovah has protected you."

~ ~ ~

Few people attended the burial service for Papa Lamech. Most of those who cared about him had died. Worse, most had become entrapped by the Destroyer in his lies and deception.

As we scattered hands full of earth over the body, dark rain clouds filled the sky.

I glanced up into the sky, expecting to see the clouds be blown away as it had many times in the last years of drought. Instead, they thickened.

Ham picked up a shovel and filled the last of the hole with the soil that had been removed in preparation to receive the body of our papa.

"He is at peace now," Grandpapa Methuselah said. "He has been sick for the past year, fighting a cough and struggling to breathe. He missed Aleeza since her death two years ago. Jehovah has taken him home."

Tiny droplets of rain fell onto our faces, mixing with our tears. Some of my tears of sorrow were for myself. I would miss Papa Lamech. He had welcomed me into the family, though I joined it much later than the others of his son's wives. Most of my tears were tears of joy. He had returned home to Jehovah and his beloved wife.

Rain fell heavier. We raced to Grandpapa Methuselah's home. One of his granddaughters, Urit, lived with him, cooking and cleaning. She had a warm stew and fresh, warm bread ready for us to eat when we returned.

We spent the rest of the day sharing stories about the love we had received from Papa Lamech. Even Basya had stories to share of the love she had received from him.

We spent the next day clearing out Lamech's room. He had moved in with Methuselah and Urit when Aleeza died. He had copies of the Book of Commandments and each of the books about the Matriarchs. I was surprised to find a thin manuscript written in Aleeza's spidery writing.

"Do you want these, Urit?" I asked, indicating the books.

"No, thank you, Imma. Grandpapa gave me Grandmama Qutarah's collection. You are welcome to them."

I lifted them from the shelf. "I have copies, as well, but Basya does not. Would you like your own copies of these books?"

Basya's jaw dropped. "I have hoped for a way to read all these books. We had a copy of the Book of Commandments, but we did not even know of the existence of these books by and about our grandmamas. I would love to have a copy of these."

I set them in her arms. "They are yours. I have not read Aleeza's story, yet. I will ask to read it when I have time."

"You will be welcome to it. Do you want to take it with you now?"

"No. It is yours. You care for it."

Noah found rolls of vellum and journals his papa kept through the years. "Do you want these?" he asked Grandpapa Methuselah.

"I have read them. I will not be alive many more years. You have more need of them than I do. You take them."

There was little more in his room of importance to us. Only clothing and other personal odds and ends remained. Urit said she would take care of them, give the clothing to someone who may need it, or just burn it.

The men spent several spans together in Grandpapa Methuselah's study, sharing important Priesthood discussions.

We women worked together in the kitchen, preparing food to eat on the way home and food for the evening meal.

We enjoyed visiting together. More importantly, I appreciated the rest from sitting on the horse.

The next morning, Noah, Ham, Basya, and I mounted our horses. I did not want to ride again so soon. It hurt to sit. I knew it would when I told Noah I could ride. But I needed to be here with him. I could manage the pain of riding home for a day and a half.

About midday, Noah signaled for us to move into some overgrown lilac bushes. We sat silently, wondering why he would send us there.

Men rode by, shouting and cursing. "We got word they left Pisgah this morning. They should be somewhere close."

"Where are they? Raghu warned us we had to get them. If not him, we have to get her. She will bring him to us. It worked before with Telemon."

I stuffed my fist in my mouth. I knew Nirit had been enticed away for a reason. Did they know where Telemon was?

Noah caught my eye and shook his head.

He was right. Now was not the time to ask them.

They rode down the path shouting and cursing. When I thought we could leave, Noah gestured for us to sit still. The raiders rode back toward us, more quietly this time. We slid from our horses and set our hands over their noses to keep them quiet.

Noah reached behind his saddle and pulled out the feed bag and poured some oats into it. He hooked it over her bridle.

The rest of us followed his example and gave our horses food, as well.

The men passed us, stabbing swords into other overgrown bushes as they searched for us. They passed, as though the lilac bush we hid in did not exist. They rode on down the path, stabbing swords into bushes and growling that we should give ourselves up.

Two spans later, Noah signaled that we could leave. We walked the horses out of the lilac bush and down the path toward Mamre.

We hid twice more on the ride home. The men passed us each time, not seeing us. We rode through the night, grateful that the rain had stopped once more.

As we returned to our home on the edge of Mamre, the clouds opened, pouring rain onto the earth once more.

CHAPTER 27

Enough Time

People danced naked in the rain in Mamre that night. It had not rained for three years. Men, women, and children had died from hunger. They still did not repent.

We joined Japeth on the wall to watch the revelers dancing in the rain. When they saw Noah, they shouted at us.

"What about your destruction now, Noah? Your drought did not kill us. It will never rain enough to drown us. You lose."

"Why is it raining now?" I asked Noah.

"Perhaps the heavens are weeping for Papa Lamech? I do not know. It will answer those who have been taunting us lately, asking how we can use an ark to float away when there is no rain."

"Is it time for us to board the ark now?" I asked.

"With the rain falling now, I would think that it is, but no. Jehovah has not sent the animals to board the ark. He will tell us when it is time. This is a normal rain."

Later, we sat in our kitchen watching the rain pound against the windows, glad that we had windows to stop it from coming in. I prepared an easy meal, enough to warm and fill our stomachs, before we fell into bed.

Sleep came easily. The past two days of riding and hiding from our attackers had exhausted both of us.

It continued to rain when we woke the next morning.

After eating, I went with Noah to the top of the wall. No more people danced naked outside our walls.

"Go back inside," Noah suggested as we climbed back down the ladder. It is not safe for you to be in the ark with Japeth, Ham, and me. Shem will guard the wall. You will be safe."

I kissed him and returned to our home, glad of the hood on my cape that kept the pounding rain from my head.

I sat down at my desk that day to write more in my book. I did not know how much more time I would have. I thought about making a copy for others when I finish, but who would read it? Who would live to care?

Amina, Basya, and Edna visited in the afternoon. Together we considered the food supply we had prepared for against the day when Jehovah called for us to enter the ark.

"We have used some of the food we planned for our time on the ark. I pray Jehovah gives us another growing time before we need to board the ark," Edna said, tapping the list.

"We are short on food for humans and grains for animals. Perhaps this is the reason Jehovah allowed the rain to fall once more," Basya said.

"It will help if we have three or four more growing times. We will be eating our seeds without time to grow more," Amina added.

"What can we do?" I asked.

"Can we ask Jehovah to give us a few more years?" Amina asked.

"We can ask. Jehovah listens to his daughters." I slipped from my chair to kneel beside it.

The other women knelt next to me and lifted their arms.

"Imma, you are the oldest here. Will you be our voice?" Edna asked.

I lifted my arms and prayed with the others, sharing with Jehovah our problems, and our need to grow more food for ourselves and any animals he would send on the ark with us. We had worked for many years to collect enough food, but with the last three years of drought, we would need at least three more years to grow sufficient to feed ourselves and the animals. Would he give us the time while the men completed the ark?

As I said Amen, the others also murmured their amen and dropped their arms.

"If Jehovah listens to his daughters, he will give us enough time to gather the food we lost during the drought," Amina said.

"He has answered my prayers before," Basya said. "He will listen to us this time."

Almost a span later, Noah and the men entered the sitting room. "We think we need to offer a prayer to Jehovah. We are not yet ready for the destruction, yet this rain is heavier than I have seen it in many years," Noah said.

"It rained like this the year I found Basya," Ham said. "If it continues, the earth will flood now."

Together, the eight of us knelt in a circle and lifted our arms into the air. Noah acted as voice for our prayer. He said many of the same things I had said earlier. When we dropped our arms, we felt the warming of our hearts in answer to our prayer.

Though the rain fell only eight weeks, enough rain fell to soak the earth and refill our water supply.

Noah and the others managed to complete all the rooms on the three lower decks. They were prepared for the larger animals. Only one more deck needed to be completed.

"I plan to complete rooms on the top deck for the humans, smallest animals, and birds," Noah told me one night before the rain ended.

"That will be nice. Why?"

"We need a place away from all those animals. The smallest animals and birds will stay in their compartments. I trust them all to behave. Jehovah will have silenced the need for meat for those who normally live on it."

Rain pattered against the window. I glanced at it. "Will we have windows?"

"Two big ones at the top will help provide light for the ark. We will set the floors back away from the edge of the ark to allow light to filter to the bottom deck of the ark. It will have to be special to withstand the storm."

"What will we do during the worst of the storm?"

"I do not know. We use candles. We would all be dipping candles for the next year to have enough for the space we would need to light. I will take the problem to Jehovah when I meet with Him once more."

"You meet with Jehovah regularly?"

"Yes. He helps me to know what I should do next. Did you not know?"

I rolled my lips in. "I suppose I knew. You come home sometimes with a glow around you and in a thoughtful mood."

"Yes. Those are the times I have spent time discussing problems with Jehovah."

"Has he allowed us more time?" I stared into his eyes.

"How could he not when his daughters prayed so earnestly for that blessing?" He put his arm around me and kissed me.

I kissed him, then leaned away. "Wait. We did not tell you of our prayer."

"Jehovah told me of your prayer. He told me to tell you he cannot deny the prayers of his faithful daughters."

~ ~ ~

Three more years passed. Noah and our sons worked every day to complete the final level of compartments for the animals.

We had grown and harvested grains for the animals and vegetables and fruits for those of us who would eat them. Some of the animals would require fruits and vegetables to keep them healthy along with the grains.

The four of us women found ourselves in the root cellar, counting the root vegetables one afternoon. Though we had it stacked almost to the ceiling, we did not have enough. Root vegetables rot over time and could not be dried and preserved as some of the other vegetables could.

"We will need to grow more of these if we have another year to grow," Basya said.

"If only we knew how to dry them and use them later," Edna lamented.

"Even if we could, I do not think the hippos and elephants would want to eat them that way," Amina said.

I sighed and looked at our tally. "We do not know for certain how many animals will join us. Noah says he will open the doors and animals will come. Jehovah will send them to us. But with all the animals I can count, we will have hundreds of different kinds of animals, from tiny mice to huge elephants and giraffes."

"Will serpents and lizards join us?" Amina asked with a shiver.

"They will need to be preserved like other animals," Basya said. "Though we are not fond of them, they have a place in our world, or Jehovah would not have created them."

"Birds as well?" Edna asked. "I love the birds."

"I suspect there will be a place for flocks of them in the upper decks," I said. "How could we live in a world without birds?"

"I know," Amina said. "It is interesting how many animals there are in our world. I suspect there are many we have never seen that will appear when the doors are opened to them."

"I trust we will be safe?" Basya asked.

"Jehovah will protect us. It will be little help to save all those animals and have all the people die. He will protect us," I said.

Our check of the other storage sheds revealed that we had almost enough of the other kinds of foods we would need.

Basya did some calculations. "If we grow as much food next year as we have each of the last three years, we should have enough for all the animals and people."

"Do you think Jehovah will give us another year?" Amina asked?

"He has been long-suffering until now. We will have to ask for another year," Basya said.

"Noah will be happy to have another year. The ark is nearly completed, but another year will give him time to finish," I said. "We should petition Jehovah."

We knelt there among the buckets of oats and rye and lifted our arms in prayer. Basya led the prayer, humbly asking for more time.

A quiet voice entered my mind. "I will give you the time you need, but do not delay."

I glanced up to see a look of surprise on each of the others' faces.

"He spoke to you, too?" I asked in an awed whisper.

"He did," Amina answered.

"Yes," Edna said.

"I never expected to hear … Was that Jehovah?" Basya asked.

I dropped my arms and sat on my heels. "Who else would it be?"

Amina lifted her arms into the air once more. We followed her example. "Thank you, Jehovah, for the answer. We will not delay."

With the knowledge we had only one more year, we rationed the food we ate. Our men received enough food for them to work hard on the ark, but we did not cook enough for food to be left over and thrown to the pigs.

We planted as much as the fields could hold during the growing time that year, hoping for a larger harvest. We worked to ensure sufficient water soaked the fields when the gentle rains did not fall.

Our efforts worked. By the end of the harvest, every storage shed had been filled to bursting. We had enough and some extra.

During the rains that year, we went through each shed and set aside seeds of every kind. These we would keep separate from the food we planned to feed to the animals and ourselves.

Ham and Shem traveled through the land for six months. When they returned, they carried bags of nuts and samples of plants and trees, many different than those we ate in our part of the land.

"I would hate to lose these plants because we forgot to gather them in," Shem said as he showed us the plants and seeds they brought back with them.

CHAPTER 28

Last of the Prophets

We women had not been allowed to tour the ark. The danger lay in the men and women who came to gawk and taunt Noah and our sons. They could not protect us while working on the ark.

One afternoon, near the end of the rain that year, Noah came to our sitting room. "I thought I would find all of you here," he said.

We were mending clothing and visiting together.

I looked up. "Is that unusual? We spend much of our time together."

"No. It is a good thing. The heavy rain kept others away from the ark today. We are finished. We want to show you through it."

As one, we stood, allowing the mending to fall on the floor.

"I have been waiting for this day," Basya said, reaching for her cloak.

The rest of us agreed and put our cloaks on.

"The rain is heavy. Do not forget to pull your hoods up and tie them. You will get wet. I hope it is worth it," Noah directed.

I pulled the hood up over my head and tightened the drawstring. The wind howled past the windows. "How will we fight that wind?"

"I will hold you up, Imma. Take hold of the hand of one of the others. We do not want to lose anyone," Noah said.

He took my hand and squeezed it. I took Amina's hand, who held onto Edna, who held onto Basya. "Do not forget to close the door," I called to Basya.

"I will shut it," she answered.

Noah opened the door and led us out. The wind whipped against me, splashing rain into my face. I wished I could pull the front of my hood down lower, but the wind would have blown it away and I would be drenched.

We walked across the green toward the gate nearest the ark. Japeth stood guard there. He opened the gate, then took Amina by the hand. Edna hurried forward to take my hand. *Is he not needed to guard the gate?*

The wind blew away any thought of questioning. Jehovah would guard our homes.

We reached the ark.

A ramp had been built that led to a small man-sized door. When we reached the door, Shem opened the door and helped us in. He took Edna's hand. Basya skipped forward and took my hand.

She looked around. "Big. Where is Ham?"

"Here." Ham stepped out of the darkness and took her hand. She let go of mine.

My hand felt strangely empty without the grip of one of the daughters of my heart gripping it.

The dim light surprised me. "How can we see?" I asked.

Noah pointed upward. A window filled a space on the wall of the upper deck. The walls of the animal compartments stood inside, away from the outer wall of the ark. "The darkness of this rainy day only allows some light in. When the rain ends, the ark will be flooded with light. There is a window on either side."

"What did you use? Will it not break in the wind?"

"It appears clear and thin, but it is made of thick stone Jehovah led me to. The one on the other side is not quite as big as this one, but it allows light in."

"I watched you put the window in and wondered about it. You have been so tired, I did not want to bother you. And then, I forgot to ask."

Noah laughed shortly. "You have had much to keep your thoughts busy. I am happy to surprise you with this."

I peered into the darkness deeper in the ark. "It is difficult to see in the center."

Ham produced a torch and a lit candle. He held the candle to one end of the torch until the torch caught fire. It illuminated much of the space.

Shem stepped forward and lit another torch from Ham's torch. The space filled with light.

"We have been making these since we saw one in Parin. Channa's brother showed me how to make them," Ham said. He glanced away, then gazed into Basya's face, begging her to understand.

"How kind of them to show you how to make them. We will need the light," Basya said. She stepped to the edge of the space. "What is this to be used for?"

"Look up," Noah advised. This is one of the tallest spaces on the ark. This will be where every animal comes on its way to the compartment set up for it. We will move the giraffes back here once all the other animals are in."

"That makes sense," I said.

The men led us through the compartments on the bottom deck. "This hall between the compartments will allow us to give the animals food during the time we wait for the rain to fall, and for the water to recede," Noah said.

Noah led the way, showing us the openings for the elephants, rhinos, aurochs, hippos, and other big animals. Shem directed us up one of the three sets of stairs that connected the bottom deck with the next deck. Beside the stairs in the center, a ramp rose from the bottom deck to the next one.

"The ramp is for the animals. We cannot expect them to climb stairs," Japeth explained. "We call the bottom space the fourth deck. We number them from the top down."

He led us down a hallway, then turned and led us back another hallway. There were three sets of compartments on this, the third deck. They were large enough for bigger animals, horses, cows, and others of that size.

Japeth pointed out the rooms where food would be stored. "We do not want to have to walk long distances to give our animal friends the food they will need."

"Is it the same on the bottom deck?" I asked.

"I did not show you, but there are rooms for food near each of the animal compartments," Noah said. "I should have known you would want to know."

My grip on his hand tightened for a breath. He turned to me and smiled.

"Lions and tigers, and other bigger cats will live on one end of this floor," Japeth told us.

We nodded, understanding the need to keep carnivores away from their prey.

Once more, Shem led us up the stairs beside a ramp that was not as wide as the ramp to the third deck.

"We expect smaller animals to reside on this second deck," Shem said, taking the lead to show us through the deck.

The compartments were not as large here as they were on the lower decks. Food rooms were set aside spaced regularly along the hallways. This time, there were four compartments, two in each hall, for the smaller animals.

One more hike up the stairs led us to the first deck. In the center were rooms much like our homes on the land.

"These rooms are for us," Ham said as he led us into the compartment set aside for people.

"I do not see any place to cook here," Amina said from the side of the room.

"We cannot build fires like in our fireplaces," Japeth told her. "We may be eating raw food."

Amina glanced at me. "Can we find another way?"

I lifted a shoulder. "Perhaps."

Beds had been built along the walls of two of the rooms. "We will want time alone, but we needed to leave enough space for all the animals, the food and the water for them," Ham said.

"Water?" Edna asked. "I had not thought of water. We cannot live without it."

"We have barrels for water. We have devised a way to direct the rainwater into some of these barrels, but we will also fill the barrels from our well," Shem said. "Look." He pulled back a curtain.

We crowded around the huge barrel behind the curtain. Water poured into the barrel through a sluice gate above.

"We can stop the water when the barrels are full," Shem said. "There are barrels like this, and bigger, on every deck where we can easily give the animals water."

"I had visions of toting buckets of water from our well to fill massive barrels," Basya said.

"We did, as well," Noah said, "until Shem thought of this. Why tote water when we can get it from the rain?"

Ham showed us the smaller compartments for the smaller animals. The compartment for birds were taller, allowing space for them to fly. Some of these compartments were stacked three high, allowing for more animals.

We strolled around the vast deck. No wonder it took so many years. Although others helped in the beginning on the outside of the ark, only four men built the insides of this huge boat, preparing it to save as many species as would come to be saved.

Shem walked to several of the rain sluices and closed them. "We have not yet called the animals to come. We do not need the water barrels to overfill."

"Now what?" I asked.

"We load the storage rooms with food," Noah said.

"Has Jehovah given you a time when the flood will come?" Edna asked.

"Not yet, but you women know the time is soon," Noah answered.

I glanced at the other women. They shrugged. We had not spoken to our men about the words we heard that day. We had talked about it only that afternoon.

"Jehovah told me," Noah said. His arm around me drew me closer to him. "I am grateful our wives are obedient."

~ ~ ~

As it neared the time when the rains ended, a messenger arrived from Pisgah. Grandpapa Methuselah had died, after living nine hundred sixty-nine years. No one had lived that long. We had been expecting this message, but still, we cried. We told him to tell Urit we would not be coming.

Before we left after Papa Lamech's burial, we told her we would send this message. We would come. How could we not? But we did not need raiders to be following us as they had for Papa Lamech's burial.

Once again, I gathered clothing and supplies. The next morning, we took our horses and slipped out the back, hidden gate for our trek to Pisgah. Japeth and Amina rode with us. Shem and Ham stayed behind with their wives. They needed to guard the ark and our homes. More importantly, they needed to make it look like we were still there, not on the path to Pisgah.

Our ruse worked. No one followed us. We arrived safely in time to bury the fragile old man who had known Adam and all the other prophets. His had been a life of watching his brothers and sisters, the men and women of earth as they descended into disobedience and wickedness.

Japeth shoveled the mud into the burial place of the old man as rain fell like tears from heaven. Of all the old prophets, only Noah lived now. He had not been given instructions to honor any of his sons with the Priesthood yet.

As we stood in the rain watching Japeth, I tucked my hand into the crook of Noah's elbow. "Do you feel alone?"

He flicked his eyes toward me, then returned to observe Japeth's sad chore. "Yes. And no. Why do you ask?"

"You are the last of the prophets."

He sucked in a deep breath through his nose. "I try not to think of that. I am certain to be asked to give Japeth or Shem or Ham that responsibility, after we survive." The last of his breath whooshed away.

"But not now?"

He twitched a shoulder in a tiny shrug. "I do not know why. I do as Jehovah commands. He has not yet commanded that I offer this great responsibility to any of my sons. I know it must be given, but when or to whom, I do not yet know."

I understood the struggle within him. As I read from the stories of the matriarchs, other prophets and their wives feared a loss of the line of prophets. Jared and Helsa waited almost two hundred years for Enoch's birth, and Enoch was second only to Adam in righteousness.

"What will the world be like with only us?" I asked.

"We have been blessed. Adam and Eve had only each other when they left Eden. They had no children. They knew nothing of this earth or its animals. They did not have fire or homes."

"They did not even know how children came. They knew nothing. We will know something about this earth." I lay my head on his wet shoulder.

He patted my hand that lay in his elbow. "We may be lonely. It will only be us for a time. Us, our sons, and their wives."

"You received word about that?"

"I did. We will be kept busy on the ark taking care of two of every animal along with the extras of the clean animals we will eat and sacrifice when this is over. But after the waters recede and we go to make our homes …"

"We could be lonely?"

"We could. Although, with Jehovah I am never alone."

"Nice for you," I murmured under my breath.

"He is with you, as well. You may not be as aware of it as I am, but He is there for you."

I gazed up toward Noah's eyes. "Are you certain?"

"I am."

Urit had a small meal prepared for us. "It is much like it was after Uncle Lamech died. So few of us to lament the passing of great men."

Noah nodded. "There are few among us who care about these men of God."

Noah spent the afternoon going through Grandpapa Methuselah's papers, claiming those that held a record of Priesthood rites and blessings. He told me later that he planned to add them to the back of Adam's Book of Commandments.

Before the sun set, the four of us mounted our horses and rode toward Mamre. We hoped to outwit any who waited to attack us.

The clouds cleared as the night deepened. A full moon lightened our path for us. About halfway home, we passed a camp of sleeping men, waiting to ambush us as we passed. We rode past them in silence. Let them think they would catch us the next day.

We did not stop to sleep. My eyes felt like dust had invaded by the time we saw the walls of our home compound. I wanted to weep, but in my exhaustion, I could not.

CHAPTER 29

Moving

As the rain decreased each day, we completed the task of moving the last of the vegetables and grains from our storage sheds to the ark. We filled all the storage rooms on all the decks. In some, we left the grain in buckets and baskets. In most, however, we dumped the grains directly onto the floor, using a board at the entrance to keep the grains inside.

We planned to plant our fields as usual, especially the grains that would be ready to harvest earlier in the heat of the year. If Jehovah had not yet instructed us to enter the ark by harvest time, we would need the extra food.

We filled an upper storage room with seeds. The small trees and plants were set where they would be bathed in the light from the window.

It took much time from when Noah and the boys showed us the inside of the ark to us to transfer all the food from storage sheds to the storage rooms within the ark. We finished late the night before a Sabbath Day.

"We are ready," I said as I lay in bed next to Noah that night. "All the food except for what is still in our homes has been transferred to the ark. I still have a few personal things I would take with me. I will want my book, the books of the stories of the matriarchs, my copy of Adam's Book of Commandments, a few sheets of vellum, ink and a pen."

"No clothing?" Noah teased.

"Well, yes. I will need clothing. Blankets and bedding are on the beds. You built seats in."

"Have you come up with a way to cook?" he asked.

"We cook with coals more than with an open flame. Can we set us a small stove with stones and keep coals alive?"

"You can, but you will not have a lot of time, I fear."

"I have a large, curved stone in my fire I use for cooking some of the time. I will take it."

"Out of the fire?" he exclaimed.

"I allow the fire to die down most nights. I will allow it to grow cold so I can take the stone. I can get fire from Amina after I remove the stone."

I felt Noah nod in the darkness. "What will you use for coals?"

"We will use smaller chunks of wood that can be kept within the stone. I have some I have been saving in a pile outside our door."

"Will it be enough for the time we are on the ark?"

"Two years? No. But the others have set aside small chunks of wood since we saw the lack of a fire space. We should have enough for more than a year, if we are careful with it."

"You have been thinking about this," Noah said, pulling me close for a kiss.

"I cannot expect you to figure everything out. You have been busy getting the ark ready for us and all those animals. When do you expect this to happen?"

"Soon," he murmured. "Sooner than we want."

"What about my mama and papa?" I asked. "They are not wicked …" I allowed my voice to drift off.

"Nor are they righteous. Have you heard from your mama lately?"

"No. I thought she stayed busy."

"She does, helping her grandchildren prepare for the up-coming cult festival."

"How did you hear this?" I turned on my side where I could see his face in the moonlight.

"I hear things." He laughed a mysterious laugh.

I thumped him on the shoulder.

"A message came from Hana today."

"And you did not tell me?" I squeaked.

"You were carrying a basket of grain. I forgot until now."

"What did it say?"

"I hear your ark is nearly finished. You need not worry about saving a place for your father and me —"

"Father? Mama never uses that word!"

"She is now. Do you want to hear the rest of her message?"

I rolled my lip inward then spit it out. "Yes. What did she say?"

"...saving a place for your father and me. We know there cannot be enough water to float that monstrosity ever in a mountain village like the one where you live. Come join us for the planting festival of Asherath next month when you grow tired of waiting for the rains. I am busily helping prepare your nieces and nephews for their part in it.

Your mother, Hana."

"She is helping the young ones prepare for a cult festival? How can she? I thought she honored Jehovah. She always did —"

"In the days you lived with her. But that was many years ago, more than a hundred. She has changed." Noah's voice echoed my sadness.

"She has. And papa, it seems. I have only my sons to go with us on the ark."

"Did you think otherwise?"

Tears dripped off my nose. I brushed them away, allowing my frustration to show. "I had hoped a daughter, a grandson, my sister, someone else I love would be eligible to join us."

Noah pushed my hand away and wiped away my tears. "I, too, hoped for more of our loved ones to join us. It cannot be. Jehovah told me, 'All your sons and all your daughters have gone astray. They choose from among the children of men and worship their false gods.' Jehovah could not be clearer. He added, 'Only your sons Japeth, Shem, and Ham live righteously enough to board the ark with their wives. None of their sons. None of their daughters.'"

"We shall be lonely," I said.

"Never lonely when I have you and you have me, and when we have Jehovah."

The next morning, I found the message from Mama. It read exactly as Noah had quoted. I allowed a few tears to fall before I brushed them away. I dropped the message into the last of the hot coals and watched it blacken around the edges before it flared into flames.

~ ~ ~

I allowed my kitchen fire to go out that morning. I did not expect to need fire in my kitchen again.

We gathered in our sitting room to worship that Sabbath morning. Our group of worshipers had shrunk from many hundred who needed a sanctuary to hold us all, to the eight of us. No more on this earth still believed in and worshiped Jehovah. I fought back the tears that threatened to fall as I thought of those I loved who had chosen to worship a false god.

I shared with them my plans for cooking on the ark. "We will want to find a few more flat stones to protect the ark. It is made of wood and will burn. We do not want to burn our refuge."

"Three flat stones lay outside my back door," Edna said. "Will that help keep us safe from fire?"

"It should," Shem said. He looked around the room at the rest of us. "How soon do you think we will be called to board the ark?"

"Soon," Noah said. "It will be soon."

Although we had been commanded not to work on the Sabbath, we carried the four stones and set them up in the living space in the human quarters.

Noah called us together the next morning. "I have heard from Jehovah. We are to board the ark and be ready to leave in seven days. The animals have been warned. They will begin to enter the ark by the end of the day. It is time."

"I saw deer and mice scurrying toward the ark this morning," Shem said. "I wondered."

"They come already? We must go." He stood. "Imma, you and I will greet the animals at the door. Can you direct the biggest animals to the compartments set up for them?"

I stood and walked toward the door. "I can do that."

"Japeth, you and Amina take the third deck. Direct the bigger animals to their compartments on that floor, and the smaller ones to move on up to the higher floors."

Japeth and Amina were close behind me. "We can do that, Papa Noah," Amina said. They hurried past me.

"Shem, you and Edna take the second deck. Guide the animals to the compartments set up for them and send the birds and the smallest animals on up to the first deck."

Shem and Edna hurried past me. "We can do that."

"We have the first deck I guess," Ham said. He and Basya hurried past me. "If the mice are already here, we have work to do."

Noah caught my hand and we followed the others across out the door and across the green.

Japeth and Ham were lowering the big door of the ark to the ground, creating a ramp for the animals to use. A small line of animals had already formed. When the ramp settled to the ground, Noah and I hiked to the top of it and faced the animals.

"Welcome. You who have responded to Jehovah's call. My wife, Imma, and my sons will direct you to your compartments. We will be bringing you food and water as soon as we can. We think you will be comfortable."

Our sons and their wives hurried to the center steps and on up to the floor to which they had been assigned. The animals started up the ramp.

Noah welcomed each pair of animals. He did not mark them off a list. He trusted Jehovah to bring the animals to him. They had seven days to arrive and settle into the compartments.

I directed the mice and deer toward the ramps. At first, it was easy to direct them toward the correct deck. By afternoon, some of the very large animals arrived. I walked with them to their compartments, opening the gates for each pair, and closing it behind them.

A mixed flock of birds flew in through the door, dipped, then swooped up the stairs toward the first deck. Basya would enjoy showing them where to rest.

A pair of crocodiles waddled up the deck. Though they were not among the biggest of animals, we had a compartment close to the center for them on the fourth deck so they could reach it easier.

Several different pair of serpents wriggled up the ramp. Edna would not be happy to be there when they wriggled past her. I waited for her scream. It did not come. Perhaps she had taken another pair of animals to their compartment home.

It went on through the day. When we had a break between animals, we hurried to fill the water and feeding troughs for them. Basya came down the stairs with bread and cheese for us to eat. We had no time for more.

That night, Basya and Ham stayed on the ark. The rest of us fell into exhausted slept in our own homes. There would be

CHAPTER 30

Animals

Each morning after that, I dragged myself from bed in time to grab a piece of cold bread and fruit before leading animals to their new home on the fourth deck of the ark.

Huge animals entered through the open door, sometimes one at a time, because they did not fit through the door together. Mastadons and aurochs were among the huge animals.

At the end of the second day, Noah suggested that we spend the night in our beds on the ark. In my exhaustion, I gratefully accepted the suggestion.

The human compartment consisted of three rooms. In the center of the middle room we had placed the cooking stones, away from any of the walls. On one side were seats for us to relax in when we were finished caring for the animals. Table and chairs were set on the other side. All this furniture had been fixed to the floor.

"We do not know why, but all the furniture is tied down," Ham had said that first day in the ark, "but we do as Papa told us to do."

"I only do as Jehovah commands," Noah said. "I suspect this ark will not always be floating smoothly on clear waters."

On either side of the main room were sleeping rooms, divided by closets. Both beds and closets were tied to the floor and unmovable.

Noah and I chose a bed in the same room as Ham and Basya, who had chosen their space the first day. I loved Basya. I would be happy in a room with her.

Noah went back to our home to retrieve the bags and baskets we had packed the night before. He had pushed me onto the bed and warned me to rest.

When he returned, he also carried with him the box that held the sacred clothing given to Adam and Eve when they left Eden. He carefully lifted and secured it into one of the closets on our side of the room.

Ham had brought Basya a kitten back when he and Shem went searching for plants to save. The little ball of fur had grown. Avi curled up in a ball beside me and slept. I slept, too.

In the next days, Japeth and Amina moved their things into the room on the other side. Shem and Edna joined us the day after.

We no longer cared to protect our homes within the compound. If people entered and took things from us, it would not matter.

Those possessions were not needed on the ark. Those we needed after could be built again or lived without. Noah could build me another loom. I would need that. But not on the ark.

I stayed busy during those last days. I stood with Noah to greet new arrivals, then led them to the compartment they would occupy. I gave them food and water, then hurried back to greet the next animals.

Noah and I were careful to settle the huge animals into compartments to balance their weight. We would not want all the heaviest on one side. They might tip us over. That would not help any of us.

Basya brought us bread and cheese in the middle of the day. Otherwise, we would not have had time to eat. Although they had many more animals to move into their compartments than the rest of us, she found time to bring us food.

Avi followed her down the steps. He would run to the animals near where I sat to eat and twined his body around them. When it was time for Basya to return to the first deck, he leapt into her arms to be carried back up to the first deck.

The sixth day after we started welcoming animals to the ark was the Sabbath. Rather than stopping to honor Jehovah, we continued to welcome and settle animals into their compartments. This activity could not be paused for worship. After the door closed, we worshiped together, remembering why we were on the ark.

"How many more animals do you think will join us?" Edna asked as we ended our worship service.

"We do not have many more compartments left on our deck," Ham said. "There are perhaps five compartments left. We have not seen eagles or ducks yet."

"We have only one on our deck," Shem added. "I do not know what animals belongs in that compartment. I hope they arrive before we close the ramp tomorrow."

"How many are missing on your deck, Japeth?" Noah asked.

"We are missing moose and polar bears. They have far to travel from the north. I hope they were warned early enough to arrive in time. We have not seen the yaks yet, either."

"And on the fourth deck, Papa?" Ham asked. "What is missing on the bottom deck?"

I thought about all the animals we had found compartments for. So many animals I had never seen nor heard of before had answered Jehovah's call. Only one compartment still waited for an occupant.

"We have not seen the bison yet. Everything else is here."

We stood waiting for the last of the animals to arrive on the seventh day. Termites entered, along with a pair of serpents hurrying up the walkways to the first deck.

A platypus pair waddled up the ramp and on up to the third deck sometime in the morning. Now we knew what Shem had missed.

The eagles flew in, circled around Noah, then flew on up to the fourth deck. The moose entered in the afternoon, along with the yak and the bison.

Japeth stood with Noah as the sun neared setting, waiting for the polar bears to arrive. Clouds began to fill the sky, making it darker than it would normally be.

"What happens if they do not make it?" Japeth asked.

Noah shrugged. "I do not know. I suspect they will be left behind." He set his hand over his eyes to shade them from the setting sun peeking through the clouds. "There. Do you see them? Here they come!"

White spots grew larger as the bears lumbered through the trees and toward the ark. They trundled up the ramp and on up to the third deck as great drops of rain began to pound the earth.

A man and a woman raced toward the ramp as Noah and Japeth began to pull it up.

"Stop!" they shouted. "We want to go with you."

"No. You may not enter," Noah replied.

"We believe," the woman shouted.

"No. You have not believed nor repented. You may not enter. It is by command of Jehovah that I say this."

The woman stopped at the end of the ramp. "I told you we could not enter," she shouted above the rain.

"No. He has to let us in." The man stumbled upward on the moving ramp.

"You may not enter!" Noah repeated.

The man became rigid, then fell off the ramp.

"I wish I could take you, but you are not worthy," Noah murmured.

The woman ran to her man and knelt beside him in tears. "I told him not to push it if you said no. I warned him you would do something to him."

"It was not me," Noah called out. "It is Jehovah who chooses. Go find a place to end your days."

He and Japeth pulled up the ramp, closing it and sealing it. The rain pounded against the ark sounding like pebbles against a window.

~ ~ ~

Noah and I walked up and down the hallways, speaking to each pair of animals in the compartments on the bottom deck. We made certain each compartment held enough food and water for the animals. By the time we finished and moved to the stairs leading to the first deck, most of the animals slept.

I gazed up at Noah. "Why do they sleep?"

"Do you not feel it?" he asked.

I stood with my eyes closed, allowing an awareness of the movement of the ark rise from my feet. Though it was gigantic, the ark lurched.

"What was that? Is there enough water already to begin to lift us?" I asked.

"Probably only a finger width," he said with a shrug. "But the ride will soon be rocky, worse than your cradle when you are angry. It is best that the animals sleep through it. Jehovah has caused them to sleep." He turned to walk toward the compartments built for us.

I followed. "And us? Will he cause us to sleep as well?"

"I do not think he will. We are needed to ensure all is well with the animals. We can understand what is happening. The animals cannot." He led me to the window. A walkway crossed between the top of the deck below and the window. There had to be a space to allow light to filter to the fourth deck.

We crossed the walkway and stood staring out at our home. Water had filled the land already. It gently rocked the ark.

"It looks like more than a finger width," I said.

"Look," Noah pointed.

The earth had separated between our well and the village well. Water spurted from the gash in the earth.

"That must be what caused the ark to lurch," Noah said. "Rain, alone, will not bring enough water to flood the earth. Jehovah must be opening all the wells."

I pointed toward the trees. People climbed into them.

"They think they can escape the flooding," Noah muttered.

"Can they?"

"No."

I shook my head and stared. I could not watch. I turned and crossed the walkway. "It is good we have a safe, dry place to live while it floods."

"While the floods fill the earth."

I bit my lower lip. "Will it fill all the earth?"

"It must, or some life will survive, proving Jehovah to be a liar. He is not."

"I grieve for Mama and Papa and our children and grandchildren." A tear dripped from my eye.

"Yes, and I grieve for the hundreds of people who refused to listen." Noah put his arms around me and leaned into me.

"How long do you think it will rain?"

"I do not know. I will keep a record."

He took my hand and we walked down the stairs to join our three sons and their wives. All our other children, all our grandchildren, all our brothers and sisters, cousins and uncles and aunts were outside, learning that they could not deny Jehovah's warnings. The lesson would be fatal.

Back in our compartment, Amina squatted next to the stones and blew on the embers. She had small bits of wood ready to move into the embers as the fire grew within them.

"She thinks we should eat," Basya said, pointing to Amina. We did not bank the fire this morning."

"I can see," Noah said. "Is there anything we can eat without fire? I am hungry."

I opened a storage cupboard and pulled out an apple. "This apple needs no cooking. Will this work?"

He took the apple and bit into it. "It is still crisp. Nice."

"It will take time for the fire to be ready then cook a meal. Who would like an apple?" I asked.

All but Amina requested an apple. I retrieved apples for the others.

"Did it!" Amina cried.

We turned toward where she had been working to see a small fire burning within the stones.

"It will not burn the floor, will it?" Shem asked.

"It should not. We will have to watch them until we are certain," Japeth said.

"If we keep the fire small, it should not be hot enough to burn the floor," Noah said.

Amina set a bowl of water into the fire. When it boiled, she sprinkled grains and vegetables into it.

Within a span, the food had cooked. We brought our bowls to the fire and held them out for Amina to fill.

"This is what I have been needing," Ham said with a sigh. "Hot food."

We moved to sit at the table in chairs that had been attached to the floor. I tried to pull my chair closer to the table, but it would not move.

"If the storms are bad, we would not want the table and chairs to slide," Shem said. "It was bad enough when the ark lurched earlier. I nearly fell."

"Good point," I said, settling into my chair.

After eating, the men walked to the window. They wanted to see how much water filled the valley.

They returned looking doleful.

"I have never seen that much rain," Japeth said as he found a seat next to Amina.

"The wind blows in circles," Ham added. "I saw men clinging to trees, but the wind blew them off. It is horrible out there."

An elephant trumpeted from the bottom deck. I went with Noah to see if there was a problem.

As we trudged down the long flights of stairs, a lion roared, and the elephant trumpeted again.

"They are not even on the same deck. I do not understand how they would be upsetting each other," Noah said.

Our steps hurried to the deck with the lions. They paced back and forth inside their compartment. Noah looked in.

The lion roared once more, then lay down and closed his eyes.

"Strange," I said.

We descended to the fourth deck where the elephants were housed. As we neared their compartment, we understood their complaint. Someone pounded on the outside of the ark. We could hear them shouting to be let in.

It was too late.

No one could enter the ark now. Even if that person had been approved earlier by Jehovah, we could not open the doors or all within would be lost.

CHAPTER 31

Rain

Early the next morning the ark jolted to the side, startling me awake. "What was that?" I yelped as I sat up in the bed.

Others in our compartment cried out. Animals throughout the ark joined in, sharing their mistrust of the movement.

"I thought they were asleep?" Ham said.

"Guess not," Noah replied as he pulled on his tunic. "I will go see what is happening."

"Are you going to the window?" I asked.

"I must if I expect to see anything."

I pulled a robe over my nightdress and followed him down the hall and across the walkway.

Muted light filtered through the windows. Lightning flashed. The ark rocked with the immediate thunder. I peered out the window seeking so see.

Water.

Wind.

I could see little else.

"Why did the ark jolt? Can you tell?"

Noah stepped close to the window and stared down.

"The tall poles we had to support the ark must have fallen. Nothing else would have caused such a jolt. We are floating."

"Already?"

He nodded.

"I thought it would take longer."

"I did, as well. Jehovah has burst open all the fountains of water. I have never seen such rain. I am grateful to be inside this ark where it is warm and dry."

"And alive," I added.

He nodded. "Yes. And alive. I do not know how much longer it will take …"

I allowed the tears for our lost family to fall. Why did they listen to the Destroyer?

We fed the animals and opened the sluice to allow water to fill our barrels. Closing them was not as easy as opening, but Ham and Shem managed.

The animals had not eaten much. They continued to sleep, mostly. The elephants stood sleeping, their feet adjusting to the rocking of the ark.

Shem told us of the monkeys. They ran around their compartment and pushed their hands through. “No, monkeys. You may not wander about the ark. You have a safe place in there. It will not be safe for you to wander,” he had told them, and locked the door closed.

We returned to our compartment to find Edna cooking a meal for us. “I should be doing that,” I said.

“No. It is my turn. You can take a turn tomorrow,” she said.

“No. Tomorrow is my turn,” Basya said. “You can cook for us on the next day.”

We sat down and worked out a schedule when we would cook and clean and who would be responsible for what sections of the ark. Basya and Ham took the first deck. She did not fear the snakes as Edna and Amina did.

Edna and Shem took responsibility for the second deck with the medium sized animals. Japeth and Amina loved horses, so they accepted responsibility for the third deck.

That left the fourth deck for Noah and me. We would care for the largest of the animals including aurochs, elephants, rhinos, giraffes, hippopotamus, and others of their size. We had bigger animals, but less of them to care for than the others. I suspect it was fair for all of us.

We fell into a daily routine. We ate our morning meal, fed the animals, cleaned out their compartments, scooped the stinking bedding and other smelly stuff into a closet for later disposal, when the rain lessened, ate a mid-day meal, visited with each other, checked on the animals, prepared and ate the evening meal, then had quiet time reading or writing, then bed.

Each day, Noah recorded the number of days we had been together on the ark and what happened during that day.

Sometimes, the ark jolted us when it bumped into something outside. At first, we hit trees. Later, we hit a hill or a mountain as the ark floated through the flood.

We could see the rain beating against the windows. After thirty days, the pounding lessened, but it did not stop.

When I could, I stood by one of the windows, gazing out at the storm. Tall trees on taller mountains lifted their tops above the water. Sometimes, an animal would gaze at us from the top of the tree. We could do nothing for it.

The animals slept through most of the rains, seldom waking even to eat. That helped us keep the smell of filthy bedding down. We had no way to dispose of the excrement while the rain fell.

"We can open the windows after the rain stops," Noah told us. "Until then, we have no way to dispose of it. We cannot burn it. We cannot dump it. We will have to hope the animals sleep and, as they sleep, they do not need to eliminate."

All those animals. Disposing of their excrement would be a huge challenge. I breathed a silent prayer of gratitude to Jehovah that it was not necessary yet. It would be, though, before long. The odor began to impinge on my senses. How much longer before the rain stopped?

We washed out many of the compartments over the next few days. That helped. The smell of the ark improved.

~ ~ ~

Forty days.

It rained constantly for forty days.

The ark floated freely above the trees, the houses, the hills, and the mountains. It had not bumped into anything that would jolt us from our seats for days.

Sun shone on the forty-first day.

We hurried to the windows and pushed them open. Sun warmed our faces. I stood with my face tilted upward allowing it to warm me.

The sun felt like heaven.

The others agreed, for they stood facing the sun for many long breaths.

I leaned out the window to look over the side. Clear water stretched as far as I could see around the ark. No trees. No rocks. No mountains. I feared I would see bodies of people or animals drowned in the flood. There were none. Only gentle waves that rocked the ark in the deep water.

"How can it be?" Edna asked. "Only water."

"This must be what they say the sea is like," Amina sighed. "I always wanted to go to the sea."

"You did not want to float on it, though. Did you?" Basya asked.

"I have heard stories of men who go out on the sea or lakes in boats. But, no. I wanted to go to the shore and watch the waves roll up the sand."

"No sand here," Basya muttered.

"No. Only water." Amina turned her back to the water and leaned against the wall beneath the window.

"Did you think it would all be gone already?" I asked.

"No. But I wanted it to be gone." Amina turned back to the unending water. "I have never seen so much water."

"Nor have I," Ham said. He had come up behind us and put his arms around Basya.

The men came from the other window and joined us. "We are not going anywhere for a time," Japeth said. "Just floating on all this water."

"But we live." Shem gazed out at the vastness of the water. "No one, nothing could live in this much water."

"Nothing but the fish," Ham added.

"We must offer thanks to Jehovah," Noah said.

We moved to the hall where we would be safe and knelt lifting our hands into the air in prayer. Noah led the pray of gratitude that the rain ended and that we lived.

"It looks like our lives will not change much for a few days," Edna said. "The animals will not feed themselves."

"Nor clean out their own compartments," Amina muttered.

I sighed. The sun would be here after I fed the animals on the fourth deck. I turned away and trudged down the steps toward the first compartment there.

Sun shone brightly through the windows, brightening up the insides of the ark. How could I be unhappy to care for the animals. They, like us, depended on the goodness of Jehovah.

I had not spent long shoveling the muck out of the first compartment when Noah joined me.

"I do not know what I thought I would find," he muttered.

"You expected something different?"

"I guess I hoped the rain would end and we could leave. But we have nowhere to go. We cannot leave the ark. The water is high enough up the sides we could never even think of opening the doors."

"To what?" I asked as I tossed more of the muck into a basket.

He shrugged and shoveled some of the muck. "I knew we would be here for a time. I do not think I understood."

"How could we know? Jehovah has never flooded the earth like this before."

"No. This is new."

We quietly scooped out the muck beneath the huge rhinoceroses, then lugged baskets of grain to them. We moved on.

"We are blessed. All the other life on earth is gone. Destroyed. Drowned. I knew it would be this way, but …" His voice trailed off.

"But you did not know it would be like this?"

"No."

We worked silently together as we cleaned out the auroch compartment. As we moved on to the hippos, Noah stopped in front of me.

"I am glad it is you who survived with me." He leaned his shovel against the wall and set his basket on the floor. He put his arms around me and hugged me close around my arms that hung by my side filled with my shovel and basket.

"Thank you." He picked up his basket and shovel and walked on down the corridor.

"You are welcome," I said, still enjoying his hug. I hurried to catch up with him.

"How long do you think it will take for the water to recede?"

He shook his head. "I have no idea. Where will all this water go? It will take time. I fear it will take longer than it took to fill it. Much longer than forty days."

"I guess you will need to continue your record."

He chuckled. "I will have to do that. Our posterity will want to know how long it took for the water to drain."

~ ~ ~

Each day we started our day with prayers. After eating and praying, I stood for a few breaths at a window, searching the water, hoping to see some indication of dry land, hoping we would someday leave the ark. Each day we continued to float, seeing nothing around us but water.

The men devised a way to bring the muck up from the lower decks so we could dump it out the windows. Even with the help of the animals, disposing of their dung and filthy bedding took much of each morning.

A wind blew, rocking us in the waves. Sometimes, the wind blew great waves that washed over the top of the ark. On those days, we could not dump the filth.

On windy days, we saw fish through the window.

"Will the window leak?" I cried. "Will that great fish come in?"

"No. The window is closed tight. Nothing but light will come through," Ham said gazing at the fish swimming past the window in a great wave.

Even the fish struggled in the rough waters. The wave receded and the big ones dove from sight.

The wind did not stop, though some days it blew harder than others. On the days that the waves did not crash into the windows and over the ark, we hoisted the waste up from the depths of the ark and dumped it out the windows into the water.

Early one morning the ark brushed up against a mountain peak. Animals woke. Brays, roars, squawks, and other animal protests echoed through the ark. We all jumped from our beds to check to be certain none had been injured.

Noah and I hurried down the steps to the fourth deck. We made our way through the large animals, examining each for injuries. The female auroch had a gash on her leg.

"Basya! Basya!" I called. "We have an injury here on the fourth deck."

Her feet soon pounded down the stairs. "Where are you, Mama Imma?" she called.

"Here with the aurochs."

She followed my voice and soon stood outside the compartment with her bag of healing supplies. She gazed through the door.

"What happened?"

"She must have been thrown into something. Her leg is cut," I said.

"Is it safe for me to enter?"

"You care for serpents and bees, yet you fear these gentle animals? Yes. Come in. Aurochs will not hurt you."

She opened the door. "They are gigantic. I do not fear them. I fear being stepped on by them."

"He will not step on you. Can you help the female?"

Basya stared past the male. "I can." She turned to Ham and asked him to get the pot of honey.

While he ran back up the stairs, she stepped inside, speaking gentle words to the big animals. The male crowded her into the wall. Avi, her cat, spit at him and yowled.

"Stop! I cannot help your mate if you do not allow me close to her," Basya cried.

I swatted the male on the shoulder and crooned, "Move aside. Basya is here to help your mate."

The big animal rumbled.

"She will help your mate, not hurt her," I comforted.

"And Avi is here to ensure I do everything right," Basya said.

The big male stepped aside and let her pass. I bent over the auroch female's leg. Blood streamed down it.

Basya dumped her bag with supplies on the floor and retrieved a clean cloth. "Can you get this wet in some clean water?" she said, handing the cloth to me.

I took it and left, pushing the big male out of the way. When I returned, the male stood near the female, watching Basya's every move. Avi sat close to the female with his tail wrapped around her lower leg.

She put four stitches into the gash in the female's leg, talking to both the female and the male as she worked. Ham returned with the honey. I retrieved it from him. I did not think the male would allow another stranger in with his mate.

Basya smeared the honey along the length of the injury, then stood and patted the big female auroch. "You will heal now. I will return each day until it is healed."

The male sniffed at the honey on his mate's leg, then snorted.

Avi ran up the male's leg and up onto his back. The cat jumped onto the auroch's head and ran to where he could look him in the eye. The big male moved closer to his mate. Avi stretched over and licked the female auroch, then leapt onto Basya's shoulder.

I giggled at the kitten's antics. Basya pushed past the big male and through the door.

She and Avi returned every day until the female auroch healed.

Forty days after the rain stopped, we stood together staring out the window, hoping to see a mountain top, a rock, anything to indicate the water had receded.

Nothing appeared. No land. No mountains. No trees. Only water. Lots of water.

In the fourth month after the rain stopped, I noticed that Amina struggled to eat her morning meal. She fought nausea with the gentle rocking of the ark.

I searched among the plants we brought to ensure they would not be lost. I found the pot filled with the peppermint plant on a ledge, growing in the sun.

I plucked two leaves and took them to Amina. "Chew on this. It will help settle your stomach."

She took the leaf and popped it into her mouth. "I did not know you brought the peppermint plant with you."

"We do not want to be without peppermint."

"Especially when you knew we would be with child."

I hugged her. "You carry a child?"

"I do. We will need children if we are to multiply and replenish this earth, if we get a chance to walk on it once more. How long much longer will we suffer this rocking ark?"

"I do not know?" I said. "We have been here many more than one hundred days. I see no change in the water."

"Nor do I. Perhaps the water is draining, and we do not know."

"That would be wonderful, but where would it drain when all the earth is covered with water?"

Before the end of another month, Basya found the peppermint leaves. She, too, carried a child.

I stared out at all the water and wondered how we would manage babies on our ark. We had enough space for all the animals and us, but not enough for children to run through the hallways and decks.

Six weeks after Basya asked for peppermint, Edna admitted she needed it, as well. All three daughters of my heart carried children.

Please, let the wind and the water abate that we may leave this ark before these babies are born, I prayed.

CHAPTER 32

Ararat

One day, as we fed the bison, the ark bumped into something. Even the huge bison were jolted and fought to stand on their feet. I did not. I fell to the floor. Grains spilled on the floor around me.

"What was that?" I yelped.

"We hit something," Noah said. He extended his hand to help me up.

I took it and pulled myself up.

The ark bounced again.

Noah wrapped his arms around me, keeping me from falling again.

"Should we go see?" I asked glancing upward toward the window.

"We should," he said. "We will return to finish cleaning your compartment," he said to the big bison.

I smiled. Noah spoke to them as though the animals understood his words.

The bison dipped their heads toward us.

As we left, they bent to the floor, licking up the grains I spilled.

"I will not have to clean up the spilled grain," I said.

Noah looked back and chuckled. "No. The bison are helping you with that."

We hurried up the stairs, meeting Amina and Japeth as we climbed past the third deck. Shem and Edna hurried ahead of us as we reached the second deck.

We reached the window behind the others.

"What was that bumping?" Edna asked.

"I hope we will be able to tell," Noah replied as he pushed to the front, closest to the window.

"I see nothing we would have hit," he said.

A great, dark blue fish rose from the water in front of the window. It gazed at us for many breaths before it slipped below the waves once more.

"A whale," Noah said. "We bumped into a whale."

"Is that what that fish is?" Amina asked.

"Yes. They are happier in the water than on the land," he replied.

"Good thing," Japeth teased. "Can you imagine finding a compartment huge enough for a pair of those? They are bigger than any animal I have seen before."

"How many would fit inside here?" Shem asked.

"None," I said. "There is no way a whale could come inside the ark."

"But if they could, maybe five would fit lengthwise," Noah said, estimating the size of the huge animals.

"One pair would take up most of the space in the fourth deck," Ham mused.

"Yes. It is good it does not need our assistance to keep them alive," Noah said.

We bumped into other big fish, but never enough to shake me off my feet after that.

Then, after one hundred fifty days on the ark, another huge bump caused me to stagger. I caught on to the elephant's leg before I fell.

"That did not feel like a whale," I said.

Noah's eyes were focused on the window. "We should see a mountain top sometime soon.

Once more, we hurried up the stairs.

A wall of rock and mud filled the window on the side opposite the doors. On the other side, we gazed out at water. Lots of water. Some water lapped along the lower edge of the window. We had lodged on against a muddy outcropping.

Through the day, the ark swung around once, then came to rest, never moving again.

The wind never stopped blowing.

Each day after that, I went with Noah to the window, watching to see how much the water went down. He marked it with a line of ink close to the edge of the window.

Each day it dropped. The first few days it dropped imperceptibly. After a few days, the water dropped faster, until it dropped below the bottom of the window.

Noah assumed we had settled near the top of a mountain. Noah named the mountain, Ararat. We watched out along the water, hoping to see other mountains.

~ ~ ~

The water dropped over time as the wind continued to blow. Some days, Noah and I were called on to help our sons feed and clean the animal compartments as their wives lay in their beds, fighting the nausea of a coming child. Our sons took breaks as often as they could to attend to their sick wives.

The stench of their sick overwhelmed us, along with the smell of the animal waste that stacked up while the waves blew over the top of the ark. We all regularly drank peppermint tea to calm our stomachs.

Between the smell and the extra work, my energy levels dropped. The other women could eat little, and I had little time to cook. I added to the stew each morning before I left to work with the animals.

Basya rose from her sick bed first. She plucked a leaf from the peppermint plant and chewed on it while she returned to help Ham feed the animals and clean their compartments. I sighed as we were relieved of this responsibility. Still, exhaustion dragged at me. I only wanted to sleep for a day, maybe two.

Soon Amina and Edna rose from their beds and joined us in cleaning the animal compartments.

Noah found me standing near the window, staring across the water, watching the waves.

"Imma?" he said. "Imma? Are you well?"

"Just tired," I said. Tired did not adequately express how I felt. Exhausted would better communicate my fatigue.

I leaned against the railing in front of the window, holding onto it to help keep me upright.

He put his arm around me. "You have worked too hard, trying to fill in for the others."

"I had no choice," I whispered.

"But you have a choice now. I do not want to lose you. You need to rest."

"But the crocodiles have not yet been fed."

"I fed them."

"The giraffes?"

"Ham fed them."

"The elephants?"

"Basya fed them."

"They are all fed?" I turned in his arms away from the window and slumped against him.

"All are fed," he said as he lifted me into his arms. "You have done more than your share in the last few days." He turned with me in his arms. "You are going to rest."

"But —"

"No. You need to rest. I do not want you to be sick next." He strode down the hallway away from the window toward our compartment.

"I am not carrying a child —" I protested.

"I do not want you to be sick," he repeated.

He pushed the door open and carried me to our bed. He lay me down and gently pulled the covers up to my chin. "Sleep. We will finish caring for the animals. Rest."

My eyes closed at his command.

The fragrance of warm bread and a savory soup tugged me awake.

Noah sat beside me on the bed. "Can you wake enough to eat? Amina made bread and Edna made a new soup."

I blinked my eyes and opened them. "It smells wonderful."

I moved from the bed to the table. "This smells wonderful," I said as Basya set a bowl of the soup with a thick slab of bread in front of me.

"You deserve a rest. You have been doing the things we should have been doing all these days."

I lifted a shoulder a bit, too tired still to lift it more. "It had to be done. We could not have hungry animals. We would not want them to find a way out of their compartments and wander freely around the ark."

"No," Basya said with a giggle. "That would be a disaster."

"We found the gorillas trying to open their door already," Noah said as he sat next to me with his own bowl of soup and slab of bread.

"And the chimpanzees cage needed two extra locks to keep them in," Ham added, sitting across from us.

"Those animals have too much time to figure those things out," Shem said, sitting next to Edna. "The lions and tigers begin to be restless. When do you think we can allow them out of their compartments?"

Noah glanced toward the windows he could not see through the walls. We had candles inside our compartment for light. "The wind continues to blow. Until we see some kind of land dry enough for us all, they will have to stay inside their compartments."

"The serpents continue to sleep," Basya whispered. "We do not have to fear they will find a way to escape."

"Oh, good," Edna said with a visible shiver.

"You still do not like serpents, Edna?" Japeth teased.

"No! I would have been happy to leave them all behind."

"They have a purpose. They help keep the vermin from multiplying and taking over the world," Basya said. "When they wake, there are many extra mice and rats for them to eat. Even with only one pair of each, they have filled their compartment with their young."

The younger people bantered about the animals and their needs. I sat with my head in my hand, elbow leaning on the table.

"Come, Imma," Noah urged. "You are sleeping. You will sleep better in our bed."

"But the dishes —" I protested.

"We will do the dishes," Amina said. "You get more rest. We need you healthy."

I nodded and allowed Noah to lead me to the bed.

I slept two more days before I could rise and return to my responsibilities helping with the biggest animals.

CHAPTER 33

Olive Twig

The mountain behind us slowed the wind some days, making life easier for all of us. Yet on other days the wind whipped around us, rocking the ark, making even the men sick.

When we investigated the condition of the animals, we expected to see a huge mess, as they would be as sickened as we were. Instead, the animals lay in their beds asleep. None of them had sickened by the motion of the boat. Jehovah had blessed us once more, helping the animals to sleep. Only the some of the birds sat on their perches, awake, and not sick.

We made our way up to the window and stared out at the wind and the water. The wind had whipped up the waves enough that they sometimes splashed on our window. I had hoped that we would not see water splashing on our window anymore.

I sighed.

"Why the sigh?" Noah asked.

"I hoped that this would be over soon."

"I fear we are less than half the way through our experience here."

"How long has it been?"

Noah scratched his beard. "We entered the ark on the seventeenth day of the second month. It is now the twenty-eighth day of the ninth month."

"We have only been here on the ark for seven months? It feels like we have been here for years."

Noah chuckled. "It does seem like longer, but it is only a few days more than seven months."

I breathed in deeply and allowed the air to escape through my nose. "How much longer do you think we will be?"

"I have no way of knowing. The water needs to recede enough we can be certain there is land to live on once more. We would not want to open the doors into water."

"No. That would not be good."

We stared out at the water. It is all we saw. Water. I had grown tired of seeing all that water. I missed dry land, our fields, my garden, and most of all, my flowers.

I walked to the shelf of growing plants and buried my nose in them. The peppermint tickled my nose. These living plants gave me joy.

We turned and walked back to our compartment. I hoped Edna had prepared wonderful bread to go with the stew. Her bread made life more bearable.

As we walked in, the fragrance of bread filled me. "Ah. As long as we can bake bread, I can live here."

"Forever if we have bread?" Noah teased.

"Until the earth dries enough, we can leave it," I said with a smile.

Noah chuckled. "I knew you were ready to leave. Too bad you cannot."

"Someday the waters will recede, and the earth will dry. I may have to wait another year. If there is bread, I will survive."

He tipped his head back and roared with laughter.

Two days later, we stood in front of the window once more. I searched across the waves, hoping to see land, a rock, a mountain! Anything except water.

The waves moved in a different way than I had seen before. I put my hand over my eyebrows to shade my eyes. Something dark sat in the middle of the waves.

I nudged Noah. "What is that?" I whispered, almost afraid to ask, fearful it would disappear.

He stepped closer to the window and peered out in the direction my finger pointed.

"I think it is … Yes, it is …"

"What? What do you think it is?"

"A mountain. A mountain has stretched above the water."

"Stretched above or the water dropped enough for it to be seen?" I asked.

He turned and took my arm, pulling me closer to the window. "Does it matter? The mountains appear once more. There is hope that the earth will dry out so that we may live on it once more."

I threw my arms around him. "When?"

"Not today. Not tomorrow. We will want to see more of the mountain than just the tops."

I turned and stared at the mountain top. "But we know the water is receding."

"We do. It may be a few more months, but we will be able to release the animals sometime and leave ourselves." Noah's voice held as much emotion as I felt. I hugged him tighter.

We watched the mountain lift out of the water every day. Other mountains appeared. The others often joined us to watch the mountains appear.

"We may get away from this smelly ark before my child is born," Amina whispered.

"Yes, it does smell. Yesterday's storm prevented removing the nasty bedding. We need to remove the animal waste again. The winds are not as strong today," Japeth said, setting his hands on her shoulders.

We left the window and tromped to our deck. There we scooped up the animal waste into the dirty, old baskets we had been using to dispose of the waste. When the baskets were filled, Noah and I each grabbed a handle and carried the basket between us and dumped it into the basket attached to the rope. The elephant walked down the long hall, tugging the basket up to the top deck where Ham and Basya dumped it out the windows.

I heard other animals walk along the hallways, pulling up the muck from the other floors. We were blessed when the men thought of this way to dispose of the animal excrement.

We loaded several more of the smelly baskets and sent them up to be dumped. We considered washing out the compartments, but rain no longer fell, we feared we would not have enough water.

"Can we drop a bucket out the window and have the animals help us pull water up?" I asked.

Noah stared into the barrel. "We probably should while water is close."

We found a bucket and climbed the steps to the first deck. Noah unfastened one basket from one rope and tied on the bucket. He tossed it over the side. It fell farther than we expected before it sunk into the water.

Noah called down to Japeth and asked him to have the horse to pull the bucket up. When it finally reached the top of the window and swung into the ark, Noah caught it. He dipped his fingers into the water and tasted it.

"Sweet. I feared it may not be. We can drink this."

After that, we spent part of each day filling the water barrels. We washed the worst smelling of the compartments. It helped.

"I wish I could set these baskets out the window to air out the stench."

"Why not?" Noah asked. "If we can drop buckets out the window, we can drop the baskets out the window and let them air out. They are attached to the ropes. They will not fall."

I stepped closer to the window and gazed toward the mountains. They looked like mountains now, not little mounds of something solid in the expanse of water.

Each evening after that, we dropped the baskets out the window and closed it. In the mornings, we opened the windows and pulled the baskets in, still attached to the ropes and ready to start dragging up the smelly mess from within the animal compartments.

~ ~ ~

Forty days after we first saw the tips of the mountains, more of them showed.

"Perhaps there is enough of them that plants are growing once more," Noah said.

"How can we tell?

He lifted a tired shoulder. "Send out birds to see if they find a home there? That would help us know that the water is dropping."

"When will we send a bird out?" I asked.

"Tomorrow. The wind blows into us today. It will be difficult for the birds to fly today."

I stared out the window until I saw more of the mountain. I hoped the winds would be gentler the next day.

Early the next morning, all eight of us stood near the window. A raven sat on Basya's arm. A dove sat on Ham's shoulder.

Japeth pushed the window open and Basya stepped close to it. The raven jumped onto the windowsill and squawked. It jumped through the window, flew in a circle around the ark, then dipped his wing toward us before soaring away.

"It is your turn to go, as well, little dove," Noah murmured to the dove. It bobbed its head, then flitted through the window.

"How long do we wait?" Shem asked.

"We can leave the window open, so if they return before we do, they can enter without a problem," Noah said. "We have animals that need food."

We stared out at the birds. I saw the raven swooping as he flew around the ark and off toward one of the mountains. "Come back with something good," I whispered.

We returned before time for our midday meal. We gazed out the window, wondering where the birds were. When the sun had crossed almost across the sky, no bird had arrived. At last, he landed on the window. His head drooped in exhaustion.

Basya found him there and brought him in.

"The dove is back," she called as she carried him toward the bird enclosure.

Everyone rushed up the stairs to welcome him home. We met outside the birds.

"Did he bring anything back to suggest there was a place for him to rest?" Noah asked.

We all held our breaths. We were ready for more good news. It did not come that day.

Basya shook her head. “He flew too far seeking a place to stay. He almost did not return safely. He is exhausted.”

“Will he live?” Edna asked.

Basya looked at bird sitting close to his mate in their nest. “I hope so.”

“Where is the raven?” Shem asked.

“He will need a place to rest, as well. Perhaps he found a place to stop. He is bigger and stronger than the dove.” Basya slumped against the door to the bird compartment.

“Perhaps he will return later,” Amina suggested.

“We will leave the window open enough he can come back in if he returns,” Noah said.

Ham and Basya fed the dove and gave him a special tea. The rest of us returned to our home for our evening meal.

Before we went to bed, we returned to stand in front of the window. A breeze blew in on us. I savored the cool, fresh air.

“Did the raven return?” Amina asked.

“No,” Basya said, shaking her head. “The raven has not returned.”

“Can we leave the window open some for it if he returns?” Ham asked.

Noah stared out into the setting sun. “Only enough for the raven to squeeze through. The wind grows stronger.”

Basya and Ham took blankets and sat near the compartments across from the window, hoping to be there to welcome the raven back.

He never did. “He must have found a place far away to perch,” she said.

By then, we had used much of the water in the barrels. We needed to be careful to use only what was necessary. We had food enough. We had stored enough for two years.

Seven days later, Noah and Basya brought the dove to the window once more. "Can you go see if there is any life out there? Is the water leaving the earth?" he asked the bird.

The bird bobbed its head and chirped before it leapt off Noah's arm and flew through the window.

We returned to the space in front of the window several times through the day, watching and waiting for the dove to return. Near midday, she returned. In her beak she carried a twig of an olive tree. On that twig were leaves.

"Trees!" we shouted.

Basya cradled the bird in her arms. "You are back earlier than your mate. Did you take time to enjoy the tree and the leaves?"

The bird chirped.

She carried it back to its compartment and fed it an extra measure of the grain. She also allowed it to take an olive leaf with it to share with its mate.

Seven days later, we tried once more. The male dove, now healthy, leapt from Noah's arm and flew out the window. Although we returned often to see if the dove returned, it did not. Early the next morning, we released his mate. Basya tried not to let us see her tears after the doves left. She loved the birds.

We continued to care for the animals. Until the land dried, we could not open the door to the ark.

Noah leaned out the window the week after the doves disappeared. "None!" he cried.

"None?" Amina asked.

"No water! I see no water down there at all."

"Can we leave?" Shem asked.

Noah shook his head. "Not yet. The earth is still much too wet."

"Can we allow the birds to leave?" Basya asked.

"You can."

She opened the door to the bird compartment. Only the raven left. The others stayed in the safety of the bird compartment.

The sun shone brightly the next month. The wind blew, joining the sun in drying out the earth.

On the first day of the new year, Noah woke us with good news. "The earth is dry. We will have to test it before we allow all the animals to leave."

We walked to the smallest door and crowded around it. Noah opened the door.

Japeth leaned out. "I see no water."

"No. Jehovah told me it had receded.

"Can we leave?" Amina asked.

Basya's cat poked his head between her legs. "Meow?"

"Not yet, Avi," she said, bending to pick him up.

Noah put his hand out. "Let him go. He is small. He will be good to see what happens when he walks on the earth."

She set Avi on the ramp. We watched him scamper down and out onto the earth. No longer a kitten, he ran across the ground until Basya called to him.

He considered ignoring her, but he returned. She picked him up and examined his feet. Small spots of mud soiled the pads of his feet, but he had been able to walk along the top of the dirt without problems.

"Horses will still sink to their knees in that," Edna muttered.

"Imagine what would happen to the mammoths and aurochs," I added.

"No," Noah said. "Close the door. The earth still needs to dry. Jehovah will let us test the earth, but we must still wait."

Ham pushed the door closed.

We trekked each week to the door to test the mud. Each time it had dried more. The second week, Noah encouraged a dog and a gazelle to walk onto the drying earth. The dog had no problems walking, but gazelle's sharp hooves pierced the crust of dry earth and had to fight to get back to the ramp. He ran back into the ark without needing encouragement.

On the third week, the dog and deer both ran across the earth without problems. Japeth led a horse out the door. He walked to a green outcropping of grass and stopped, allowing the horse to eat. The weight of the horse cracked through the drying crust of mud.

Japeth led him back in and both the dog and deer returned, not yet ready to leave the ark. We stood on the ramp in the sunshine, watching the animals. When Ham and Shcm lifted the ramp and closed the door, I sighed.

"Soon," Noah said. "Soon we can leave and let all the animals out."

"Maybe next week?" Amina said, voicing all our hopes.

The following week, I led out a giraffe. She represented the big animals of the fourth deck, although she did not weigh as much as the huge aurochs or mammoths.

Ham and Seth unwrapped the ropes that held the door closed. They held them to allow it to open smoothly.

It did not. Japeth had to climb up and reset one of the ropes along the grooves that allowed it to move smoothly. When he returned to the deck and stepped out of the way, Ham and Shem slowly and carefully allowed the door to open outward until the top of the door rested on the nearly dry mud.

I led a giraffe down the ramp, stopping to lift her nose and smell the fresh air of a world only recently covered by many more than thirty cubits of water. Her splayed feet did not break through the dry crust. She wandered to a tall tree and nibbled at the leaves. She turned and stared toward the ark, seeking her mate.

I patted her long neck. "Not today, sweet one. The earth is not quite dry enough. I fear the bigger animals will break through."

She huffed and walked back into the ark. Her head drooped.

CHAPTER 34

Land

On the twenty-seventh day of the second month, after testing the earth once more, Noah led the aurochs through the huge doorway and down the ramp, one after the other.

They walked across the earth a distance before they stopped. They turned to look at Noah. He walked forward and put his arms around their big heads. When he dropped his arms, the big animals turned and trundled away.

He returned to the ramp. "It is time. Mama and I will release the animals on the fourth deck. Each of you return to your deck and open the compartments. Help the animals to leave the ark."

While the other couples hurried up the stairs to open the compartments, Noah and I went to each compartment on the fourth deck. We opened the doors and went inside. Some of the big animals carried young. Noah and I wrapped our arms around most of the animals and wished them well, thanking them for their service and the help they were to us in the past year plus ten days.

We walked with each couple down the hall to the huge door. We watched them walk across the valley before we went back for the next pair of animals. While we opened the doors, the others opened the doors of their compartments and walked with them to the doors of the ark.

Most of the animals walked slowly down the ramp, hesitating when they set their feet on the dirt. When they did not fall through, many of them kicked up their heels and raced across the valley, disappearing around a bend.

Noah opened the doors to allow the alligators and crocodiles to leave. "I am sorry, friend alligators and crocodiles. I am not giving you a hug. I will pat your head."

The crocodiles bent and allowed him to pat their head. The alligators opened their mouths wide. Noah patted their head as they waddled past.

All the other animals walked, waddled, or slithered past us down the ramp and out into the new world. Birds flew out the window and down through the open door. They flew into the open and out across the valley. Some little ones stopped on a branch of the nearby tree before flying on away.

Basya and Ham walked down the stairs carrying a beehive and a hornet's nest. They returned several times with some of the smaller animals, turtles, newts, and others, who struggled on to run down the ramps.

It took all the next four days to release and accept the gratitude of the rest of the animals. Most of the animals trotted down the ramp and moved away. We did not see some of them ever again. Others, we saw occasionally.

Animals like horses, cows, goats, and sheep stayed near us. They had become used to living with people from the days of Eve and Adam. Dogs and cats, chickens and ducks, and other animals chose to stay with us.

On the sixth day, we stepped down the ramp to explore the land around where the ark had settled. We were still higher in the mountains, much like we had been in Mamre. We would need to plant our seeds soon if they were going to have time to grow and feed us later in the year.

The men built a large home for us all to live in that first year. It had a room for each couple and their children. We would want to split up after that. Each couple would search for a place to build a home.

We had spent a year living close together. We had not fought because we always had animals to feed and care for. Now, we needed to work together to grow food and offer the support we would need to survive life in this strange new world, a world much like the one we left the year before, but different.

The ark carried us away from the land we had lived in. Nothing looked familiar. Noah told me that the water had changed the look of the earth.

We were here. It became our new home.

A clear stream flowed along the side of the valley below the ark. This gave us fresh water. We had rationed our water for more than a month.

I knelt next to the stream and drank deeply of it. Its clear purity tasted sweet. I dipped more from the stream and drank it until my thirst had quenched.

The others had bent to drink, as well. The water in the barrels had become stale and nasty. We had to drink it. We had nothing else.

Noah joined me at the stream to drink. After we had quenched our thirst, I stared around at the valley. "What do we do now?"

Noah smiled. "Build an altar and make an offering to Jehovah in gratitude for bringing us safely to a new world."

I nodded my head. "You are right. We will need to offer a sacrifice and give thanks to Jehovah."

He strolled around the space and chose a place on a ridge above the valley. He bent to gather stones and lay them together.

Japeth, Shem, and Ham joined us. When they understood what their papa did, they joined him gathering stones and laying them together to create an altar. It took less than a span with all four of them working to complete it.

Noah searched among the animals that stayed with us for an appropriate sacrifice. He found a young ram sheep, pure and without spots. Shem helped him wash the ram, then led him to a grassy place to dry while Noah washed and prayed in preparation for this important first sacrifice here in … the new world.

It is a new world, clean and new. Cleansed from all the wickedness and sin of those who soiled it before. It is the same earth, but different. We are pioneers, new to this clean earth. I pray we can keep it clean and pure.

I climbed the stairs to our living quarters behind Noah to help him dress for the sacrifice. He pulled out the box he had brought with him to the ark.

Inside were robes made of skin. A faint musty smell rose from the depths of the box.

"What are these?" I asked.

"This is the sacred clothing given to Adam before he left Eden."

I had heard of this clothing. I knew both Adam and Eve were given sacred clothing, but I had not seen it before. "What animal provided this skin? I have not seen anything like this."

"I believe it was a mastodon."

"Oh." We had carried mastodons with us on the ark, huge elephant-like creatures. "I would never think of using their skin as clothing."

"Or food," Noah said. "I have heard of men eating the mastodon."

He pulled on the sacred clothing, gently tucking and tying it until it fit.

"It could have been made for you."

"They are made for the prophets. I found them with Grandpapa Methuselah's things. I need to wear them today."

I found a torch we had not yet lit and carried it and a lit candle down the stairs behind Noah as we descended from the ark. I glanced at the sun. It stood only a finger width from the zenith. We had time to offer this sacrifice. I lit the torch and handed it to Noah. I blew out the candle and tucked it inside my pocket.

Coals had been retrieved and placed in the fire space of the new home. For now, however, Noah would use the torch for the sacrifice.

I followed Noah across the distance to the new altar and joined the others. They saw us leave the ark and came to sit where we could observe this sacred rite.

In the end, Noah pulled the torch from where he had stabbed it into the soil and lit the offering. We watched it burn until nothing remained.

A gentle mist of rain fell on us.

Edna flinched.

"Look!" Noah commanded. "We followed his pointing arm and gazed toward the sun.

A colorful bow of light crossed from one side of the valley to the other.

"With this token of the bow, Jehovah promises he will never again destroy all life from the earth by flooding it with water. We may become wicked. We may forget His laws and promises. But He will never again destroy all life on the earth. This is His promise."

I sighed, and heard the others sigh with me.

"From this day forward," Noah continued with a light surrounding him as it did when he spoke for Jehovah, "seed time and harvest, cold and heat, summer and winter, and day and night shall not cease. Life will continue until that great day when Jehovah shall determine it is enough and shall roll the earth together as a scroll."

I tried to envision the earth rolling together as a scroll. I could not.

"You are commanded by our loving God, even Jehovah, to multiply and replenish this earth once more. Teach your children of His commandments and His love. Help them know that only in obedience will we find joy."

Many other commandments came from Jehovah that day. Most had been written before. I remembered them from the Book of Commandments that Adam wrote. Truly, Jehovah is the same yesterday, today, and forever.

When Noah ended his teaching, he handed the portion of the ram to me. "This is for us to eat. Can you prepare it for our evening meal?"

I nodded. "I will need some assistance gathering wood for the fire. There are still grains and vegetables stored on the ark."

~ ~ ~

I gazed across the field at the growing crops and at the women and their men who worked to water them. Each of the women carried a child. From them, would come more children to populate the earth once more.

I had not been called on to carry the burden of childbirth, but I would be here for them as their children came into the world, for a time.

My eyes turned toward the home our men had built to protect us from the weather. The animals we feared were gone, for now. Would they remember our kindness in their year on the ark? The original pair may, but would their children? I doubted it.

Our home and our fires would keep them far from us. We were the beginning of a new world, a new people in a new land. We had come out of the darkness of a land filled with wickedness and evil into a clean and pure land filled with light.

A colorful bow arched above the remnants of the gentle rain, a promise that Jehovah would never destroy all life from this earth again. Could these grandchildren of ours, those waiting in their mama's bellies and those yet unborn keep the land filled with this brightness?

A cool breeze caused me to shiver. We were here. The Destroyer could not be drowned in the depths of the flood. He would be here, as well.

Help us teach our little ones better, I prayed within my heart. *Help us teach them obedience so they will not be overcome by wickedness as our families were — before.*

The call of the Destroyer is strong. He will bend his lies to fit the needs of the people. Jehovah could not take away their right to choose. We would lose children to the Destroyer. I only hoped that more would see the light.

Perhaps, since these children would not live so many years, they would not have the time to become as wicked as they had in the past. I prayed it would be so.

With a sigh, I bent to pull weeds from my garden. Weeds, like darkness, could be pulled out, allowing the light to help us grow. Would that we could always live in that light.

Back Matter

Acknowledgements:

As I complete another story in the lives of the Ancient Matriarchs, I am always amazed how many people are involved in the creation of a book. Much of the writing is done in the silence of my mind. Still, others are involved in the completion.

I have enjoyed participating in writing sprints with other ANWA members each evening, pushing me to write better and faster.

My husband sits beside me, as always, helping me with ideas and words. His patience is never-ending.

Danica Page and Dar Albert helped make this a beautiful book, with great editing and a beautiful cover. Thanks go, too, to the members of my AngelCAST team who read the book a final time for errors, problems, and typos! When you find one, however, (and there seems to be one all the time!) the blame is mine.

As always, my parents have helped and supported me in my efforts to write. I love and appreciate them.

Last, but never least, I thank you, the reader, who has chosen this book to spend your time and money on. I have loved working on this work of fiction. I would love to hear how you liked it.

Angelique@AngeliqueCongerAuthor.com

Dear Reader,

I have waited many years to write this concluding story to the lives of the early matriarchs. Truly, Imma and Noah were the couple who led the family of man from the world of wickedness and evil to a clean new world.

I wrote these words as the world shut down in the Covid-19 pandemic. I listened to others who worried about not having enough toilet paper, then seeing there was little else on the shelves in the stores, when allowed to enter.

Lives changed. We wear masks and stay far apart, fearing the disaster of a virus that spread throughout the world.

I read many comments that Noah stayed on the ark 40 days. Yes. And then, he and his family continued to be locked there until the waters dispersed — more than a year after they entered the ark.

I hope we do not have to be separated from our loved ones a whole year!

As I write this, the world begins to open once more. Stores and restaurants are opening. There is hope we may regain a new normalcy. I hope this includes greater kindness, love, and gentleness towards others.

I hope you have enjoyed this book. One more is on the way: We Stood with Them, a book of short stories and novellas detailing the lives of those other women who stood beside the early prophets.

Angelique

Did You Enjoy This Book?

If you did, will you do something for me?

I'm an independent author, publishing my books without the backing of a major publisher. That means no six-figure advances and no advertising budget. This makes it difficult to promote my novels and put them in places new readers can find them. But you can help me.

Honest reviews and genuine "word-of-mouth" advertising makes all the difference. I'm not asking for one of those awful book reports I used to try not to sleep through, as a teacher. What will help me is for you to leave an honest star rating and a couple of sentences on Amazon or Goodreads. Or a short review on your blog. Or tell your friends about it on Facebook or Twitter.

Let people know what you liked about this book and why they might like it, too. And, if there was something you didn't like, you can say that, as well. Constructive criticism helps me write a better book next time.

But, please. No spoilers!

Thanks for reading.

Books by Angelique Conger

Ancient Matriarchs:

*Eve, First Matriarch
Into the Storms: Ganet: Wife of Seth
Finding Peace: Rebecca, Wife of Enos
Moving into Light: Zehira, Wife of Enoch
Out of Darkness: Imma,Wife of Noah
We Stood with Them: Other Wives of the Prophets
(August 2020)

Lost Children of the Prophet

Lost Children of the Prophet
Captured Freedom
Abandoned Hope
Brotherly Havoc
Betrayed Trust
Convicted Deliverance
Trouble Escaped
Contrary Devotion
Impassioned Grief
Love Defied
Hidden Purpose
Concealed Innocence

Would You Like More?

If you enjoyed this story, you may enjoy a **Free Micro Story**, written about Eve in her travels with Adam, later in their lives. Eve must find a way to rescue Adam after he was taken by servants of the Destroyer. No one else is near and it is up to her.

Avenging Angel is **free** and only available when you subscribe to my **Ancient Historical Fiction Reader.**

Go to: http://www.AngeliqueCongerAuthor.com to get your **free copy.**

OR, if you would rather have a **Free Short Story** that tells how Shamgar, the healer who helped Crites and the Red Guard, and later taught all the best healers, please go to: https://dl.bookfunnel.com/ldg1thkpcj

To get your copy of **Damaged Healer**.

Both stories will add you to my weekly newsletter, where you will receive news of upcoming books, sales, and other fun things.

If you have something to share with me after reading, you are welcome to email me:

Angelique@AngeliqueCongerAuthor.com

ABOUT THE AUTHOR

Angelique Conger writes historical fiction about the earliest days of our earth between Eden and the flood. Many consider her books Christian focused, and they are because they focus on events in the Bible. She writes of a people's beliefs in Jehovah. However, though she's read in much of the Bible and searched for more about these stories, there isn't much there. Her imagination fills in the missing information, which is most of it.

Angelique followed her Navy husband around the world and later worked as a teacher in the years her children were growing. Writing about the earliest days of our earth, those days between the Garden of Eden and Noah's flood, helps in her efforts to change the world.

Angelique lives in Southern Nevada with her husband, turtles, and a cat. Her favorite times are visiting children and grandchildren.

<<<<>>>>

Made in the USA
Monee, IL
11 March 2023

29642581R00197